Catalyst

CATALYST

Mark Eklid

Independently published.

ISBN: 978-1-8384179-0-1

To my dad, Alf, and in memory of my mum, Norma.
Behind me at every step.

1

'Seriously, these are really good.'

In case there was any doubt Anna was sincere in her appreciation for the food Martin had laid on for the meeting, she leaned forward and helped herself to another snack-sized piece from the large plate on the table around which the seven of them were gathered.

Across the table, Diane watched as Anna hungrily took a bite from the green-topped rectangular slice and silently envied her youthful nonchalance when it came to casual food consumption. How nice it must be to be free of the perpetual concerns suffered by the more mature woman and eat how much you like whenever you like. The group had felt the need to attract younger activists for a while and Anna had been a breath of fresh air. Oh, to have such energy again! Oh, to have that metabolism!

'Mmm, what's this one?'

Martin tucked his collar-length straight dark hair behind his ears and a broad grin wrinkled the lines of his face behind a straggly beard. He loved seeing people eat his food with such enthusiasm. It was one of his passions. It was his living.

'That's my toasty tofu. It's basically spinach leaves,

fresh basil and breadcrumbs on a fried tofu slice and finished under the grill to make it crispy. What you had before that was one of my aubergine balls.'

'Delicious,' Anna concluded, chewing on the last of the slice. 'And all this is from your café?'

Martin nodded, his eyes skirting around the cosily snug confines of the *Better World* café. They were crowded in the booth at the end of the room, furthest away from the front door. The busiest time of the afternoon had passed and only four customers remained: an older couple who often dropped by for a soya latte and a shared cake and two women in their mid-twenties who were cramming in as much catch-up conversation as they could before it was time to pick up the kids from school.

'All made on the premises. Much of it by my own fair hand,' he replied, proudly.

'I will *so* have to come here with my house-mates some time,' said Anna.

'I do ten per cent discount for students and I'm open until seven every day except Sunday. We do gourmet evenings every two weeks, which are extremely popular and tend to be booked up quickly, but if you just want to drop in one day, it'd be great to see you.'

'Anyway,' interrupted Vivienne, in her best school mistress tone. As chair of the group, she often drew on her experience of how to deal with unruly seven to eleven-year-olds when the focus of the meeting broadened into a wider discussion of policy or an ethical debate. The cause of disruption was not usually the buffet, however.

'Sorry Vivienne,' whispered Martin, suitably chastised.

Anna offered nothing as she scanned what remained on the plate, silently debating the important issue of what to try next.

'Are we all clear on our roles for the Climate Emergency rally on the fourteenth?' asked Vivienne. Slow nods around the table indicated that everyone was, indeed, comfortable with their assignments.

'Good. Any further issues anyone wants to raise?'

The slow nods turned to slow shakes.

'I think we're done, then.' Vivienne gathered the papers in front of her to officially signal the meeting over.

Anna turned to check the time on the large clock on the wall behind the café counter. She jumped to her feet, draped her colourful knitted scarf around her slim neck and pulled her long dark hair free of it.

'I have to go. I literally have a sociology lecture in quarter of an hour,' she said, snatching up her canvas shoulder bag and grabbing a chickpea bite before heading for the door with a hasty goodbye wave.

'You're OK with recruiting other members of the XR Students' Society to take part in the march?' called Vivienne after her.

'Totally,' replied the retreating figure and she was gone.

The rush of activity left a lull around the table in its wake, like they had just sailed out of a storm and into a pocket of calm.

Richard, the most senior member of the group, broke the brief silence. 'I sometimes wonder if she ever eats apart from when she comes to the meetings.'

'I wish we could bring a lot more like her into the

3

group,' responded David, who was now the youngest of those around the table, despite being in his mid-thirties, and was never slow to scent the opportunity for a confrontation.

'So do I,' Richard swiftly clarified. He was a veteran of the cause and should have known better. He had seen so many times before how an innocent remark could be construed as offensive if someone like David tried hard enough to see the hidden meaning.

'I just meant she's so slim. Not that there's anything wrong with that, of course.'

But David's fervour was now stirred. He shuffled forward in his seat, ready to emphasise his point, and pushed the bridge of his round, red-rimmed glasses further up his nose with his index finger. That meant only one thing. Vivienne laid her papers back down on the table.

'When are we going to drag this group into the new age?' David demanded. 'I mean, we've been going for nearly two decades and people have never been more aware of the climate emergency the world is now in and yet Anna is the first new face we've had around this table for months – years even. How long will it be until she realises we've become nothing but a gathering of blustering old farts who don't actually *do* anything? I mean, we talk, we make placards, we wave them from the town hall steps and we go home, deluding ourselves into thinking that we've made a difference. People sign our petitions to feel good about themselves, but they still drive their big cars, eat mountains of red meat and fly abroad for their fortnight in Spain. They don't realise or don't care that they're part of the problem. Meanwhile, the people in power make a few sympathetic noises and then ignore us. That's what we are. We're ignored. It's too easy for them to disregard us. What we have to do is make ourselves impossible to ignore. We need to disrupt. We need to occupy buildings and public spaces. We need to draw attention to ourselves by locking ourselves to railings, gluing ourselves to doors, staging a naked protest if we have to.'

Diane shot him a look of silent horror at the prospect of being required to glue herself naked to a public building.

'We have to make the media notice us – and I'm not talking about a small picture on page 50 of the local rag. We have to do something spectacular to make them acknowledge us and shock the public into realising that these are drastic measures because we are in the middle of a drastic situation. We have to wake them up from their complacent, comfortable lives and make them realise that it's everybody's responsibility to bring about change – now!'

David thumped his fist down on the table, startling the older couple close to the door.

The final word reverberated around the room long after the crockery on the table had settled and the two young mums had picked up the flow of their conversation. Vivienne composed herself, ready to lead the response to David's outburst.

'With respect, David,' she began, 'there are people around this table who have been promoting the cause of climate change awareness for a long time and have achieved many successes and concessions over the years by lobbying and educating and –'

'Besides,' interrupted Richard, whose sense of irritation had been steadily growing through his younger colleague's tirade, 'the general public – not to mention the people in authority – don't respond well to the kind of disruption you're talking about. Supergluing yourself to a building, stopping people going about their normal business – all that does is turn people against us, makes it possible for them to regard us as fanatics, extremists. The sort of action you're talking about harms the cause.'

'Can you not see?' David held his head in his hands, an edge of despair in his voice. 'What we've been doing for years has not worked. The world is slipping deeper and deeper towards oblivion and that demands more than nice words and gentle protest. What we need is non-violent direct action. That's the only solution. That's the only way we're going to bring about real change. How many more years do you think there would have been gross inequality if the civil rights movement had limited its activities to handing out leaflets? How much longer would there have been atrocities committed in Middle East if the Stop the War Coalition had just written strongly-worded letters to *The Times*?'

He raised his head. 'Look at us. Why do you think it is that we can't attract dynamic, young activists? Where's our diversity? We're white, middle-aged and middle class. If people saw us gathered and didn't read the placards, they'd think we were on our way to a Trump rally.'

The accusation stirred a wave of indignation around the table.

'Steady on,' said Frank, whose contributions to the

gatherings were rare.

'The debate has moved on. We either change our focus to start actually doing something or we're going to become irrelevant.'

David stared intently at the faces around him. Richard and Vivienne met his eye. The rest could not. David shot to his feet.

'You know what? Forget it. If you can't see it, maybe you're all irrelevant already. I'm going to join another group. One that isn't afraid to take action.'

Pausing only to mutter 'excuse me' to Rachel as she edged back her chair to allow him to get past, he stormed out of the café.

'Prick,' said Richard.

Several of the others gave him reproachful glances.

'Sorry, but he is. Always has been. We're better off without him. Anyhow, I've got to go. See you all soon.'

Richard pulled on his jacket and stood to leave, bubbling with umbrage. The rest of the group also gathered their belongings along with their bruised sensitivities and wandered away, until only Vivienne and Martin remained.

'He was out of order,' offered Martin as she pushed her papers into a bag.

'But he was also right,' Vivienne replied. 'The cause has moved on. The mass of the population has stopped listening – I mean, *really* listening. We've done a lot of great work over the years to raise awareness, but awareness only gets you so far. The small concessions we win aren't enough anymore because the situation is getting worse and the people with the power to change that aren't being put under enough pressure to force them to take meaningful steps towards halting the slide. Our form of protest has become the faint noise in the background they can block out. They need to be made to listen. Disruption and direct action might truly be the only way forward.'

Martin was stunned into silence.

Vivienne sighed and rolled her eyes in resignation, then walked quietly, ruefully, out of the café.

2

The bike seemed slightly too big for him, like it had been bought for a child with a view to his growing into it one day.

But Martin was well beyond the age where he might be expected to get any taller. People in their mid-forties rarely experience growth spurts. It wasn't the bike that was oversized; he had always been undersized.

When people occasionally, insensitively, asked him exactly how tall he was, he would tell them he was five foot one. He couldn't recall having been measured since he was very young when his parents, who were both a little above average height, were concerned that their son might have some sort of disorder and so had taken him to see people. Specialists. Five foot one seemed about right as an estimate now, though, and satisfied the curiosity of those who asked. It was rarely an issue for him. Not these days. Not since school, really. There were more important matters in the world.

Martin comfortably pedalled his bike up the gentle incline of Marlborough Road, between the rows of solidly majestic gabled stone houses set behind old stone walls that ran, broken only by the gaps for driveways, along the length of the long, straight road. It was a bright, warm March day and this was one of his favourite roads to cycle along, away from the fumes and fury of the major arteries, but something troubled Martin as he rode it this time.

It wasn't so much what David said. David was always a bit of a hothead who much preferred the sound of his own voice to listening to anyone with a contrary opinion and had often been the cause of too much unnecessary tension in meetings. They wouldn't miss him if David, this time, was to carry out his threat to quit so he could impose his rigid, uncompromising views on some other unsuspecting group.

No. What bothered Martin was Vivienne's reaction. She had practically agreed with him. Vivienne never allowed anyone to get under her skin. That was why the group had elected her chair. Vivienne was strong, unwavering, unflappable. Vivienne was totally committed to what they were striving to achieve.

He and Vivienne had been with the group from the start. They had never doubted that their cause was fundamentally right, even when their views were very much in the minority. They had stayed resolute, celebrated small victories when they could and looked on with relieved satisfaction as gradually, across the world, the voices of the doubters had grown quieter. The cause for which they had lain themselves open to vilification was now in the mainstream. It was cool to be a climate activist.

It was only right that the younger generation should take up the fight to halt the crisis. They were the ones who would inherit the mess created by previous generations, after all. Sure, their methods could be different, more challenging, but perhaps that was a good thing. The situation is escalating. Time is running out. It's good that greater immediacy is being injected into the fight to save the planet and the younger generation, with the global reach advantage given to them by social media, is adding plenty to the cause. Perhaps direct action is the answer. Perhaps the less committed – the lip-service sympathisers and the complacent policy-makers – do need shaking up.

But that doesn't mean groups like Sheffield Environmental Action Network, with their more moderate methods, should step aside and leave them to it. They had been promoting the cause since Greta Thunberg was in biodegradable nappies and had the experience to help everybody achieve their goals.

We still have a voice. We can still achieve. We are still relevant.

Martin still believed that. So did Vivienne, he was sure. She had just been caught in a bad moment by David's outburst. Everybody struggles with their frustrations occasionally.

He turned at the end of the street and rose in the saddle to take on Northumberland Road. Inconsiderate motorists and inadequate cycle lane provision were not the only problems faced by cyclists in the city. Regularly getting around Sheffield by bike tested your fitness and Martin's short, strong legs handled the hill easily.

He stopped at the crossroads at the top and peered warily to his left before attempting the right turn. It was not a great junction. The view to the left was always obstructed by parked cars and a high-sided van on his side of the road was not helping today. Nothing was coming from the two other directions and so Martin set off. He had reached the far side of the road when he was startled by the blast of a horn as a silver car closed down on him. It was going far too fast. The car missed him by inches but the disturbance of the air as it whooshed so close and the shock of the blaring horn caused Martin to lose his balance.

He wobbled, his left foot slipping off the pedal, and the front wheel hit the kerb. Though he had barely built up any forward momentum out of the junction, the contact with the kerb was enough to make him topple on to the hard pavement, narrowly missing a black and white bollard.

He lay still for a second, disorientated; stunned by the suddenness of the incident and winded by the fall. His bike lay, its front wheel pointing skywards, on his leg and he sat up to lift the handlebars and ease himself free of it. Martin was aware he had hit his head against the pavement as he landed but the helmet appeared to have done its job. However, he was in pain from his left hip and his left elbow. He inspected his arm. His new bright yellow safety jacket was torn.

'Why don't you watch where you're fucking going?'

The driver of the silver car, an angry-faced younger man with sunglasses perched on his close-cropped head, had climbed from his seat but stayed by the side of his vehicle. He did not appear to have any intention of walking over to see if Martin was all right.

Martin was still dazed and there was a moment's time delay as he processed the insensitivity of the driver's rebuke.

He's saying it was my fault?

'You were going too fast. This is a thirty zone,' he called back, almost despairingly.

'Fucking cyclists. You're a fucking menace.' The driver spat out his words with venom.

Martin felt his indignation rise. 'I've as much right to be on the road as you have.'

The driver pulled a disparaging face and began to lower himself back into the car but only after delivering his final shot.

'Tell me that when you start paying road tax.'

With a heavy step on the accelerator pedal, he sped away, leaving Martin to gingerly climb to his feet and brush himself down. He picked up the bike to see if it was damaged and winced at the scrape across the blue paint of the frame where it had caught the kerb.

He looked up to where the silver car had long since disappeared from view and regretted not having noted the registration number so he could make a complaint. It had happened too fast to think of such a detail.

The rest of the bike appeared undamaged, but Martin decided to push it the rest of the way to his home. It was only a five-minute walk. He took hold of the handlebars for support and limped away, a sorry figure. His left hip hurt a lot.

The sight along Spring Hill Road was always one to lift the spirits. It was an avenue of mature trees, their upper branches swaying in the gentle wind and the sunlight making dappled patterns on the road around their shadows.

It had taken a three-year fight to save these trees from being part of the city council's now infamous felling programme. It was a policy that seemed to Martin and many other like-minded people arbitrary and needless. His group, SEAN, had campaigned against it and had been part of the victory. Martin felt the sense of triumph every time he walked along the road and gazed at the trees, glorious and bursting with new life.

This time, though, he was distracted by the activity at the far end of the road. People were gathered. Some of them were wearing orange and yellow high-viz gear and hard hats. There was a council truck too. The scene was wearily familiar and Martin increased the pace of his limping progress towards it.

The closer he got, the more clearly he could hear the raised voices. Several neighbours were making their enraged point to a man in orange jacket and trousers who seemed to be drawing their attention while the other council workmen unloaded gear from the back of the truck. This was all happening outside Martin's home.

'Samir, what's going on?' he asked the man from next door as he reached the edge of the group.

'They say they're going to chop that one down,' he replied, gesturing with a nod of his head towards the large tree to their left. The one directly outside Martin's home. The one he regularly stood and watched from his bedroom window. One of the trees he had helped to save.

'Could you look after my bike for a minute?' he asked and, without waiting for an answer, strode purposefully towards the man who, it seemed, was in charge.

'Excuse me,' he said and the words proved enough to

14

stall the neighbours in their business of haranguing the unwavering man before them. Martin had become their self-appointed leader through past campaigns to save the trees.

Maybe it was the jacket, possibly the cycle helmet or perhaps it was the reaction of the neighbours, but the council man also fell obediently quiet and diverted his attention to the short figure who now stood before him.

'These trees are protected under the Street Tree Working Partnership, agreed between the city council and citizens' environmental protection groups to prevent a return to the illegal felling that took place three years ago. Can I ask what authority you have to be here?'

The council man's eyes narrowed beneath the peak of his hard hat and his hands clenched into fists inside his heavy-duty black gloves. He loathed protesters. They got in the way, with their bleeding hearts and small-minded indignation. He had a job to do and he hated having to deal with these time-wasters.

'We have an order to cut down that tree,' he said, pointing towards the unfortunate intended victim. 'It's in a dangerous condition and there have been complaints that the damage caused by its roots to the footpath are a potential tripping hazard, as well as an obstruction to people with mobility scooters.'

'Rubbish,' said a young woman from the grim-faced crowd opposite him.

Martin held up his hand to quieten any further protest. He knew the best way to deal with people like this was to speak their language.

'This tree has been examined recently and it is perfectly

healthy. It's over a century old and it will still be there long after you and I are gone. As for these alleged complaints – who has made a complaint? Can you show us these complaints? I'm not aware of any complaints and I live here. Does anyone else here know about complaints?'

The huddle behind him shook their heads in unison.

'So where is your evidence to back up your claim of an unsafe tree and complaints?'

The council man drew a deep breath. His patience was wearing thin.

'Look, it's only a tree. What does it matter?'

That was the wrong thing to say to an experienced environmental campaigner.

'*Only* a tree? Trees are the earth's lungs. Sheffield has more trees per person than any city in Europe and there are 35,000 street trees like this which remove three tonnes of air pollutants every year and store 12,000 tonnes of carbon. This city would choke without its trees and that's before we even consider the amount of wildlife they support. *Only* a tree?'

'35,000 of them, you say?' The council man nodded his head and looked up at the tree with a mocking new-found respect.

'I guess that means we won't miss this one.'

He jabbed his finger into Martin's chest. 'This tree is coming down and either you get out of our way or I get the police in to have you all arrested.'

He turned, ignoring the angry calls of the disgruntled group, to head towards the truck, which now had metal mesh fencing leaning against it, ready to cordon off the area around the tree. One of the workers wore a helmet with a curved Perspex visor and was checking over a fearsome chainsaw.

Martin said nothing. He was not a man often stirred to anger but neither was he easily intimidated. He was weighing up his next move. David's stinging criticism rang in his ears again.

It was time to show he could still make a difference.

It was time to take direct action.

'Right,' he declared to himself and returned to where he had left his bike. He unravelled the heavy-duty security chain, with its blue PVC coating, from where he had wrapped it around the frame.

'Give me a hand will you please, Samir?' he asked and his neighbour followed him to the endangered tree. Martin coiled one end of the chain around his right wrist and then reached both of his arms around the substantial trunk of the old tree.

'Wrap the chain around my other wrist and click the two ends of the combination lock together, will you?'

Samir did as he was asked and then scrambled the four-digit combination code, locking it in place. The gathered crowd watched as Martin was secured in his embrace of the tree and cheered loudly when the operation was complete.

The head of the council workers heard the cheer and turned to see what the cause of it was.

'Oh, for fuck's sake,' he cursed, under his breath, and sighed heavily.

The symbolic expression of defiance drew all the onlookers together. They gathered around where Martin and the tree were now joined and clapped, goading the council workers with the joyous support of their new hero. Some of them took out their mobile phones to preserve the scene on video. As the beginnings of a chorus of 'We Shall Overcome' started to gather momentum, the worker with the chainsaw looked to the boss.

'What are we going to do?' he asked.

A mixture of malice and despair filled the older man's expression. The situation had become complicated. Instinctively, he wanted to instruct his men to force the crowd out of the way, cut the tree-hugger free and get the job done but that would make it even messier.

'I don't need this,' he responded, finally.

'Let somebody else sort this one out. Pack up. We're heading back to the depot.'

bearer of such bad news was the hardest part of his job as the council officer assigned to assist the leader.

'Yes sir,' he said, attempting a calm smile and preparing to, again, feel the blast of Hardstaff's fury for a matter that was, most certainly, not his fault or of his making.

'Why the fuck was I not informed about this?' Hardstaff demanded, leaning his hefty frame back into his black leather executive chair with a low creak.

Perkins had been seeking to find the answer to that question since he had, with a heavy heart, realised the report was a matter that the boss needed to be made aware of.

'I've been looking into it, sir, and I believe it was simply a basic health and safety issue. The tree in question had been examined and parts of it were found to be diseased, so the decision was taken to send out a team to make it safe. Unfortunately, it wasn't realised at the time that this was one of the trees identified for felling in our previous programme and that's the reason for the public outcry this time. Parks and Recreation still have the matter in hand, sir. The tree still needs to be cut back, at least. This isn't quite the end of the matter.'

'The fucker on the interview seemed to think it was,' spluttered Hardstaff, pointing accusingly at his phone where it had come to rest by a pile of papers on his desk. 'Who the fuck is he, anyway?'

'I haven't yet established that, sir,' Perkins replied.

'Well, find out! I'm going to have his balls. If the fucker thinks he can take me on, he's got another think coming.'

***

'We defeated the council in their programme of slaughter three years ago to win protection under the Street Tree Working Partnership and we have won here again. What I would say to Cranford Hardstaff is, don't challenge the will of the people. Your job is to do what the people want you to do, not to impose the misguided beliefs of you and your cronies upon us. Listen to us because the ordinary people will never be defeated!'

Evelyn Dawes pressed the button on her TV remote control with a contemptuous curl of her lip. She had seen enough of that jumped-up bigmouth and the rest of her no-good neighbours over the last five days without having to listen to them on the local news programme as well. Who did they think they were, making an exhibition of themselves and causing such a disturbance in the street like that? What a rabble! And all over some tree!

It was a good job she didn't leave her house much these days because she would hardly have been able to get out of the door for all the neighbours with their placards and the camera crews and the other fools creating such nonsense.

Thank goodness it had all died down now. She had something important to do.

Evelyn carefully eased back the edge of the grubby net curtain in her living room with her spindly fingers to peer outside.

The wind was really getting up now. The forecast had said that Storm Daphne would be sweeping through in the late afternoon and into the evening and, for once, they hadn't been wrong. Storm Daphne! Whoever thinks of these silly names?

The bare branches of the trees on Spring Hill Road – all the trees, not just the one that had been the centre of all that fuss – were being buffeted by the strong gusts of wind and the long TV aerial on the house opposite was being bent and shaken. It was a wild evening but at least it wasn't raining.

Evelyn allowed the curtain to fall back into place and took a deep breath. She wanted to do this and a bit of bad weather wasn't going to stop her. She had wanted to do it since she had found out his address in the letter from her solicitor and had thought out her plan. It was time he faced the consequences for what he had done to her.

She drew on a long winter cardigan and then put on a well-worn thick black coat, adding protective bulk to her stick-thin aged body. She then picked up a mustard-coloured woollen hat and pulled it down over her straggly grey hair before easing her feet into a pair of scruffy black boots.

All ready.

She had left the most important part of her preparations for last. Evelyn went to the dark oak sideboard and took out an old biscuit tin from the bottom drawer, placing it on the top surface and opening the lid. She lifted out an object wrapped in a blue shawl and carefully peeled back the folds of material, knowing fully what it concealed but needing to check anyway.

As the last fold fell away, Evelyn looked down on what had been hidden at its centre. A pistol. A vintage World War Two German Luger pistol, its black paintwork chipped and its brown wooden handle dulled but still a formidable looking weapon.

It hadn't seen action for more than seven decades but all that was about to end tonight.

She wrapped the shawl around it again, almost reverently, and carried it on her two flat palms, like a divine offering, to her fawn shoulder bag, placing it carefully inside and zipping it closed. She looped the strap of the bag over her bony shoulder and set off into the faded light of the evening.

The first blast of strong wind, as she trod carefully down the steps from her front door, was almost enough to knock her over. Evelyn steadied her tiny frame and set out again. It was even wilder than she had thought from looking through her window.

She checked to make sure there were no cars coming up or down the street and stooped her head against another powerful gust as she began to cross.

The noise of the wind meant she did not hear the cracking sound above her head but, seconds later, as she had almost reached the pavement on the other side, she felt the impact of the heavy branch as it broke from the tree and landed, with a sickening thud, on the back of Evelyn's neck.

She crumpled under the weight of it, like a plastic cup that someone had stamped on, and it pinned her to the road, face down. Evelyn gazed, her eyes wide, stunned by the blow and gasping for breath against the crushing force of the limb, her cheek pressed against the road.

She attempted a pitiful cry for help but made no sound and could do no more before slipping, swirling into unconsciousness.

4

Martin opened the lounge door and was startled by the blue light as it flashed through the window, lighting up his front room. He had been baking in the kitchen at the back. The two women who regularly helped out had been so understanding, working extra hours to make sure the café stayed open while his attention was diverted by the tree protection protest, but it was time to get back to normal now and stocks of the fresh goods his customers loved had run low.

Without bothering to switch on the main light, Martin walked straight to the window to find out what was happening. He saw the ambulance and a small gathering of concerned neighbours.

My Lord! Has somebody been knocked down?

He hurried to the front door, slipping on his canvas shoes and pulling on a waterproof jacket, to join them.

The path was littered with twigs and leaves left by the storm, which had all but passed now and was offering only a few short belligerent blasts as a reminder.

A figure was being carefully lifted into the back of the ambulance by the two paramedics. Martin could not make out who was on the stretcher. Their face was hidden by the two bright orange blocks that had been fixed on either side of their head.

'What happened?' Martin asked the first neighbour he recognised. She was one of the people who had helped out in the protest.

She sighed and rolled her eyes, pointing towards the large branch which still lay in the middle of the road.

'What do you think?' she said, curtly, and moved away.

Martin stared at it, still not able to fully comprehend the situation. He saw Samir.

'Samir, what's going on?' he asked.

Samir paused for a moment, as if working out the best explanation. He appeared shaken.

'A tree branch broke off in the storm and hit the old lady from across the road,' he replied at last.

'Oh, Lord!' Martin, shocked, struck by the seriousness of it all, looked towards the back of the ambulance. The stretcher was now inside and the paramedics were securing it, getting ready to take the old lady away.

'How is she?'

Samir shrugged. 'She was unconscious when they found her.'

'This is awful,' said Martin, feeling sick.

The two of them stood in silence as the paramedics finished their preparations and watched as the ambulance was driven away. The blue lights coloured the houses as it moved steadily down the road and the crowd began to disperse.

A group moved past Martin and Samir with their heads bowed but one of their number turned back, unable to restrain his need to say what was on his mind.

'Nice one, Martin. How's your victory feel now? Looks like the council might have got it right this time, eh?'

Martin was crestfallen. Only a few hours earlier, these same neighbours had shared with him the joy of their apparent success in saving the tree and now an old lady was – what? Dying? Critically injured? It was all his fault. If he hadn't been so quick to pick a fight with the council workers, who were only trying to do their jobs, none of this would have happened.

I've been so stupid.

'We weren't to know,' offered Samir, seeming to understand what was going through his friend's mind. He laid his hand on Martin's arm.

Martin nodded to acknowledge the gesture, though it was no comfort.

They stayed a few moments longer until they were the last on the street. It began to rain.

'Anyway, I shall see you soon,' said Samir with a sympathetic smile and then he, too, turned to go home.

'Yeah, see you later, Samir.'

The rain was coming down heavier but Martin stood still on the quiet road. The branch had been dragged away, so that it could do no more damage this night. He looked up, to where it had broken off the large, treacherous tree.

He sighed. Sometimes nature reminded us that it is still our master.

It was time to head back inside but, just as he turned to go, Martin saw something, leaning against the tyre of a parked car. He moved towards it. It was a light-brown shoulder bag.

Martin glanced up and down the road. No one was hurrying back to reclaim it.

Then he thought, maybe it was the old lady's and the paramedics forgot to take it in the ambulance with them.

Either way, he reckoned, he should not leave it there. Martin picked it up and carried it into his home, for safe keeping.

***

Wearing his cycle helmet and now repaired bright yellow safety jacket, Martin pushed his bike down his path. He was already aware the council workers had arrived and cordoned off the area in preparation. This time, there were no protestors to delay them.

He had absolutely no desire to engage with the workers again and deliberately avoided looking towards them. He hoped they did not recognise him. As Martin jumped on his bike and prepared to pedal away – up the hill so that he did not have to ride past their lorry – he noticed the sound of the chainsaw chugging into life.

It had been two days since the accident. He made several calls to the hospital to check how the old lady was and was relieved to hear she was fully conscious and expected to make a total recovery. His self-chastisement had been brutal enough without having to deal with further burdens on his conscience.

Now it was time to try to make amends. Martin decided he should visit her in hospital, to apologise and to see what he could do to help her.

The four-mile ride to the Northern General Hospital was as relatively straightforward as it gets when you are cycling in a hilly city while competing for space with cars, vans and buses. Martin arrived there without ever really being in danger of completing his trip in an ambulance.

The spinal injuries unit was on the far side of the sprawling complex of specialist departments and he stopped to buy fruit after securing his bike in the shelter.

'I'm here to visit Mrs Dawes,' he whispered to the nurse at the station on the ward. He had never had to go to a hospital before and was painfully wary of making the slightest sound, in case he should disturb some terribly poorly patient.

The nurse briskly checked her list. 'Bay three,' she said. 'Just there to the left.'

Martin looked towards where he had been directed but turned back to the nurse, feeling slightly awkward.

'Would you mind,' he asked, grimacing. 'It's just that... I don't actually know who she is. I'm a neighbour, you see, and I knew about her accident, but we don't, err, know each other. Could you tell me which one she is?'

The nurse smiled. 'Certainly. Mrs Dawes is in the far bed on the right.'

'Oh, great, thank you.'

Martin hesitated and shuffled uncomfortably from foot to foot.

'Sorry to keep bothering you, but is there anybody else in there with her? I don't want to barge in if she's being visited by family or friends.'

'That's perfectly all right. No, Mrs Dawes does not have any other visitor today. In fact, we've not been able to trace any family or friends to contact since she came to us. I'm afraid Mrs Dawes has not been very communicative.'

'Oh!' Martin absorbed the information and it made him feel worse. He had only been vaguely aware of her, even though they had lived opposite each other for at least a couple of years, and had not known her name until he called the hospital for the first time to ask about the 'old lady who was hit by a falling tree branch on Spring Hill Road'. Now he had been told she had no family or friends and he had not so much as bothered to knock on her door to say hello all this time. Would it really have been so much of an effort to be a better neighbour? Shame stabbed at his already raw sense of guilt.

He said his thanks to the nurse and walked, hesitantly, toward the bay. The far bed on the right. That had to be good. Don't they say they put the most ill patients closest to the nurses' desk?

The old lady lay still in the bed, her eyes closed, looking frail and vulnerable. She wore a hospital gown and a white neck brace but, apart from that and the cannula attached to a drip, which pierced the thin skin on the back of her bony hand, she appeared fairly unscathed. That was a relief.

Martin tightly gripped the brown paper bag of grapes and three satsumas, holding them in front of him like a protective shield, as he stepped softly towards the bed. He stood at the foot of it and looked at her, trying not to be overcome by the guilt he felt. She hadn't noticed his arrival. She must be asleep. Martin briefly considered tiptoeing away and leaving the fruit at the nurses' station but her eyes slowly opened and she stared at the short figure in a yellow coat and cycle helmet.

'Hello, Mrs Dawes,' he said. His mouth was dry. 'How

are you?'

She did not answer. Her eyes narrowed into a glare.

'I'm Martin. I live across the road from you.'

Again, she said nothing. She knew who he was.

'I wanted to come to see you, to see if there was anything I could do for you. Anything at all. And to say how sorry I am for what happened the other night. I'm just so...' His voice tailed off and tears sprang to his eyes.

'Anyway, I brought you these,' he said, suddenly aware again of the bag he was grasping and thrust them towards the old lady. She did not move and his discomfort grew. He laid it uneasily down on a table at the side of the bed.

'I'll just leave them here for you.'

She stared back at him, giving up no ground in her displeasure.

He stood a few moments longer, shrinking in her scrutiny, and decided he should go.

'As I said, if there's anything I can do for you – anything – don't hesitate to ask. I can bring back whatever you'd like me to from your house, if you'd like. Oh, actually...'

Martin suddenly recalled an important point he had told himself he should not forget.

'I found a light brown bag on the road on the night of the accident and I thought it must be yours. Would you like me to bring that in for you?'

Evelyn's expression immediately changed and she spat out the word 'No!' with close to horror in her eyes. The urgency of her reaction made Martin jump.

'Leave the bag! Don't touch the bag!'

33

He was dazzled by the sudden change of mood.

'OK,' he replied, meekly. 'I'll just keep it safe until you're well enough to come home.'

She was glaring at him again. There was fury in her eyes. Martin began to back away and then turned, walking much more briskly from the bay than he had going on to it.

The same nurse was still at the station and he stopped, flustered but still in need of more information.

'Could I just ask,' he said, and she looked up at him again, 'Mrs Dawes, do you think she will be kept in for long?'

'I shouldn't think so,' she replied. 'Mrs Dawes suffered a slight concussion and a little trauma to her spine which we will need to keep an eye on, but the MRI showed no lasting damage and I think, with a little physiotherapy, she should be well enough to go home in a week or two.'

She set down her pen. 'It depends a little on how she reacts to the physio. At the moment, I must say she's showed no great willingness to want to work with us but it's early days. She's an old lady and she's had a nasty experience. I'm sure it would be a big help if you came back to visit her a time or two more, just to help her come to terms with getting back to normal. She can soon be back on her feet once she gets over the initial shock of it all.'

Martin nodded and said, 'thank you', before turning for the exit. He was not at all convinced his presence would help Mrs Dawes' progress but perhaps he should be willing to try. Until she was ready to show him some other way he could make it up to her, maybe that was the least he could do.

5

Colin Perkins gathered his courage with his papers and stood, readying himself to step into Cranford Hardstaff's office again. For whatever reason, the council leader had been particularly short-tempered of late, as if he were under mounting pressure. As the boss wound down towards the end of his tenure in just less than two months, Perkins had thought there might be more of a mellowing in the old man's manner, but it seemed the opposite might be the case.

He tapped on the slightly open door and poked his head around it. Hardstaff glanced over the top of his glasses.

'Yes. What is it?' he asked, wearily.

'The agenda for next week's Cabinet meeting for your final approval, sir,' said Perkins, holding up half a dozen sheets of paper like a white flag of peace.

Hardstaff gestured for his assistant to bring the documents to him without lifting his head from studying the other documents already before him.

Perkins timidly laid the new papers where he found a small space on the large desk.

'There was one more thing, sir,' he said, backing off as he spoke.

Hardstaff looked up, his eyes challenging the officer to make sure this new information was worth his while.

'The man you asked me to find out about – the one in the tree protest video?'

'Oh, yes!' The memory and his amusement at the news that followed the next day appeared to lighten his mood and a broad grin broke his surly expression. 'Karma was on good form with that little twat, wasn't it? What about him?'

'His name is Martin Bestwick, sir. He is the owner of a vegan café called *Better World* in Broomhill.'

'Vegan? Ughh!' Hardstaff pulled a face like he had stepped in something nasty. He hadn't much time for lifestyle choices which were not in line with his preference for eating a 'proper' cooked breakfast most mornings.

'He's also a member of a group called the Sheffield Environmental Action Network.'

'An eco-mentalist. I might have guessed,' Hardstaff added, with contempt.

'They are the group hosting the Climate Emergency rally in the Peace Gardens on Saturday, sir,' Perkins prompted. Hardstaff's eyes widened as the penny dropped.

'That's right. I'm going to give a speech about how the city council has led the way on green issues etc. The city council has spent a bloody fortune on all that stuff in the last decade or so. There's no way I'm going to let those buggers steal the moral high ground.'

'Precisely, sir.' Perkins allowed himself a smile.

'Yes, I'll put them straight. That bastard Bestwick had better keep out of my way, that's all.'

***

Martin looked out from his lofty position towards the top of the steps by the town hall and smiled. There must have been 300, maybe more, official protesters in the Peace Gardens and plenty of interested onlookers were milling around the information stalls to swell the numbers further. The fountain glistened in the sunshine and a carnival atmosphere was building, with a steel band playing on the grass and the smell of whole food cooking in the air. The weather had been kind to them, but still, he could not remember such a well-attended rally.

He clutched his 'Declare A Climate Emergency Now!' placard with pride.

'Great sight isn't it?' said Vivienne, who had moved to stand beside him.

'It certainly is. I didn't think we'd get this many.'

Vivienne nodded her head. The turn-out had surpassed her hopes, too.

'A lot of this is down to you, you know, Martin,' she said.

He gazed back at her, puzzled.

'The stand you took over the tree. I know it had an unfortunate ending, but it caught the attention of a lot of people. Anna said so many of her student friends saw you on social media and it kind of struck a chord with them. A lot of the people here are students and they are precisely the type of people we'd love to attract into the group.'

'Wow!' said Martin, looking out over the crowd again.

'It's not only the students as well,' Vivienne added. 'You gave those of us in the group a real boost, too. Personally, I found your brave decision to take a stand in the face of aggression rather... inspirational, and I thank you for that, Martin.'

She took his hand and squeezed, smiling.

He was moved and nodded gratefully. 'Thanks, Vivienne. That means a lot.'

She released her hold and looked at her watch.

'Almost time for the speeches. We're giving Cranford Hardstaff the chance to speak first. No doubt, he'll want to shoot off as soon as possible and it's a good tactic to keep the council on side as much as possible.'

Martin agreed.

'Might be a good idea if you stayed in the background for that one,' Vivienne looked at him, knowingly, 'bearing in mind your little challenge to him the other day. If he wants to bury the hatchet with you, great, but we'll let him make the first move on that one.'

Martin agreed again. He didn't want to confront the council leader face to face if he could avoid it.

Vivienne gave the introductory remarks, thanking people for joining the rally to show their support for what she soberly called the biggest crisis facing the planet. The people in the Peace Gardens took their cue to shuffle closer to where she was speaking from, midway up the steps, and the band took a break. Martin looked down on it all from the top of the steps, from where he felt he could stay unnoticed while the council leader gave his speech.

Hardstaff was there now, standing beside Vivienne. He seemed to have taken his lead from the *Countryfile* weather presenters and had decided that dressing down was the suitable look for this occasion. His large belly hung heavily over the beltline of his blue jeans, into which was tucked a red and black checked shirt, and his sleeves were rolled up. He beamed at the crowd in feigned affinity and waited for his chance to give them the benefit of a few key platitudes.

'So here is the first of our speakers today. We are incredibly grateful to be joined by the leader of Sheffield City Council, Councillor Cranford Hardstaff,' Vivienne announced.

The crowd reaction was mostly polite applause but there were a few jeers among them. Hardstaff pretended not to hear them as he waved and took the microphone.

'Thank you, ladies and gentlemen – and how wonderful it is to see so many young people here today because the future is yours and, looking around me, I believe our planet is in good hands,' he began, to another smattering of applause.

'As the leader of Sheffield City Council, I am proud of our record as protectors of the environment through our ground-breaking Green City Strategy, which sets out our aim to make this a zero-carbon city by 2050 by initiating significant reductions year-on-year and making this great city a responsible and safe place to live for many generations to come.'

'What about the trees?' called out someone from the back of the gathered crowd, winning a few cheers of support. Hardstaff ignored the intervention. Martin shrank a little further into the shadows.

'We will make Sheffield a climate-resilient city for all, offering sustainable and affordable energy for homes and businesses, modern, reliable and clean journeys for everyone and a green and innovative economy.'

From behind him, Martin heard a lone voice yell out 'Bollocks!' and was pushed forward as someone leaned on his shoulder. Whoever it was pressing down on his small frame then propelled an object with their spare hand.

A lager can fizzed through the air, spitting out some of its contents over the people in its path until it hit the council leader on the side of his head, just as he was about to outline how, under his guidance, the authority was tackling the causes of pollution. He winced from the unseen blow as audible gasps sounded around him, the lager soaking his red and black checked shirt and the microphone giving a loud whistle through the PA system as he dropped it.

'What the fuck–' he said as he recoiled with the shock, holding up his arms for protection in case the rest of the four-pack was soon to be hurled his way.

As the people closest to him recovered their own poise and turned to assist the soaked leader, Hardstaff spun to face where the can had been thrown from. There were at least ten people in the vicinity but Hardstaff saw only one face.

'You!' he growled, glaring at where Martin was still steadying himself from the push in the back and wondering what had just happened.

Their eyes met. Hardstaff hateful, Martin bewildered. Then a couple of council security men bundled the councillor away to safety.

***

Hardstaff had the rest of the weekend to stew over the assault and to plan his retribution against the eco activist who clearly had a vendetta. Two could play that game.

'Perkins!' his voice roared out before the hapless assistant had even been given the chance to take off his coat. Of course, Perkins had seen the coverage of the incident on the news and hardly needed this early reminder that it might be a challenging start to the new working week.

'Yes, sir,' he said, tentatively edging into the lion's cage.

'Bestwick's café,' he barked.

'The *Better World* café in Broomhill, yes sir.'

'I want Environmental Health around there to give it a hygiene inspection and I want them there first thing tomorrow. Tell them we've had an anonymous tip that they're breaking the law.'

Perkins looked confused. 'Tomorrow, sir?'

'Tomorrow!' shouted Hardstaff. 'First thing. No excuses. Tell them it has to be done on my orders.'

There was no margin for doubt. Perkins slipped away to make a strong coffee and consider the best way to communicate the council leader's wishes.

Hardstaff growled to himself.

'I'll have you, you bastard,' he hissed under his breath.

He had a plan to make sure the health inspectors found exactly what he wanted them to find.

***

The instruction had been clear enough. The target was the *Better World* café, which was the second from the left in a terraced row of four shops on Hampshire Street. He was to find a way to access the building around the back, where the kitchen was, and to deposit the load there.

With a rucksack slung over his shoulder, his well-worn

jeans and the grey woollen hat on his head, the young man could have passed for one of the thousands of students who lived in this part of town. He took no chances of being noticed by anyone, though, and approached the job from the back streets, which took him straight to the rear of the terraced block.

He stopped, pretending to check his phone, as he took a last look around to make sure there was no one to see his next move. It was well after two in the morning and the streets were quiet, with only the noise of an occasional car on the main road a hundred yards away breaking the still silence of the night.

Two black and two blue wheelie bins narrowed a driveway between the block of shops and a row of terraced houses, and he quickly slipped past them. It was unlit down the driveway, which was helpful. A wall, around seven feet high, protected the back yards of the shops and this presented a momentary concern, but there were also doorways built into the wall. He worked out which of the shops was his target and tried the corresponding door. The knob turned and the door opened. No lock. Trusting.

The back yard was shallow and bare, save for three bins and a pile of loose bricks. He closed the door behind him quietly and scanned the back of the shop. This might be the trickiest part.

There was a square window. It was made of white PVC and might not be as easy to force as one of the older wooden ones. He looked at the door, which was older and – bingo! – had a letterbox.

He smiled and began to think this might be the easiest £100 he had ever made.

Prising the letterbox open with his gloved fingers, he kneeled to make sure there was nothing obstructing it on the other side and took out a short length of plastic pipe from his rucksack, jamming it into the letterbox. He picked up a small stone from the yard and dropped it into the pipe, hearing it roll down the length of it and fall with a small clunk onto the floor inside. Perfect!

Reaching into his bag again, he tugged on the tied brown sack and felt the contents jump and wriggle as he pulled it out. He untied the sack, wrapped the opening over the end of the pipe, holding it firmly, and slowly tipped the bottom of the sack until sixteen mice were sent scurrying down the pipe to plop on to the floor of the kitchen.

He jiggled the sack to make sure they had all gone and pulled the pipe from the letterbox, packing it and the sack into his bag again.

At the door in the wall he stopped and looked back, allowing himself satisfaction at a job well done. He had no idea who wanted this carried out. The instructions had come from the bloke who occasionally paid him a few quid, cash in hand, to collect and distribute stuff, on the understanding that it wasn't his place to ask questions.

Whoever it was, though, he reflected, really didn't like this café.

6

Evelyn Dawes glanced again towards the entrance of the six-bed bay when she heard more footsteps approaching, attempting nonchalance again but unable to hide the slight trace of disappointment in her eyes when the sound proved to be another false alarm.

He was late. He had been there every day since the one after they had brought her to the hospital and he always arrived for his next visit by the time he had promised. Until today.

Maybe he had grown tired of coming to see her. Maybe her cold silence had scared him off at last. That had been the aim at first, when he turned up at her bedside with his hair too long, that awful scruffy beard and always in jeans and a T-shirt. Didn't he have any proper clothes? She didn't want him to visit, not at first, and had barely spoken a word to him. She had definitely not said a kind word to him – about how she was quite touched by his concern (even though it was largely, by his own admission, his fault she was here in the first place) and how she enjoyed the fact that someone was taking the trouble to spend a little time just chatting to her. She hadn't experienced that for a long time. He did all the talking.

He had even brought her some food the day before last. Made it himself, apparently. He said he ran a café, only it wasn't a real café; it was one of those vegan ones. She didn't know much about vegans, except that they seemed, from the telly, to enjoy making a lot of noise telling ordinary people why they should be vegans as well and she didn't like that. Like those Jehovah's Witness people, turning up on your doorstep unannounced and wanting to talk about God and things. They all seemed a bit too full of their own importance for her, but Martin wasn't like that. Not really. She turned up her nose when he told her about what was in the food and wouldn't touch it while he was there but she had some after he left and it was quite nice, even though she didn't normally eat that sort of thing.

Evelyn felt completely justified in her hostility at first because if he hadn't made such a fuss about that tree and had let the council people cut it down, then the branch wouldn't have broken off and hit her. She was cross with him for that and he deserved to be made to feel bad about it.

But she hadn't put him off. He would turn up, all cheery, pull up a chair and just chat. He'd always start by asking how she was, never seeming to mind that she wouldn't specifically answer him but would roll her eyes or pull a face or something. He always seemed to have been given a briefing by the nurses anyway, so he was more aware of her progress than she would have liked him to be. Then he would usually say something irritatingly upbeat to her, like: 'I hear you've been able to get to your feet today, Mrs Dawes. That's great!'

Then he would start talking about his day. He told her all about the rally in the Peace Gardens and how such a lot of people came, about how they all had a great time and about how somebody threw a beer can at the council leader. He seemed a little upset at this, but it made her smile. She never liked that man when she saw him on the telly. It's a good job for him he wasn't her councillor because she wouldn't vote for him. Shifty bugger.

Martin also told her a lot about the people who came to the café. It sounded such a happy place. She was beginning to feel as though she knew some of these customers. She thought it might be nice to go there one day, when she was out of hospital.

At times, especially at first, she would occasionally close her eyes and pretend to be going to sleep, but even that didn't stop him talking, telling her his little stories. She would always listen. Perhaps he knew she was listening really. She would never tell him, but secretly she really enjoyed hearing him talk.

She couldn't just start being nice to Martin, even though she wanted to. Her antipathy was too entrenched now and Evelyn felt she would lose face if she started being friendly to him, after digging in her heels so deeply at first. Besides, what would she say? She never got out of the house these days, apart from to go to the shop, and never spoke to anybody. She certainly never interesting conversations, not like the people at the café did. All she ever did was sleep and watch telly.

There was no point in her saying anything. He would find it boring and would stop coming. It was better if she stayed silent; left all the talking to him.

But she was starting to look forward to his visits more than she cared to admit and now she might have spoiled it for herself. He might have taken the hint and decided not to bother coming any more.

He was never late.

But then, there he was, bustling into the bay with his cycle helmet on, carrying a dark blue drawstring bag, and her heart lifted. Inside, she was beaming.

'I am *so* sorry I'm late, Mrs Dawes, but I have had a morning like you would not believe,' he said as he straight away pulled open the bag to take out two apples and two pears. He added them to the bowl on the window ledge and rooted out the grapes that were shrivelling in the dry heat of the hospital ward.

He did not so much as attempt to prompt her into an acknowledgement of appreciation for the gift and she offered none. Instead, she looked towards the clock on the wall opposite her and pretended that she was not especially aware what time it was, let alone what time he had said he would arrive. Martin was so busy with the fruit that he missed the show.

'I'd literally only just opened the café door this morning when I had a visit from the council health inspectors. They never let you know when they're going to do an inspection but they only did my place three and a half months ago and it's usually only once a year but that was no problem. I always keep everywhere spotless because high standards are so important, don't you think, and I always get a five-star rating.

'Anyway, we've got one of our gourmet evenings tonight and the visit set me back with everything I wanted to get on with because the first customers arrived while the inspectors were in the kitchen and Maggie, one of my assistants, phoned in to say she'd got child-care issues and that she was going to be a bit late and… nightmare! Anyway, we managed and the inspectors seemed happy when they left, but that's why I'm running a bit late. Oh, and there was another strange thing happened this morning.'

He finished with the fruit and collected a brown plastic bucket seat from the stack in the corner of the bay, placing it down by the side of Evelyn's bed.

'Pete from *Original Spin*, the record shop next door, usually comes to the café at about eleven for a coffee and to pick up a sandwich for his lunch. Well, he came in today and looked as if he'd had an even more difficult morning than I'd had. He told me he'd opened up and his stockroom was infested – I mean, like, full – of mice! It's a good job they didn't manage to get into my place, with the inspectors coming around. That would have been unfortunate timing. Anyway, Pete had spent all morning trying to find somebody who could lay some humane traps to catch the mice before they got anywhere else in the shop. God knows where they'd got in from!

'Anyway, enough of all that – how are you today?' Martin leaned in and smiled, encouragingly.

Evelyn had been bursting to react to his tale of woe but maintained her veneer of disinterest and pulled another of her faces.

'I'm told the physio is going well, which is excellent. Well done, you. The nurse said if you carry on making good progress, they could have you home in a week.'

She didn't want that. She was enjoying being taken care of in hospital. She was getting used to being given attention. Maybe she would have to pull back a little on what she allowed the physio to put her through.

'Oh, I was going to tell you something else before I forget. You know I've mentioned Mr and Mrs Miller from Whitham Road, two of my regulars – lovely couple – anyway, I was telling them about you, and they said to pass on their regards.'

Talking to someone about me? Strangers passing on their regards?

Evelyn was touched and though she said nothing, this apparent concern of a couple she had never met warmed her. She listened as Martin chatted and fussed for 25 minutes more and thought about the day when she would pay a visit to the café and have a cuppa with Mr and Mrs Miller.

***

Martin wheeled his bike through the front door and into the hallway.

What a day that had been! Maggie's continuing child-care difficulties meant that she had to leave mid-afternoon, not long after he had got back from seeing Mrs Dawes at the hospital, and she hadn't been able to do the late shift for the gourmet evening. So, as well as assisting Justin the chef, he'd also had to wait on all the tables. They were fully booked, as usual, and it had been hectic, though he never liked to complain about being busy.

It was almost half past ten and Martin realised, as he cycled home, that he had not eaten since snatching a late lunch. He was almost beyond hungry but decided he should, at least, have a couple of slices of wholemeal toast and a jasmine tea before heading for bed.

He unclipped his helmet and unzipped his jacket, hanging both on the handlebar of the bike, ready for the next morning. The house seemed particularly quiet after so much interaction with so many people at the café. The quiet was kind of soothing at the end of such a busy day, but it would have been nice for there to be someone waiting for him at home; someone to listen to him say how busy it had been and to tell him to put his feet up for a minute while they made him a couple of slices of wholemeal toast and a jasmine tea.

Martin sighed. There hadn't been a special person in his life for 19 months, two weeks and three days. He wondered where Jody was now.

He sighed again. Better not to go there.

The photos. Martin had been telling Mrs Dawes about his trip down part of the Cleveland Way, walking from Saltburn along the North Yorkshire coast to Scarborough in four blissful days, and he had been so happy with the photos he took along the way that he had a set of prints made. He'd described the walk and the sights – Staithes was always a favourite and he had an overnight stay there – and had told her he would bring in the pictures to show her.

For a moment, he thought he saw a flicker of enthusiasm to encourage him when he suggested it to her, but he might have been imagining it.

He was still not sure what to make of Mrs Dawes. She appeared not to want him to be there at all, but the nurses said she was always happier after he had been and that they had noticed a general improvement in her spirits in recent days. They told him he was doing a great job.

That was good. Despite her lack of communication skills, he was developing a bit of a soft spot for Mrs Dawes. He could tell she was a real character and found it so easy to talk to her. Perhaps she would be more forthcoming when she has fully recovered from the trauma and was back at home. Maybe then they would pop over to each other's houses, for chats.

The photos. Martin remembered he had put them away upstairs, in the spare room. He skipped up the narrow staircase, finding an extra surge of energy at the thought of sharing his happy memories of the Cleveland Way, and opened the door to the spare room, making a mental note to tidy up one day as he switched on the light.

Where did I leave them?

The wardrobe. He was fairly sure he had put the photos on the top shelf in the wardrobe. All his walking gear was in there and, as he opened the door, he noticed something he had forgotten he had also decided to store there. The shoulder bag he was keeping safe for Mrs Dawes. The one she had with her on the night of the accident.

Martin looked at it and the memory of her reaction, when he asked her if she would like him to bring the bag to her in hospital, washed back over him.

She was so angry! Scared, almost, shouting at him to leave the bag alone. What *was* that all about?

He thought again. Were those the only words she had spoken to him over these last few days? He could not recall hearing her speak at all apart from that, which made her reaction even more bizarre.

Martin picked up the bag and stared at it, as if trying to figure out its secret just by taking it in his hands. He sat on the spare bed with it on his knees and his hand moved to the zip.

He hesitated. He shouldn't do this. It wasn't his bag and Mrs Dawes had the right to ask him not to look inside, but he was intrigued.

He unzipped the bag and took out the one thing within it, wrapped in blue material. Whatever was concealed within was heavy and solid, like something metal. He put the bag to one side and began to peel back the folds of material.

He saw it and his eyes opened wide.

7

'I said I didn't want you to touch the bag.'

Evelyn pursed her lips to confirm her disapproval.

'But,' Martin shuffled his chair closer to the side of her bed, the legs making a squeal as he dragged them across the hard floor, 'there was a…' He checked to make sure no one was close enough to hear and reduced his voice to a whisper.

'There was a *gun* in the bag! What were you doing with a gun in your bag?'

Evelyn turned her head from him to show that she had no intention of responding to his question, like a child refusing to take their medicine.

'Why were you going out with *that* in your bag? You weren't going to do something to yourself, were you?'

She glanced back towards him, quizzically, and then realised what he was asking.

'No!' she replied with indignation. 'I could never do something like that. How messy!'

Martin continued to stare at her with alarm written all over his face, waiting for her to provide him with a logical explanation to counter-balance the many wild and frightening theories that had dominated his thoughts since the previous night.

She remained stubbornly silent.

'So?' he prompted at last. 'What were you doing? Where did you get it from?'

Evelyn sighed. She could see he was not going to let it drop.

'It was my father's,' she said. 'He took it from a German captain who surrendered to him at a town called Belzig, just outside Berlin, in 1945. He smuggled it back with him, as a souvenir. It's sort of a family heirloom.'

That was not enough information to ease Martin's agitation.

'And?' he added. 'Why did you have it in your bag? Don't tell me you were going to show it to somebody on the *Antiques Roadshow*. Where were you going?'

'I was going to my ex-husband's house, if you must know,' she relented. Evelyn was growing irritated at his questioning but could see no way of stopping it other than to provide a few answers.

'Your ex-husband! You weren't going to shoot him, were you?'

'Of course not,' she answered, a hint of regret in her tone. 'It isn't loaded. I just wanted to... scare him a bit.'

Martin's head and shoulders drooped. This was altogether too bizarre for him to comprehend at the moment, but he began to feel as if he was tapping into a deep-seated story that was sad, rather than dangerous, at its origins.

He raised his head and reached over to take her hand.

'Oh, Mrs Dawes. Why?'

Her resistance was broken. Despite herself, tears

sprang to her eyes. She wanted to tell him now. She had never told anyone before, and it weighed heavily on her.

'He deserved it,' she said. 'He ruined my life.'

Martin leaned to take a box of tissues from the top of the bedside cabinet and offered her one. She pulled it from the box and blew her nose.

'We were married for forty-eight years. He was the love of my life. We were so happy together but then he changed. He became moody, remote. He wouldn't talk to me anymore and it became like he hated me, all of a sudden. He started getting, I don't know – spiteful, nasty. He wasn't my Frank anymore. I couldn't work out what it was I'd done wrong. I didn't think he'd found somebody else, not at our age, but there was this poison in him and all he wanted to do was to take it out on me, whatever it was that was controlling him.'

Martin took her hand again. 'You poor love,' he said, sympathetically.

'He told me he was divorcing me, and I was shattered. Married life with Frank was all I'd known for so long, and I didn't know what I was going to do. I was scared – but that wasn't the worst part. We have a daughter, Tanya, and he turned her against me. I have no idea what he told her but, all of a sudden, she stopped coming round, wouldn't even answer my calls. I tried going to her house, many times, but she wasn't there anymore. I haven't seen or heard from my only daughter in more than three years and it's all because of him.'

The tears pooled in her eyes and dribbled slowly down her sullen cheeks as her tormented mind drifted deeper into the pain of the memory. Martin felt a lump in his throat and tried to swallow it down. He allowed the silence to settle between them as he composed himself.

'That's such a terrible story. What must you have gone through?' he said. 'But what did you expect to achieve by going to his house and threatening him with a gun?'

Evelyn shook her head. 'I was at my wit's end, I suppose. We sold our house as part of the divorce and I had no idea where he was living until I had a letter from my solicitor a week or so ago and that had his address on it. I thought if I went there and threatened him I could scare him into telling me where Tanya was now and then I could go to her and show her that, whatever it was he told her I'd done, it wasn't true. I thought it might be my only chance of seeing my daughter again.'

There was nothing Martin could think to say. It was such a pitifully desperate plot that to point out the inevitable futility of it would have almost been cruel. He could not imagine how low an ebb someone must have stumbled into for them to hatch such a plan. It truly must have been a last resort.

'But then I was hit by a falling branch from the tree you saved and I never got the chance,' added Evelyn, the tone of her voice changing. The resentment she had felt towards Martin in the days after the accident came bubbling back to the surface.

So, too, did his overbearing sense of guilt.

'I told you how sorry I am for what happened and if I could…' He broke off. There was no point wishing it had not happened. 'I promised you that I'll do anything to make it up to you.'

An awkward quiet fell on the corner of the hospital bay.

'You should do it,' she said suddenly, decisively.

Martin did not understand. He looked for a clue in her expression and saw none.

'Do... what? What do you want me to do?'

'You should go to my ex-husband's house and get him to tell you where my daughter is.'

He attempted to absorb the information and process it in a way that could possibly make it a good idea.

'You want *me* to go to see your ex-husband?' he repeated, needing to be sure he had heard correctly.

'That's right,' she said, firmly.

'But why on earth should your ex-husband tell me, a total stranger, where I can find your daughter?'

She looked at him and spoke with the tolerance a teacher would allow a slow child.

'Because you will have the gun, of course.'

For a second or two, the full realisation did not dawn. Then, with the impact of a cup of cold water to the face, it did.

'No!' he said, recoiling. 'No, no, no, no, no, no, no! You cannot be serious. That is such a bad idea.'

She shrugged, clearly satisfied, in her mind, with the plan.

'It's quite simple. I give you the address, you say you are an associate of mine and let him know that he's not going to get away with it anymore. He gives you the information, you go to see my daughter and explain the situation, then you bring her to me in hospital. What could go wrong?'

'What could go wrong?' Martin raised his voice so much that the old man at the opposite far end of the bay and his two visitors turned to look at him.

'What could go wrong?' he repeated in more hushed tones. 'Where do I start? Apart from the fact that you'd be asking me to do something that is totally illegal, it's also highly dangerous to threaten someone with a gun...'

'It's not loaded,' she reminded him. 'Check the magazine in the handle. There are no bullets in it. It's not been fired for seventy-five years, so it probably wouldn't work even if there were any bullets for it. It's not dangerous at all.'

'It's definitely illegal,' he retorted, though he still wasn't willing to totally concede the possibility of no danger attached.

'Oh, come on!' she chided. 'Are you telling me you've never done anything that wasn't legal? You're not suggesting to me you didn't realise you might be arrested when you chained yourself to that tree.'

'That was different,' he replied. 'That was taking a stand for a just cause. It was an acceptable risk.' Martin realised he might have implied that Mrs Dawes' cause was not a worthy one.

'I'll happily call around to see him. I'll tell him about the accident and that you want to see your daughter again. I'll appeal to his better nature. I'll reason with him.'

'He has no better nature,' she said, bitterly. 'Unless you threaten him with the gun, he'll never give you the address and then he'll tell Tanya more lies and I'll be even worse off than I am now. I know my husband. Believe me, I've thought this through. There is no other way.'

'I won't do it.' All the firm resolve Martin could muster was put into those four words. He meant it. The argument had already gone much further than reasonable logic demanded it should have.

She softened, slumping back into her pillow, defeated. She dabbed at her eyes with the tissue and reverted to vulnerable little old lady mode.

'You said you would do anything to make up for what happened to me,' she reminded him, a pitiable tremor in her voice. 'This is the one thing I ask. I know I haven't much longer in this world and all I want is to see my daughter for one last time, then I can die contentedly. This is my only chance. You are the only one who can grant a poor, lost soul her dying wish.'

She turned her head slowly to him, as if the effort of it demanded all that remained of her strength.

'Please do this for me, Martin. It's all I need.'

His heart was crumbling. He was powerless.

'He lives at number fifty-two, Silverwood Close. It's not far away. Only a half-hour walk.'

Her head sank deeper into the pillow.

'Martin,' she pleaded. 'I'm begging you.'

8

Of course, he knew it was emotional blackmail and, of course, he knew he should not have given in to it. He had always been what some might uncharitably term a 'soft touch', though he preferred to think of it as a sign of his caring, empathic nature.

Either way, Martin already regretted telling Mrs Dawes that he would pay a visit to her volatile ex-husband Frank and that he would play it her way. With the gun. Even though he knew the chances of the plan succeeding were none to zero and that he would, quite frankly, regard the mission as a success if he could get away without Mr Dawes collapsing from a heart attack and dying on the spot.

Oh god! What if that actually happened?

Much of the rest of his afternoon was spent thinking through how to fulfil his promise to Mrs Dawes with minimal risk to himself, as well as his intended victim.

It was ludicrous to contemplate doing it the way Mrs Dawes wanted him to. It was highly illegal, hugely dangerous, completely reckless, utterly nonsensical and probably completely counter-productive, too, even if – and this was a big 'if' – he went through with it and somehow managed to walk away with the information he wanted.

There had to be a better way.

The best option would have been to cut out the whole gun confrontation thing altogether. Martin knew that if he could somehow find the daughter himself, he could try to deliver the desired outcome without having to behave like an undersized mobster.

He tried Google-searching for any trace of a Tanya Dawes in the Sheffield area but drew a blank. Nobody of that name in the phone directory or the electoral register search, no likely matches on social media. Perhaps she had taken on a married name. Perhaps she had moved away. Martin regretted not having asked Mrs Dawes for any more information that could have helped his search.

Reluctantly, and after pursuing all the possible alternative options he could think of, he allowed his thoughts to return to the original plan and decided his best starting point would be to reassure himself that the gun was harmless.

After the horrifying first moment he discovered the Luger the previous night, Martin had hurriedly rewrapped it in the material, zipped it into the shoulder bag and had pushed it as far back in the wardrobe as he could. For extra peace of mind, he had also concealed it beneath a mass of spare clothing, boxes and whatever else came to hand. No amount of precautions, however, had been unable to crush his illogical fear that the police might telepathically pick up on the panic within his soul and decide this was the time to conduct a random search of his home.

After carefully removing the pile of jumble, he

unwrapped the blue cloth again and stared at the gun. The shock of seeing it for the first time was so great that he had not taken in the detail of it, but he dared to touch it now and feel the weight of it as its wooden grip slipped snugly into the palm of his hand. He raised and extended his arm, squinting one-eyed down the length of the barrel as if taking aim at the face of an otter on the 2012 Yorkshire Ecology Conference poster on the far wall of the room and curled his forefinger around the trigger.

A sensation of power surged through his body, frightening Martin and compelling him to quickly lay the gun down on the bed. He deplored violence and had told himself that he could never imagine firing a weapon at another living creature, in anger or in defence, in peacetime or at war. But he had felt the adrenal kick and had heard the whispered seductive call of the gun, enticing him to embrace the dark thrill of its menace. He shuddered.

So that's what it feels like to hold the balance of life and death in your hand.

Martin tried for half an hour to figure out how to remove the magazine from the handle before resorting to finding a YouTube video in which a scary-looking American man with a large beard performed the function with easy nonchalance in less than a second. Five minutes later, he had the magazine in his fingers and had satisfied himself, by peering at it from every conceivable angle, that it did not contain bullets, as Mrs Dawes had assured him. That was a relief. He clicked the magazine back into place.

Mrs Dawes had grossly underestimated the time it

would take to get to the address at Silverwood Close. The computer map told him it was reachable in twenty-four minutes by bike and would take him almost an hour to walk there. Cycling was the better option. He worked out he could leave his bike at a large Asda store and cut through a small park to get to the house, satisfying himself the plan would offer a good chance of slipping away unnoticed after completing the task.

He closed his eyes. How the hell did it come to the point where he was devising a plan to sneak halfway across Sheffield to threaten an old man with a gun, all at the request of a woman he barely knew? This is madness!

But then he thought about what poor Mrs Dawes must have been through. Not only did she have to cope with the shattering impact, the humiliation, brought about by the forced ending of her marriage, the man she had loved and trusted for more than half a century had twisted the knife by taking their daughter from her too. What sort of a person would do that? He should not be allowed to get away with treating her like that. Mrs Dawes should be reunited with her Tanya and if there was a chance that he could bring that about, however unconventional the method, then he would have done a good deed. He would have righted a wrong.

He owed it to Mrs Dawes to at least try.

Steeling himself, Martin made a decision. He would do it tonight when it went dark. That way, he would cut down his chances of adding to the many perfectly good reasons to back out he had already come up with. Once it was done, he would be able to get rid of the gun from his home.

That had to go. Family heirloom or not, he would come

up with a way of disposing of it so that it could never be traced back to him. That was the condition Mrs Dawes would simply have to accept.

***

Martin walked briskly along the asphalt path on the outer edge of the small park and tried to give the impression there was absolutely no reason to believe he was doing anything out of the ordinary whatsoever. No one was around to confirm whether he had succeeded in his aim but, deep within, he felt far from ordinary.

The sun had set an hour ago and the park was shielded from the housing estate that ran beside it by a thick band of mature trees and bushes, so that the only light in the park fell from the dim, far-distanced street lamps alongside the path. Martin was grateful for all the anonymity he could get. He hunched under the hood of his black sweat top, a black scarf tucked within it, and buried his gloved hands into the pouch of its front. It was a chilly enough night to justify the look and he was showing no distinguishing logos to give away his identity. He had never been one for designer gear. There were too many horror stories of developing nations and their exploitative production culture to tolerate buying from the big brands.

His cycle helmet and jacket – and the gun – were tucked away in the dark rucksack on his back and he felt it heavier than normal, weighing down his progress with the awareness of what lay within.

Close to the end of the path, he ducked into the shadows and slipped the rucksack off his shoulders, opening it and taking out the gun. He stood and quickly pushed the barrel of it down the front of his jeans, pulled his hoodie down to hide the handle from sight and resumed his walk.

The road he wanted was left out of the park and then a first right. Martin lifted his head just high enough to check if there was anyone around as he exited the park and he saw a man walking a dog to his right, but he was heading in the opposite direction and was too absorbed by checking whatever was on the screen of his phone to have noticed the figure in black.

Less than a hundred yards ahead, he saw the opening he knew was the one he was looking for and fear growled deep inside his guts. Martin crossed the road and read the street sign. Silverwood Close. He almost wished he had got it wrong and that the sign had told him he was at the bottom of a completely different street, but there it was. Only a short distance ahead was number fifty-two. This was his last chance to back out, submit to good sense and go home. He would have to tell Mrs Dawes he could not go through with it. She would understand.

Would she? He dragged back the mental image of Mrs Dawes in the arms of her daughter and pooled the last remains of his resolve. It had to be done. He trudged forward again.

The even numbers were on the right and he counted down – twenty-four, twenty-six, twenty-eight. Almost there. At forty-eight, he stopped and pulled the dark scarf over his nose so that only his eyes could be seen under the hood. He drew a long, deep breath. The detached houses along the road, neat and respectable with their tidy front lawns, were all built to the same template and had their main doors set into the side wall, providing welcome shelter from exposure to the road. Anything that might hide what he was about to do was welcome.

Martin spoke quietly to himself.

'This is the most ridiculously stupid thing you have ever…' he scolded and walked on anyway.

***

Darrell Morrison lounged on his sofa and eased a hand down the front of his black cotton shorts to scratch a sudden itch. Within reach of his other hand, next to the empty beer bottle on the laminated flooring in front of him, was the lesson plan he was due to deliver the following day, examining the underlying pessimism of TS Elliot's *The Wasteland*, but he had been far too easily distracted by the dull Premier League football match on the TV to give it a great deal of attention.

The overwhelming majority of his Year Ten English Literature class had no interest in the work anyway and, honestly, neither did he, but the GCSE mocks were coming up and it was on the curriculum. They still had a fair bit to get through, but Darrell was not panicking. He had been a teacher for almost fifteen years and could reel off Elliot's underlying influences and imagery references in his sleep.

The doorbell rang and he turned to look suspiciously towards where the sound had come from. He picked up his phone to check the time. Just after quarter past nine. Who the hell would ring the doorbell at quarter past nine? It was almost certainly not for him but Helena was working in the study and he knew she would be pissed off with him if he made her break off from what she was doing to trail downstairs to get the door herself, so Darrell hauled himself to his feet, slipped on his flip-flops and lumbered lethargically to the bottom of the stairs.

'You expecting anybody, babe?' he yelled. Helena had an important job at the council, and it was not entirely unknown for her to receive visitors at odd hours.

'No,' she called back. 'Who is it?'

He looked at the closed front door and thought about saying something sarcastic in response but stopped himself. It wouldn't go down well.

'I don't know,' he said.

'Better answer it then,' came the terse reply and he shuffled to the door.

'I'd figured that bit out for myself,' he muttered, turning the key in the lock and gripping the handle.

At first, he didn't fully take in what was before him but as he stood in the open doorway and his eyes adjusted from the brightness of the house to the gloom outside, he realised there was a short figure whose features were almost entirely obscured by dark clothing around ten feet in front of him and that what appeared to be a gun was being pointed at his chest.

'Jesus fucking shit!' he yelped. A shockwave of terror made his heart leap as, almost involuntarily, his hands shot to head height, palms open.

'OK, stay cool, stay cool,' he said, attempting to regain his poise even though every nerve was being stretched to its limits. 'Nobody do anything silly here, let's just take this nice and easy. What do you want?'

The dark figure said nothing. It appeared even more agitated than he was. It was twitching its head jerkily, as if it were desperately searching for the way out of a trap.

Darrell turned from horror-struck to confused.

What the fuck is going on here?

A new calmness settled over him and he squinted, attempting to gaze deeply into those frightened eyes. There was something there he thought was familiar.

'Is that you, Daniel Renshaw?' he asked. He lowered his hands. He realised what was going on. He was being pranked.

Darrell peered towards the street.

'Where's the rest of the gang, eh? Are they hiding in the bushes filming this?'

He stepped out of the house, cutting off the direct route of escape. The dark figure backed away, its breathing growing noticeably shallower, the shaking of the gun in its outstretched hands betraying its increasing anxiety.

'Give it to me,' said Darrell, firmly, holding out his left hand and chancing another short step closer towards the figure.

'I can tell it's only a toy. Give it to me.'

He inched forward again and the figure retreated further, until its back was almost touching the garage door.

'Come on. You're already in big trouble and it's only going to get worse for you unless you give that to me. Come on. Now!'

The figure was quaking uncontrollably now. Darrell took another short step until his hand was no more than a foot from touching the end of the gun barrel.

'Give it to me. Come on.'

He lurched suddenly forward, making a grab for the end of the barrel. The movement caught the figure by surprise and his whole body tensed in total alarm.

What neither of them expected was the bang.

The noise rang in their ears and, for a moment, they were frozen together in suspended time. It seemed to last an age, but it was only moments. That was how long it took for Darrell to feel the searing pain in his right foot, the full gruesome realisation of what had just happened confirmed as he stared, wide-eyed, at the mess of blood covering his flip-flopped foot and splashed up the dark skin of his legs.

He screamed, his cry piercing the night and waking the dark figure from his paralysis. Darrell fell to the ground, rolling and gripping his injured bloody foot in overwhelming agony.

'Fuuuuck! Fuuuuck! Jesus fuuuuck!'

The figure stood and stared. He wanted to help but he knew he had to get away from there as quickly as he could. He heard a woman's voice from within the house, getting closer.

'Darrell! Darrell! What's happened?'

He ran. The figure ran as fast as he could, before the woman or whoever else had been alerted by the sound of the shot and the screams arrived at the scene to stop him running. He ran towards the park, ran along the path, pausing only to frantically shove the gun into the rucksack and pull out his cycling gear to disguise himself, then he ran the rest of the way to the Asda. He slowed to a walk, attempting to not attract attention or suspicion from shoppers, before he fumbled the bike security lock open and cycled away into the night, as fast as he could pedal.

9

The nurse at the station glanced up but had to look twice before she recognised him. He wore a green cap, pulled hard over his head, and dark sunglasses. When she arrived for the beginning of her shift, several hours earlier, there was no reason to anticipate a gloriously sunny day and nobody had suggested since that it had turned into one.

'Hello, Martin,' she said. 'Everything all right?'

He appeared on edge, nothing like the bright and breezy Martin who had become such a regular and welcome sight on the ward for the last week or so, making such a difference to the old lady he visited every day and supplying the staff with tasty food.

He attempted a fleeting, thin smile. 'Fine, thanks, fine,' he replied, unconvincingly.

'Rough night?' asked the nurse playfully.

He cleared his throat and shuffled uncomfortably. He had hardly slept, his mind constantly playing back the horrible incident with the gun and all that blood and that poor man who, for all he knew, might be emotionally scarred for life and may never walk again. All night he had run over and over what happened and had concocted an ever-worsening list of grave ramifications, while, all the time, he had listened for, anticipating, the heavy thud of the police hammering on his door to arrest him, ever more damned by self-condemnation to believe that he deserved whatever punishment came his way.

'You could say that,' he answered.

'Is there…' he looked nervously from side to side in case there was anyone close who might overhear. 'Is there a private room where I can talk to Mrs Dawes today? I need to talk to her privately.'

The nurse realised their usual friendly rapport might not be appropriate this time. Something was clearly bothering him.

'Sure,' she said, checking the list of patient names on the whiteboard at the side of the station. 'One of the side rooms is available. Shall I get a porter to take Mrs Dawes through in a wheelchair?'

'Yes please,' he replied, pulling on the peak of his cap. 'Thank you.'

He watched from the entrance to the bay as the porter helped the old lady into the wheelchair and followed behind them as she was steered to the side room. The porter left the door open after making sure the brakes of the chair were on, but Martin moved quickly across the room to shut it.

Evelyn's face was alive with eager expectation. 'Did you see him?'

Martin was still on the move, pacing by the end of the bed.

'No,' was his flat reply.

Disappointment overwhelmed her. 'You didn't go.'

'Oh, I went,' he responded, still pacing.

'He wasn't there?' Her eyes followed his agitated movements. Something was wrong.

'He wasn't. He doesn't live there. Not unless Frank is in his mid-thirties, about six foot four and is of Afro-Caribbean ethnic origin, that is.'

She was confused. 'Did you go to the right address?'

'I went to the address you gave me. Exactly the address you gave me. Fifty-two Silverwood Close.'

'Court,' she said, almost attempting to retrieve the word back into her throat as soon as it escaped, realising in a moment *exactly* what was wrong.

'What?' He stopped pacing.

'Fifty-two Silverwood Court.'

'You *said* Close.'

'I *meant* Court.' She glanced at him sheepishly from the top of her eyes, unable to meet his incredulous stare. 'I was upset. You upset me.'

'Jesus Christ!' Martin leaned against the bars at the end of the bed and his head sank into his chest. He held the pose as he attempted to compose his thoughts, then slowly rose and meandered a few steps towards the window, taking off his sunglasses with his right hand and rubbing his eyes with his left.

'I shot him,' he said.

The delivery of the words was flat and was directed away from where Evelyn was sitting. She thought she heard what he said but if that was what he was really saying it didn't make any sense. He must have said something else.

'What did you say?'

He spun quickly to face her. 'I shot him. The man at

the house. The man who wasn't Frank.'

'With *my* gun?'

'Of course with *your* gun. How many other guns do you think I have access to? He tried to take it off me and I must have pulled on the trigger in trying to stop him and it went off. I shot him. In the foot.'

Martin turned again towards the window. He hadn't intended to be so short with Mrs Dawes but could not help himself. His nerves felt so tightly wrapped that he feared they may snap at any moment.

'Thank god it was only his foot. I could have shot him through the heart or through the head or… Oh, god!'

Evelyn sat quietly, trying to process the information. 'But the gun wasn't loaded,' she tentatively suggested.

Martin took off his cap and ran his fingers through his hair.

'Well, evidently, it was,' he replied, in a calmer tone. 'I looked it up when I got home. There weren't any bullets in the magazine – I know that because I checked – but apparently that type of gun stores a bullet in the barrel behind the firing pin thing. It must have been there since 1945 and, clearly, everything was still in full working order.'

'Well, I'll…' Evelyn eased back in her wheelchair. 'Say what you like about the Germans, they certainly made things to last.'

Martin was not in the mood to endorse her new-found admiration for the high standards of German small arms manufacture. He sat on the bed and slumped forward, his head in his hands.

'What am I going to do? I shot a man. I can't just

pretend it didn't happen. I should turn myself in. I should go to the police and confess before they trace me and come to get me. At least that would look better when it comes to the trial. I might even get a lighter sentence. I've not got a proper criminal record – just a few minor convictions for trespass and obstruction, nothing like this. If I confess now, they might be lenient. I might get out in a few years.'

Evelyn stared at the pathetic, crushed figure. 'You can't go to the police,' she said, firmly. 'If you tell them what you did, they'll want to know where you got the gun from and then they'll want to know why I had the gun in the first place and why I sent you round to that house with it and then I'll be in trouble. I'll be a whatchacallit – accessory. I can't go to prison, not at my age. I'd die there. I'll never see my daughter again and Frank will have won.'

He shook his head. 'Then what should I do?'

'This man you shot, did he know who you were?'

Martin sighed. 'I don't think so.'

'Did he get a good look at your face?'

'No. I wore a scarf over my face, like a mask.'

'Did you leave anything at the scene that they might be able to use to trace you? Did anybody else see you? Could anybody have noticed you going to the house or have seen you getting away?'

'I don't think so. There was a man walking his dog, but he was going in the opposite direction and I don't think he noticed me at all.'

Evelyn preened triumphantly. All those afternoons spent watching repeats of *Midsomer Murders* and *Miss Marple* were paying off.

'Well then,' she said. 'You've nothing to worry about. How could they know it was you as long as you don't go to them and tell them?'

He sat still, considering the point. He had tried to take precautions and wasn't aware of any potential snags. He couldn't think of any reason for the police to suspect he was the gunman. He'd just kind of assumed the police *knew* these things, like it was obvious.

'But what about the gun?' he asked at last.

'You'll have to get rid of it,' said Evelyn. She was seeing it all so clearly now. It was a plan that would even fox John Nettles.

'Wipe it clean, really thoroughly, so that there are no prints on it and get rid of it, somewhere it will never be found. Bury it. Throw it in a lake. And the clothes you were wearing last night – you'll have to get rid of them as well. Burn them and bury the ashes.'

She reflected that the last bit might have been a little overcautious, but she was in the zone.

It had worked. Martin was on his feet again, no longer beaten. No longer the condemned man.

'You're right,' he said. 'I did go out first thing this morning – I couldn't sleep – to pop some money through the letterbox at a florist near where the man lives so that they could deliver a bunch of flowers, anonymously, by way of an apology – let him know it was an accident. I thought that would be the right thing to do. I'll keep an eye open for news about him and his foot and, as long as it's not too serious, it might be best if I leave it at sending the flowers and keep quiet about it from now on. I don't deserve to go to prison. I'm a good man and I don't deserve to be punished for one mistake when I was trying to do a good thing. It's not as if I *meant* to shoot him. I'll get rid of the gun. I'll not do it tonight. I'll leave it a day or two, just until the initial heat dies down, and then I'll get rid of it.'

'That's the spirit!' said Evelyn, adding a flourish with a small punch of the air.

'Then you can go to the proper address and sort Frank out. You can take something else to threaten him with – like one of those baseball bats.'

Martin stared at the old lady in the wheelchair. Was she *really* suggesting…?

'There is no way I am ever going to threaten anybody with any sort of weapon ever again,' he said, leaving no room for misinterpretation. 'I will find Frank for you and then I will bring your daughter to you. I promise you that, Mrs Dawes, but this time we will play it my way. I'll do it as soon as I've cleaned up this mess.'

***

That morning, Pam had pushed open the door to *Pam's Petals* flower shop and the bell above the door gave her a welcoming tinkle-tinkle. Her entrance also activated the harsher buzz of the intruder alarm and she stepped purposefully across the floor of the shop to key in the passcode before it could burst into full-blown jarring siren.

The inside of the shop was cold, almost as cold as the early morning outside. Warm environments were not great for cut flowers. It was forty minutes until they would normally be open for business and it was going to be a busy day, but Pam was not stopping. She had finally given in to her husband's suggestion of the long weekend away they had been promising each other for too long, but had decided to pop in to the shop before they left, just so that she could open up and prepare as much as she could for when Aleesha, her young assistant, arrived to take over.

Pam stood for a moment while she made up her mind what needed to be done first. There was so much. She was looking forward to spending a couple of days in the Lake District, but the timing was not ideal. It always seemed to be that there would be a flurry of orders just before either of them took time off. Sod's law. There was nothing she could do about that and she knew Aleesha was perfectly capable of taking care of everything, but Pam still felt guilty for abandoning her.

A gust of wind through the open door stirred the bell into action again, reminding Pam that she should begin by closing it. Then she saw the envelope on the floor.

She closed the door and picked up the envelope. There was no name or address on the outside. It must have been pushed through the letterbox by someone who was passing by.

The knife they used to open the mail was in the drawer behind the counter. Pam took it and slit the top of the envelope open.

Inside was a folded A4 sheet of paper and, as she unwrapped it, she saw that it contained six £10 notes. She put them on the counter and read the note, which was typed on a computer rather than written by hand.

'Please could you deliver a suitable display to 52 Silverwood Close as soon as possible. I do not wish there to be a card attached. The recipient will understand what it is for.'

Pam smiled to herself. Someone's got some making-up to do.

She looked on the back of the note. There was nothing else. Strange, she thought, but whatever. An order's an order.

The bell tinkled again and in walked Aleesha.

'Morning Pam. What are you doing here? I thought you were leaving this morning.'

The younger woman pulled the strap of her handbag over her head of short blonde hair and began to unbutton her dark coat, revealing her green tabard. She walked to hang up them in the back room.

'I am. I just thought I should…'

Aleesha stepped back into the shop. 'There's no need, you know. I can manage.'

Pam sighed. 'I know you can, love, but we've got all those orders to prepare for the two funerals and that's on top of all the other stuff and I just feel bad for leaving you with it all like this. We could set off this afternoon if you need me to…'

'Don't be daft,' she interrupted. 'You deserve this break. You've not had any time off for ages. I'll be fine. Just go!'

'Thanks, love.' Pam smiled. She should trust Aleesha more. She will be fine. It was just that she was so used to taking on the responsibility herself. She walked to her assistant and they hugged.

'You know it's the Atkinson funeral tomorrow morning and I told the funeral directors we would have everything to them by three, so Theo will be here by half-two to make the delivery. He'll be picking up everything we need from the wholesalers about now, I'd guess, and there's the arrangements in the back ready for him to take out this morning. We haven't got any more deliveries to go out this afternoon at the moment, so that should be fine and then...' Pam's eye flicked around the shop, completing her mental checklist.

Aleesha smiled at her, tolerantly. 'Have you finished dithering?' she asked.

'I'm going, I'm going!' Pam replied, realising she was simply repeating details for her own benefit. She turned to leave but noticed the six £10 notes on the counter.

'Oh, and there was this that had been pushed through the letterbox this morning,' she said, snatching up the money and the sheet it had been wrapped in.

'You can do this with the Atkinson order so that Theo can take it with him this afternoon. There's an address on the sheet.'

'No probs,' said Aleesha, taking the small bundle. 'I hope you have a lovely time.'

'We will.' They hugged again and Pam hurried away before she gave herself the excuse to delay her exit any further.

10

It had been a long night. They had spent almost eighteen hours in hospital while the doctors cleaned and patched up Darrell's foot, removing all the traces of metal splinters, dirt particles and flip-flop fragments they could find and assessing the damage the bullet had left in its wake as it tore through the mass of bone and soft tissue. It was a long process.

They told him he had been fortunate. His fourth metatarsal was fractured, but it would heal and would not give him a long-term problem, he had been assured. It otherwise looked as if the bullet has passed through cleanly. They told him he must have had his foot slightly off the ground at the moment of impact, which was a good thing.

Darrell did not feel fortunate. He felt exceptionally tired from having not slept a wink, hungry from having only had a pre-packaged cheese sandwich and a cup of tea since his evening meal the previous day and cold from having shivered in the back of the taxi completely inappropriately prepared to face the chilly March day, in his thin t-shirt and black cotton shorts.

Most of all, he felt scared.

The sight of the scene of the incident, as he struggled to get used to manoeuvring himself on hospital-issue crutches from the taxi to his front door, brought it all back.

The police had clearly finished doing whatever they needed to do on the drive, but they had not attempted to wash away the large dark blotch of dried blood on the black asphalt. Though Darrell needed to put all his attention into his awkward progress on the crutches, he could not help but notice the bloody stain and the dent, about the size of a 10p piece, at the heart of it where the bullet had ripped through his foot and burrowed into the surface of the drive. He shuddered and, this time, a gust of cold wind was not the cause.

Have you any idea why anyone would want to do this?

That was one of the questions the police had asked in hospital when they arrived to take his initial statement.

Has anyone previously made a threat against you? Do you have any reason to suspect anyone of carrying out this assault? Have you, at any time, become involved, directly or indirectly, with people who are engaged in criminal activity and might have cause to resort to violence?

No, no, of course not, he had told them, an edge of exasperation in his replies. I'm a schoolteacher, for Christ's sake. I've never been involved in gangs or any of that stuff. I've not got myself messed up with loan sharks or druggies or anything like that. Maybe they were going to try to rob me, I don't know. I honestly don't know why anybody would want to do this.

He knew they were only asking the questions they needed to ask – eliminate all the possibilities for their enquiries, right? – but he truly had no idea why a gunman had appeared at his door late at night and had shot him through the foot.

That was the most frightening part.

Darrell had mentioned to the police that his initial thought was some fifteen-year-olds were pulling a prank to get video material to show their mates how they had managed to scare the shit out of Mr Morrison, but he had added that he no longer considered this likely. Would a fifteen-year-old carry a loaded gun just to prank a teacher? Even Daniel Renshaw wasn't *that* stupid.

So, who was it? He was scared and felt completely vulnerable. What if they came back?

Helena Morrison filled the kettle and flicked the switch. After helping her husband to the sofa in the front room and fussing around him until he was comfortable, with his foot up, she had decided her next job should be to make them both the hot drink they badly needed.

She leaned, her palms flat against the work surface, and bowed her head so that her long, auburn hair fell forward to mask her pale, pained face. She suddenly felt emotionally, as well as physically, exhausted. A single tear plopped against the surface. She quickly wiped it away and attempted to rally herself to prevent further tears from forming in the corners of her green eyes, but she could not. Apart from when she had to briefly leave his bedside to go to the toilet at twenty past four in the morning, this was the first moment Helena had had to herself since it happened and the first time she had been able to lower the veneer of calm support she had needed to keep up for the last 18 hours. After all that effort, she had no more energy left for holding her shattered emotions in check. She needed a good cry.

The kettle began to boil and Helena rallied herself to turn it off. She tore off a piece of kitchen roll to dab at her eyes and then blew her nose, trying to do it as quietly as she could so it would not be obviously heard in the front room, before diverting herself with the task of making tea.

Her hand was shaking. She noticed it as she stirred the tea bag in the mug, clinking against its sides, and though she tried to keep it still when she pulled the spoon out of the hot liquid, the hand would not obey her. Helena tried to convince herself it was because her blood sugars must be low but she knew she was still in the grip of the terror that had overtaken her the previous night, when she heard the loud crack of the gunfire followed by the piercing screams of her husband and when she ran down the stairs to see him there – in all that pain, with all that blood.

It had taken her what felt like an age to realise what had happened. That sort of thing just never occurs on a nice estate like theirs. She stood in the doorway and could do nothing. It was too much. It was beyond anything her mind could process.

Darrell was on the ground, on his side, his large frame wrapped up almost into a small ball. He was hardly moving, just rocking slightly, rhythmically, with both hands wrapped around his right foot, his fingers glistening in the faint light coming from inside the house because of the dark liquid which was spilling, all the time, on to the hard surface of the drive.

She stood, wide-eyed and helpless, just staring at him like he was an image from a grisly TV drama brought to life, and it was only when he threw his head back to release another loud, anguished, primal cry into the night that her trance was broken and she was jolted into action.

'Darrell! Darrell! What happened?'

It felt like a stupid thing to ask now but she could think of nothing else. *This makes no sense.*

'I've been shot! Oh, god! Oh, god!'

Helena had never seen anyone in so much distress.

What do I do? What do I do?

Towels. Try to stop the bleeding. Call an ambulance.

She rushed back inside, into the downstairs loo, to grab the two hand towels from the rail and picked up the handset from the landline, trying to control her panic enough to press the 'nine' button three times. As it rang, she dropped beside her husband and thrust the towels at his hands.

'Darrell! Take these. Wrap them around your foot and press hard. Come on! Do it!'

He did as he was told as the operator, calmly, tried to get a response from the frenzied voice at the other end of the line.

'Ambulance – please. My husband has a gunshot wound to the foot. Somebody shot him. We're at number fifty-two, Silverwood Close at Bent's Green. Come quickly, please. He's losing a lot of blood.'

By then, the first neighbours had begun to tentatively peer from the end of the driveway, alarmed by the noises that had disturbed their peaceful evenings, curious to find out what had caused it. One or two ventured further, to offer what support and comfort they could, and it was not long before the paramedics arrived to take over.

The memories flashed back before Helena again as she helped Darrell from the taxi to the familiar comfort of their home and she could see the same was going through his mind too. It was no less shocking to them for having had eighteen hours to try to come to terms with what had happened.

And now in the kitchen she gazed at her shaking hand, holding the spoon, and wondered what she should do.

Poor Darrell had been unable to comprehend what he had just been through. The police asked him all sorts of questions to see if there was any reason he could give them – anything – to suggest why a gunman had appeared at his door, but there was nothing he could tell them. Of course he couldn't. Why would anybody want to attack Darrell? There wasn't an ounce of spite in him and he didn't have an enemy in the world.

Helena kept quiet while the police asked their questions. She was beginning to realise Darrell might not have been the gunman's intended target.

The doorbell rang. Such an everyday noise but its familiarity now tainted by the trauma of the last time they heard that sound. It made Helena jump, fear catching in the back of her throat as she wondered who it might be.

She stood stock still for a moment, as if any movement might give an unwanted confirmation to whoever was outside that they were at home. Should she just ignore it? She considered the option but her rational mind kicked in.

Don't be silly. It's probably just a neighbour who had seen the taxi bringing them home and was coming around to see if everything is OK and ask if there was anything they could do to help.

Helena stirred herself and edged, reluctantly, towards the door, easing down on the handle and pulling the door slowly back until she could see who was outside.

It was a young man and he had his head bowed, checking whatever was written on the piece of paper in his hand. When he saw the door open, he glanced up and shot the nervous face peering around it a friendly, comforting smile. He wore a dark green rainproof jacket that was slightly too big for his slender frame and was holding something by his side.

'Hi. I have a delivery for you from *Pam's Petals*,' he said and raised his arm to present, with both hands, a circular arrangement of flowers.

Helena stared at it. She was dumbfounded. It was gorgeous, with purple irises, white roses, white chrysanthemums and crisp green leaves, but her heart was far from raised by it. It's a funeral wreath. It's definitely a funeral wreath.

'What the…' Helena stammered.

The young man continued to offer it to her, but she would not take it.

'Why… I mean, who sent this? Have you got the wrong address? You must have the wrong address.'

He released his hold on the wreath with one hand to check his piece of paper.

'Fifty-two Silverwood Close. This is number fifty-two Silverwood Close, isn't it?' His smile had given way to a slightly concerned expression. Was he at the wrong address?

'It is, but… Who sent this? It must have come from somebody.'

'I'm afraid I can't tell you,' said the young man.

Helena was even more alarmed. *What the hell is going on here?*

'I mean, there was no name given,' he added. 'It was just an envelope with money in it and a note saying that we should deliver the arrangement to number fifty-two Silverwood Close. I didn't see it myself, but apparently whoever it was asked that it should be sent anonymously. They said you would know what it meant.'

He offered the wreath again and, this time, Helena took it, almost involuntarily, automatically. She stared at it in her hands.

They said you would know what it meant.

The young man began to back away, noticing for the first time the dark, dried puddle on the drive but without seeming to understand what it was. He took three steps towards his delivery van as Helena stood, unmoving. Transfixed.

'Oh,' he turned back to her as a thought occurred. She tipped her head to look at him.

'Please accept the condolences of us all at *Pam's Petals*,' he added solemnly.

11

Helena Morrison slammed the door shut and stood with her back against it, as if to form a barricade against an outside world that was becoming increasingly strange and threatening.

She was breathing hard, her mind swimming. The haunting fear that had invaded her thoughts through the long night in the hospital accident and emergency department might not be such an irrational one after all. Perhaps trauma and sleep deprivation were not entirely to blame for the dark theories which had begun to take seed. Maybe there really was someone out there who wanted to get inside her head. They wanted to show her that they knew. They wanted to warn her that there would be consequences for what she was doing.

Oh, god! What made me think I could get away with it?

She became suddenly aware again of the circle of fresh flowers in her hands and was alarmed, throwing the wreath to the floor as if to hold on to it any longer would allow it to release living, growing tentacles which would crawl into her veins and poison her body with guilt. It lay on the wooden floor, a scattering of white petals having now fallen loose from the impact of being cast down.

'Who was it, babe?'

The voice from the front room made her flinch. How would she tell Darrell? She couldn't tell Darrell.

'It was the florist. A delivery,' she replied, trying to sound calm.

'Oh, yeah. Who are they from?'

Who *are* they from? That's the question.

'Dunno. There's no card with it.'

There was quiet for a moment.

'That's a bit strange. Bring them in, babe. I'd like to see them.'

He'd like to see them. She wanted to grab them and throw them back up the driveway and hope they would just disappear but if she did that, it might appear odd. Darrell might wonder what was going on.

So she bent to pick up the wreath, hesitating before convincing herself that they were only flowers and that they could not hurt her.

She took them into the front room. Darrell was as she had left him, laying on the sofa with his heavily bandaged foot resting on three cushions. He was responding to messages on his phone as she walked in but then looked up and his thumbs fell still.

'Jesus, is that them?'

She nodded.

'But it's a…'

She nodded again.

'Who the hell would send a wreath?'

She shrugged. 'As I said, there was no card.'

'What did the delivery person say?'

'He said somebody put money in an envelope and

wrote a note asking them to send this to our address.'

'No name?'

'No name. Just a note saying we would know what it means.'

Darrell felt a chill run through his body.

'Jesus!' He reached to put his phone down on the floor. 'What kind of a sick fuck…'

They were both motionless, their minds churning, their thoughts mulling the same conundrum but leading them in separate directions.

'Do you think it might be the same person? The one with the gun?' he asked, tentatively.

'How should I know?' she snapped, her anxiety showing in her unintended sharpness.

'We need to get in touch with the florist. They might still have the note. Which one was it?'

'*Pam's Petals*. The one on the main road.'

It had been so long since Darrell last surprised her with flowers that she had to assume he did not know where the shop was.

'Should we tell the police? It might be connected to…'

She considered this. If the source of all this led back to where she feared it might, it may not be such a good idea to have the police investigating it too closely. That might prove more than awkward. It could prove costly.

'Yeah, we probably should,' she replied, attempting to sound like there could not possibly be anything to hide but that she was not exactly sold on the idea.

'Maybe in the morning, eh? Maybe we've both had enough of all this for one day and we should leave it. Get a good night's sleep and then think about letting the police know. They'll be very busy anyway.'

Darrell said nothing. His mind had started to race. The big question that had tormented him all night in the hospital – who could have done this? Who would want to do this to me? – had so far failed to produce an answer, but now he felt as if he might have one. He did not like to face that possibility but could not dismiss it. Could it be?

'Yeah, in the morning,' he said. 'We can tell them in the morning.'

'It's for the best,' said Helena. 'I'll go and put this in the garage, shall I? Out of the way. Then I'll bring us that tea in. It'll be going cold.'

She hurried out of the room.

'Yeah, put it in the garage,' Darrell muttered to himself. He was barely conscious of having said the words. His thoughts were rampaging away on a frightening course.

Helena ignored the two mugs of cooling tea. She went straight to the drawer where they kept keys in a pot and picked up the one for the back door and the one for the garage side door, then snatched up her phone off the kitchen surface on her way outside.

The chilly air was welcome. It had made her feel nothing other than more desperate to get home when she left the hospital, but it was soothing now, easing the bubbling anxiety within that was overwhelming her. She sucked in a deep lungful and released it again with a low, suppressed tormented call. She wanted to scream out loud but did not want to alert anyone to the turmoil she felt. There was only one person she could tell.

Unlocking the wooden side door, she tossed the wreath into the gap between their car and the garage wall, then quickly closed and locked it again. Practically in the same motion, Helena unlocked the screen to her phone and scrolled down her list of contacts to the only entry under the letter 'Y'. Yuvraj Patel.

Yuvraj was the city council's Senior Scientific Officer. As the Head of Planning and Regeneration, Helena had worked closely with Yuvraj in her own job with the council, especially in the last months while the Swarbrook Hill project gathered pace. The Swarbrook Hill project had taken up a huge proportion of their and many other council officers' workloads over the last months – a multi-million-pound housing development on the edge of the city on which so much rested, for the authority, the local economy and for themselves personally. It was at a delicate stage and much more work was needed to see it over the line. It had been a stressful time for them all, but Helena knew it would be worth it in the end.

If it were not for Yuvraj, she would not have got the job as the city council's Head of Planning and Regeneration in the first place. She was in no doubt about that.

Yuvraj was a trusted colleague.

He had also been her lover for the last eight months.

She pressed the green call button.

'Yuvie, it's me,' she said, as soon as he answered.

'Hold on. Let me find somewhere private,' he replied. She heard the commotion of a crowded room fade, followed by silence apart from the echoing sound of his footsteps as a heavy door squeaked closed behind him.

'I heard what happened. Hell, are you all right?'

Just hearing his voice made her feel better but she was starting to cry again.

'Yeah, I'm OK. Just really tired,' she said.

'How's Darrell?'

She was glad he had asked. Neither of them wished ill of Darrell. It wasn't his fault they had fallen in love. All they wanted was an opportunity to come clean – get out of their marriages with as little damage done to their other halves as possible and make a fresh start somewhere else. That was what made Cranford Hardstaff's proposal so attractive.

Darrell was the victim here and now he had been victimised in a way neither of them could have imagined.

'He's going to be OK, but Yuvie, I'm so scared. This is all my fault.'

The tears were beyond control now. Yuvraj's heart sank as he had to listen to the sound of her sobbing at the other end of the phone. He had to give her time to let the worst of it out.

'Try to be calm. This is not your fault. Just take your time and tell me what happened.'

Helena battled to regain her composure and breathed deeply.

'It was a man at the door, just after nine o'clock. We think it was a man but he was apparently quite short and he was all in black, with his face covered. Darrell thought it might be one of his Year Tens at first. He tried to get the gun off him, but he was shot in the foot. Oh, Yuvie, there was so much blood and he was in so much pain and I realise now it was all because of me. I was upstairs, working, which was why Darrell went to answer the door, but I think it was me they were after. Darrell had to take a bullet for me.'

Yuvraj heard another wail down the line. This was hard to listen to and even harder because he could not understand why Helena had taken the blame on her shoulders.

'It's OK, it's OK. Why do you think someone would want to threaten you with a gun? No one knows about us and no one knows about our deal. No one has any reason to come for you. This sounds to me like a random incident. Perhaps this person was looking for money. Perhaps he was a drug addict or something. You can't assume this was a planned attack.'

'Oh, but I can!' she hissed back. 'This afternoon, not long after we got back from the hospital, we had a delivery from a florist. Someone had sent us a funeral wreath, Yuvie.'

'Jesus!' His blood ran cold.

'The boy who delivered it said it was paid for anonymously by someone pushing an envelope through their door and a note said to pass on the message that we would know what it means.'

Yuvraj was struggling to provide a rational counter to her hysteria.

'Just hold on, hold on,' he stammered. 'That doesn't necessarily mean…'

'It was a fucking funeral wreath, Yuvraj. The note said we would know what it means. What the fuck else could it mean? It means they know we've taken money to get Swarbrook Hill through to approval, despite everything.

Somebody is on to us. This is a fucking death threat. They're saying next time it will be a bullet through the head, not the foot.'

Yuvraj's throat went dry. His head was spinning, but he had to try to calm the situation. He had to say something to get her thinking straight again. They both needed to think straight.

'There has to be another explanation. Nobody apart from the three of us and the top man at the property development company knows about this and it's in all of our interests to keep it that way. I don't know how to explain the wreath, but it must be some sort of misunderstanding. This has to be a random incident. We've just got to keep our heads and the truth will out. There has to be another explanation.'

Helena listened but she was not swayed. She knew. He just didn't want to face the ugly truth.

'No, Yuvie. This is serious. We have to call Cranford and put an end to this straight away, while we still have time. The development will have to be radically remediated or scrapped altogether because you know as well as I do that there is no way it should go to approval in its current form anyway. People will die if we let it through. We'll be exposing them to cancer and all sorts of deadly poisons, and we could be signing off irreversible damage to the environment as well. I know we both agreed to take the money and turn a blind eye to the facts because it was the way to secure our future together and I still want that more than anything, but we can't just ignore this warning. Somebody is on to us. We have to call Cranford. This must stop.'

He sighed. 'You know Cranford isn't going to do that.'

'He has to!' she cried. 'He can't do this without us. He'll have to listen to us.'

The line fell quiet for a few seconds. She was clearly terrified. That was understandable, but he had to buy time so that she might see things differently in the cold light of a new day.

'Let's just take a breath before we do anything drastic. You've had a tough day but, I promise you, you won't see this the same way tomorrow. If you do and we don't just find that this was all about a random druggie looking for money for his next fix, then we'll… look at our options. But it would be wrong to act now while emotions are running so high.'

Helena rubbed her brow to ease the thumping chaos inside her skull. She wanted to believe that Yuvraj was right. She wanted there to be another, less scary, explanation.

'OK, we leave it for now,' she conceded. 'But unless it comes to light that this was not what I think it is, we go to Cranford and we call the whole thing off. I don't care if we lose the money. I don't care if we all end up on corruption charges. This is serious shit, Yuvraj.'

He was relieved. They both needed time to get their heads around what had happened. He had helped to steer Helena away from a potentially huge mistake, but he could not ignore the nagging fear in the pit of his stomach telling him she might be right.

'Agreed. If it looks like you are right, we go to Cranford and we get out. Look, I have to get back now. We'll speak tomorrow, right?'

'Right.' She rang off. She had better get back too. Darrell would be wondering where she had got to.

Darrell heard the back door closing with a slam as Helena headed outside with the wreath and picked up his phone off the floor. He stared at the screen, his thumb hovering over the controls, pondering his next move.

Should he call Beth? Was it too early to raise the alarm when all he had was an instinctive feeling? Could he be right?

He hadn't thought so much about it since, but the conversation, a few weeks earlier, came back to him. He and Beth were in bed. Helena was on some sort of council planners' thing in Harrogate for the weekend and Beth had been able to convince her husband that an old friend had got in touch and they had arranged a night out with an overnight stay in Birmingham. She did go to Birmingham, but it was to meet up with Darrell.

They had worked together since Beth arrived to teach modern languages at the start of the new academic year and they had been tiptoeing around a covert, energetic and tremendously exciting sexual relationship for just over two months. They had set about the business of concealing their liaisons from their partners and, more trickily, from everyone at school with the efficiency of a pair of double agents. They had needed to become inventive in finding their opportunities to indulge their considerable lustful appetites for each other. The back seat of her car at the 24-hour Asda had become a bit of a go-to. In a small storage cupboard adjoining the school library while a geography lesson was going on in the next room was the most daring.

She was eight years younger than him. He loved her firm, supple, heavily-inked body and her short hair, dyed vivid orange, which was the perfect frame for her lively hazel eyes and elfin features, and he loved every snatched illicit moment they shared together. But it wasn't just that she was much more sexually adventurous than Helena had ever been. Sure, finding such a willing partner to live out so many fantasies had provided a massive boost to his ego, but he was also drawn to Beth's lack of complication, her plain speaking, her spirit. The world was a more straightforward, happier, satisfying place when he was with Beth.

He and Helena hardly ever seemed to have time for each other anymore, especially since she started her new job. It was all work and career with her. Their marriage had become staid and dull. He was not ready for steady, repetitive, boring middle age. All Helena seemed to want was to make her name at the council. That was her passion now. Their sex life was dead. It was like she had gone off it completely.

That day and night with Beth in Birmingham was bliss.

The only time they left the room was to grab some food and a couple of drinks – recoup a little energy – in the early evening. They made the most of the rest of their time together.

He remembered now how she lay with her head on his chest, twiddling his gold necklace in her fingers and letting it fall again against his ebony skin as they bathed in the rapture of their complete shared carnal gratification.

It had become a bit of an unspoken rule that they didn't talk about each other's spouses but, for whatever reason at that particular time, he was curious. One of their other rules was that if either of them had something on their minds they should not be afraid to bring it into the open – just say it, be honest – so he decided to ask.

'Babe?' he said, tentatively.

'Hmm,' she purred, as lost as if she was floating in the middle of the ocean.

'Your old man.'

'Hmm.'

'Tell me about him. What does he do?'

She stirred and stretched in a suppressed yawn that stiffened and straightened her body down to the ends of her toes.

'You don't wanna know,' she said, sleepily.

He considered her reply for a moment.

'Yeah, I'd like to. I'm curious.'

'Honestly, lover, it's best that you don't.'

He thought about it again.

'Yeah, I would. Tell me about him.'

She sighed, irritated at being stirred from her state of joyful abandonment.

'Don't spoil the moment, Darrell. What do you want to know that for?'

'I just do. You said we should always be open with each other. No secrets.'

Beth sighed again. 'OK,' she said. 'He's a little arsehole who makes a shitload of money from a wide variety of shady and illegal activities but stashes it all away because he says it would bring too much attention on him to spend it. He's morally bankrupt, incapable of showing compassion to another human being and dead from the waist down, but if he ever had cause to protect what was his I have no doubt that he would be as savage as a hyena with a goat's carcass. Wesley is a self-absorbed, unscrupulous, uncaring bastard who lives his life scurrying in the shadows like a sewer rat. That's who my husband is.'

Darrell lay in stunned silence.

'He's a fixer. His criminal friends use him to do the dirty work they don't want to risk doing themselves because they know he's very good at it. He's clean, he's untraceable and there are no depths he wouldn't go to in order to get the job done properly. When they occasionally fuck up, he's there to clean up their mess. In the underworld, he's the man who keeps thieves, gangsters and other such scum out of jail.'

'Shit,' he said, finally. 'How the hell did you end up married to a man like that?'

'Fuck knows,' she spat out, anger and regret in her tone. 'I suppose I was in a bad place myself, mixed up in stuff I shouldn't have been, and I'd lost myself. I'd certainly lost all sense. I met Wesley through this other girl who was even more seriously fucked up than I was, about three years ago, and we got married four months later – just because I decided we should. It was as impetuous as that. I soon realised what a mistake it was. I think the shock of it woke me up. I've been getting my life back together since then and part of that was deciding to train to be a teacher.'

'But why did you stay with him?' He half-wished he had not asked about her marriage at all but was so wrapped in the absurdity of what he was hearing that he had to know more.

'I guess I'm still not completely sure I'm ready to stand alone,' she replied. 'Besides, he's filthy rich and I know where he's hidden some of it. When someone bumps him off or he gets thrown in jail, as will inevitably happen one day before too long, I'll be made. Then I'll be able to do whatever I want to do, with whoever I want to do, for the rest of my life.'

She threw back the sheets and pounced on him, her naked body astride his, leaning forward so that her breasts brushed against his chest as she pressed her hands down on his broad shoulders.

'Would you like to be the one, lover boy? Would you like to spend the rest of your life in bed with me and live off my husband's ill-gotten gains? Would you want that?'

Darrell checked the time. It was long after the final bell would have signalled the end of the school day. Beth would be free now, unless she had been roped in to supervise detention. It should be a good time to call. He might not have long until Helena came back indoors. If he didn't call now, he might not get the chance to be alone for a while and Beth might not be able to get away from her husband to talk without raising suspicion. It had to be now, or this would start eating him up.

'Hey, babe.'

'Shit, Darrell, it's been all around the school today. Are you going to be OK? What the fuck was that all about? I wanted to call you or text you all day, but I presumed she would be with you. This is just absolutely fucked up. Are you OK?'

He smiled. No nonsense Beth. He craved that all the while Helena was trying – but failing miserably – to stop herself from becoming a totally frenzied emotional wreck through the night. He had badly wanted to text to let her know he was thinking about her and that he was going to be fine, but it would have been too risky.

'I'm going to be all right, I think, babe, but there's something I need to know.'

There was something wrong. She could tell.

'Sure. What is it?'

'Your husband. Does he know? About us, I mean. Does he know?'

The suggestion quietened her. She had no reason to think so, but why would Darrell make a suggestion like that, out of the blue?

'I don't… I can't see how. Why are you asking?'

'The man who shot me, he was a short guy – about five foot tall. Your husband's a short guy too, isn't he?'

'He is, but I still don't see…'

'The thing is, I can't think of anybody I know of who might even own a gun, let alone anybody who might use one. I've been thinking about this. I don't know of anybody who has reason to come to my house at night and threaten me with a gun and then threaten me again today. Somebody sent a funeral wreath to my home, Beth. No way of tracing who it came from, just some message about I should know what it means. I think I do know what it means. I think it means they know where I live and that they're coming for me and they aren't afraid to kill me. I think it's your husband. You told me yourself he's got it in him to do anything if somebody is trying to take away what's his. I think he's found out about us. I think this is a final warning to me.'

Beth listened intently, digesting the possibility Darrell could have worked it out correctly and that he was in danger. Moreover, if Wesley knew, they were both in danger. He was no killer. He was the one who followed in the trail of killers and fed off their carrion, but he didn't pull the trigger himself. Had he cause to, however, she had no doubt that he was capable.

'I think we'll have to cool it, babe,' Darrell added. 'We won't have much of a choice for a while because I'll be stuck here with my foot up, but we might have to lay off seeing each other for some time beyond that – at least until we know it's not him. You have to find that out. Be careful but you'll have to see if he knows.'

She was calm but knew this was serious enough for her to be concerned. She would have to tread carefully but she had to find out.

'Yeah, I will. Stay safe.'

Darrell heard the back door opening. Helena was coming back.

'Gotta go, babe. Stay in touch, yeah?'

He hung up and put his phone on the floor just as Helena walked back into the front room with a painted smile and two mugs of cold tea.

12

Evelyn sat up in the hospital bed, propped up by pillows that absorbed her frail body as if it was a delicate ornament being prepared to be packed and posted. On her head was a pair of large black headphones, making her look like the world's least likely DJ, and she stared, wide-eyed, through old-fashioned plastic-rimmed spectacles at the screen of a phone.

It was Martin's phone. They were also his headphones. He had brought them with him to show her the regional news report of the shooting two days earlier which had left local residents shocked and frightened, though not so shocked and frightened that they were unable to share how they felt with a TV audience.

Martin was still nervous about the whole business and felt exceptionally wary about giving anyone any reason at all to believe that he was connected with the shooting. He had read that the man's injuries were not considered serious, which was a relief, though the high-ranking police officer they rolled out to face the cameras stressed that the authorities were treating the incident extremely seriously, which was worrying.

He hadn't wanted to worry Mrs Dawes, but he thought

she would be interested to see the report for herself. He also hoped it would underline to her the importance of not sharing information, inadvertently or otherwise, which might lead to others suspecting they were involved. It had to stay their dark little secret. He hoped he could rely on Mrs Dawes' discretion but was not completely sure. They still did not know each other that well.

The short recording ended with a grave-faced reporter handing back to the studio and Mrs Dawes kept looking at the screen, as if wondering what would happen next.

'Would you like to watch it again?' Martin asked.

She saw him gesture to attract her attention and saw his lips move but that was it.

'What?' she called back to him, far louder than was necessary.

'Would you...'

She screwed up her face. 'I can't hear you,' she yelled and the nurse seeing to the lady in the bed opposite turned to give Martin an amused glance.

He smiled back, apologetically, and stood to ease the headphones off Mrs Dawes' ears.

'I wondered if you would like to watch it again.'

She stared back at him, quizzically, still holding the phone in front of her with two hands.

'Don't we have to wait until the next time the news is on?'

Martin found the suggestion sort of charming but did not want to show it and risk embarrassing Mrs Dawes with his reaction.

'No, it's all there on demand, through the website.'

'Really?' She gripped the phone and looked at it in

wonder. 'What else can you watch on this?'

'Anything really,' replied Martin, not expecting to be the standard-bearer of modern technological achievement with someone who, it seemed, was stuck in a bygone era. 'TV shows, films, documentaries – anything. You can access lots of other stuff through YouTube or listen to music as well, if you like.'

'What type of music?'

'Any type. Anything you like. It's all available.'

Evelyn was open-mouthed. She had observed people constantly paying attention to their mobile telephones but had been too wrapped up in disdain for them to really question why everyone seemed to find them so fascinating. This was a revelation.

'All on this little thing? Well, I'll be...'

Martin leaned forward to reclaim the phone from her bony fingers.

'Anyway, what did you think?'

'About what?'

'About the news. The report.'

She waved dismissively at him. 'It'll all blow over.'

He exhaled and looked to the skies. 'I wish I had your confidence. The police officer said they were taking it extremely seriously.'

'You see it on the news all the time,' she added. 'Things happen and everybody makes a big fuss for a few days but unless they catch somebody straight away, that's the last you hear about it. Everybody forgets about it and they move on to something else.'

Martin was not prepared to accept that the situation was quite so straightforward but had to admit to himself that she might have a point. He knew from his involvement with the environmental group how important it was to constantly press their issues when they were supporting a major campaign, or the attention span of the general public soon wavered. Commitment was in short supply these days. Maybe that might work in his favour this time.

'I hope you're right.'

'Of course I am,' she said with certainty. 'Have they said anything about the man's injuries yet?'

He winced. The screams of that poor man still echoed around his brain like a trapped bird struggling to escape a small room.

'All I've seen is that he's not seriously hurt. The report in the paper said he's expected to make a full recovery. I just wish there were something I could do.'

Evelyn shook her head. 'There is nothing you can do. Not without giving yourself away and I don't think that's what either of us want, is it?'

'No, you're right,' he conceded. 'I did send him flowers the next day, like I told you. I was careful to make sure there was nothing that could lead them to working out where the money had come from. I even wore gloves to make sure there were no fingerprints. I felt so low, like a criminal, but at least the flowers might make him understand that I didn't mean to hurt him. I hope so.'

'That's a lovely thing to do, but leave it there,' said Evelyn, sternly. 'Don't get involved anymore and the trail will go cold. You keep your head down, the man will get better and the police will go back to looking for proper criminals, just you see.'

Evelyn crossed her arms and appeared pleased with

herself for quickly putting their situation back into perspective. Martin was less convinced, his lingering concern betrayed by his silence.

'When are you going to find my Tanya for me? That's what I really need to know,' she asked, suddenly vulnerable again.

He looked up and saw the sorrow in her eyes.

'I promise I will track her down soon,' he said, reaching out to take Mrs Dawes' hand. 'I just need to take care of a few things from the other night first.'

He knew that she knew the priority was now to make sure neither of them could be implicated in the shooting, but he recognised the pain that caused.

'I tried looking for her on the internet the other day, but it was only when I started searching that I realised I knew nothing about her. Tell me about Tanya. What is she like?'

As he put the question, Martin realised it was a gamble. He had risked sending Mrs Dawes into a deeper melancholy, but he saw the twinkle in her eyes and the edges of her mouth curl up in fond recollection and he knew it was the right thing to ask.

'She was such a lovely little girl,' she said, her thoughts drifting back to a lost time.

'Tanya was our only child and we loved her so much. She was perfect – a joy – from the day she was born. People always warned me – you know what people are like, always looking to drag you down with gloom and doom – they warned me that when she grew up from being the most adorable little girl into a teenager that she would change and that me and her would clash like nobody's business, but it never happened. She grew up into a gorgeous, loving, considerate young woman and we were so close. We were like sisters.

'Oh, and she was so hard-working. When all her friends were getting distracted by boys and all that, Tanya made up her mind that she was going to put everything into her school work so that she could get top grades and go to university to learn to be a solicitor. It upset her that there was so much unfairness in the world and she decided to study law so that she could go on to do something about that in her working life. That was my Tanya in a nutshell. Always putting others first.

'She worked her way up to become one of the partners of a firm in Manchester – only a small firm, but they took on a lot of work for practically nothing to help people and, you know, charities and stuff who couldn't afford to pay big legal fees, but that was what she wanted to do. Then she started seeing one of the other partners at the firm, a nice lad called Ryan, and I've never seen her as happy as she was the time she brought Ryan over to Sheffield to meet us. They were talking about getting married and they had plans to take off and have such adventures. You know what young people are like these days. The world is their playground. Anyway, that time she brought Ryan to meet us was the last time I saw her.'

Martin watched the light in her eyes die. She seemed to melt into her pillows before him.

'I still don't know what Frank told her to turn her against me and I have no idea why he would do such a thing. She just cut me off, like I was a disease. She never answered my calls on the phone, nothing. No explanation. I even caught the train to Manchester to go to the last address I had for her, but the house was empty and there was a 'For Sale' sign in the garden. She and Ryan must have moved in together. Perhaps they're married now as well. They never invited me.'

She stared desperately at Martin, pleading her case. 'I did nothing wrong. I was so happy for her – for both of them – so why did she believe whatever her father told her I did without even asking for my side of the story? Why did he have to tell her whatever terrible things he said? If he thought our marriage was over, fine. It hurt me and it wasn't what I wanted, but I would have given him his divorce. He didn't have to do the rest. He didn't have to break my heart as well by taking my Tanya from me. I don't understand. How could they all be so cruel? If only I could find her and talk to her, I know we could make it right again.'

All through her agonised tale, Martin had squeezed Evelyn's hand but now he had to release it so that he could wipe away his tears.

'I promise you I will do everything I can to help you find Tanya,' he said, with as much assertiveness as he could muster.

'I know you will,' she smiled at him. 'You're a good man, Martin.'

They sat, each reflecting on the emotional drain of the moment they had just shared. A few days ago, before the accident with the tree branch, they did not know each other at all. Now they shared a bond – and not only one of mutual complicity in the shooting of an innocent man. It was much more than that. They had tapped into each other's souls.

'Anyway,' Evelyn suddenly declared, breaking the spell. 'That's my story – what about yours? I know about your café and your friends in the group, but I've never heard you mention about your home life. Is there a Mrs Bestwick?'

He grinned, amusing himself with the thought.

'No, there isn't,' he said, dismissively.

She was not about to let it drop. There was so much she had given up about herself that she felt it gave her the right to push back the boundaries of his privacy. Caring less about the niceties was one of the privileges of being old.

'Is there anyone special then?'

Martin hesitated.

'I was in a relationship. A serious relationship, but we split up. About a year and a half ago – just over a year and a half ago.'

It hurt to say the words. He never talked about it.

'I see,' she said. She could tell the feelings were still raw, but she wanted to show she cared.

'What was her name?'

'Jody,' he replied. '*His* name was Jody.'

'His?' She was startled. She hadn't expected that.

'So you're…'

He nodded confirmation. She fell quiet.

'Oh!'

Martin allowed the silence to gather. He had to let her come to terms with the knowledge in her own way. Different people reacted in different ways. Older people sometimes found it harder to accept. They saw things through another perspective in their day.

'I see,' Evelyn said at last. 'Well that's…'

She offered no further indication as to exactly what she thought it was for a few more seconds, but then smiled and reached with her left hand to where he still cupped her right hand on the bed and tapped him reassuringly.

'That's perfectly fine. I had no idea. I don't think I've ever known a… you know. But that's… fine.'

Her awkwardness was endearing, but Martin believed that she had negotiated what was, for some, the difficult first step of understanding.

'Good,' he replied.

'I wouldn't have been able to tell,' she confessed, as if she perhaps should.

'I've never felt the need to wear my sexuality like a badge,' he said. 'It's just who I am.'

'Right.' She nodded, pleased with herself for how well she had accepted this. It was the first time she had experienced such a conversation first hand. People were far less up front about it in her day. There was an invisible barrier of persecution and misunderstanding which discouraged such honesty and that was the way it was.

'Good for you,' she said. 'It's who you are. That's all that matters. If anybody has a problem with that, well they can just… fuck off!'

Her unexpected burst of candour stunned Martin momentarily. It felt strange to hear that word coming from her mouth. But then he laughed out loud and they giggled together, feeding off each other's inability to stop like a couple of teenagers on the back row of a bus. They were helpless.

They laughed until it hurt. Evelyn took off her glasses to dab at her damp eyes. She hadn't laughed like that in so many years.

Martin, when he could muster the control to make his body do as he wanted it to again, stood and planted a soft kiss in the middle of her forehead. He looked at her with real affection.

'Mrs Dawes,' he said, 'you are priceless.'

13

It was not the Environment Agency's fault. Their report was no drier or more tedious than most of the other reports that ended up on his desk. It was not as if he did not appreciate their perspective on the issue of groundwater protection. Its findings were truly relevant to the report he was due to present to the council in a matter of days. He had to stay on top of the latest official guidance if he were to provide a compelling argument for why the Swarbrook Hill project should be allowed to progress smoothly through the planning processes, but the words of the report simply could not complete the journey from the eye to the brain.

Yuvraj Patel stood up from his armchair and meandered slowly to the French doors. He pulled open one of the heavy full-length curtains to gaze out into the dim half-light that had settled over his back garden and sent a startled fox scurrying away in retreat.

He barely noticed the fox's flight. He stood for minutes, not moving at all, looking but not seeing. His mind was elsewhere. It was certainly not on the Environment Agency report.

The phone call with Helena that afternoon had been

long and difficult. It would have been better if they had been able to meet face to face, so that he would have been able to physically comfort her and attempt to calm her with his presence, but she had not wanted to leave Darrell alone. She said she feared that the gunman would come back.

Helena sounded like her nerves had gone through the shredder. At times, she was barely making sense, going round in circles about how 'they' were on to their plan and about how 'they' would clearly stop at nothing to prevent them from allowing Swarbrook Hill to proceed. Not only was she unmoved in her opinion that they ought to go to Cranford Hardstaff straight away and demand that he immediately end their arrangement with the developers and damn the money, she was now talking in terms of fleeing the country until it was safe to return.

Clearly, Yuvraj's suggestion that the situation would look so much better after a good night's sleep had been intrinsically flawed. Neither of them had been able to sleep.

Yuvraj still believed that to call it off would be a mistake. It would blow apart all the plans they had laid, for the two of them, because they needed that money. Proclaiming their love to the world and heading into the sunset to start a new life together would be a gloriously romantic gesture but they could not live on nothing. The money they would make as part of Hardstaff's scheme was crucial.

At one point, at least forty minutes into the call, in his exasperation he had suggested she was being paranoid. He immediately regretted using the word. It was not so much the anger it provoked. It was the silence. Worse still, it was silent anger. He could tell. He tried to withdraw from the word and convince her that he hadn't meant it, but it was too late. The remaining fifteen minutes of the conversation were frosty, as well as difficult, and had brought no compromise over what they should do next. They had only agreed to discuss it all again tomorrow. A further deferral was the best he had been able to manage and he still had no idea what he was going to say to Helena tomorrow which could possibly make this whole situation better.

He dragged the curtain closed again and ambled back to his chair, picked up the blue and white covered report from where he had left it open over the chair arm and sat down. In the next room, he could faintly hear the trashy TV show his wife and their two children were watching together and, just for a moment, he wanted nothing more than to join them as they abandoned themselves in the artificial unimportant dramas of whatever awful soap opera was drifting in front of their consciousness. It seemed a far simpler option.

Instead, he opened the report to attempt to read it again but quickly gave up again and laid it to rest on his rounded belly. It was hopeless.

The lounge door was nudged open wider and in came the family's border collie, trotting enthusiastically to his chair before sitting in front of him, ears pricked, demanding his attention.

'Hey, Buddy.' He leaned forward and tousled the dog's black and white head. 'What are you after then?'

He need not have asked. Yuvraj looked at the clock. How did they know, to such a degree of accuracy, it was that time of the evening every day?

'Oh, I see,' he said. 'Come on then.'

The dog jumped to its paws again and trotted off towards to the front door.

Yuvraj rose slowly to his feet. *It might be a good time to go for a walk*, he thought. *It might clear my head.*

***

The rest of the afternoon at the café had been busy after Martin got back from visiting Mrs Dawes at the hospital and he was weary. Perhaps the last couple of days had taken more of a toll than he had realised.

He wheeled his bike through the front door of his home and into the hallway but did not take off his helmet and jacket this time. He was heading straight back out. It was time to get rid of that damned gun.

After the incident, Martin had decided the wardrobe in the spare room was not a secure enough hiding place for the pistol and so he headed upstairs to get the stepladders, so that he could retrieve it from the loft.

He began to climb the steps but then stopped and climbed down again. Gloves. The previous evening, before putting it in the loft, he had rubbed at every millimetre of the gun with a cloth to convince himself, as far as he could, there was no trace of evidence to suggest he had ever touched it, let alone fired it. He also stuffed the clothes he was wearing that night into a black plastic bag and had pushed them into the loft too. The realisation that spots of the man's blood were spattered on both legs of his trousers and his shoes had turned his stomach. He would burn them all when he had the chance but, for now, it was the only all-black clothing he had and so he reasoned that he might as well wear them again for this next stage of the clean-up operation.

Martin pulled on the black thermal gloves he wore for winter cycling and climbed the steps again so that he could reach and push open the loft hatch.

With the gun, still wrapped in the blue material, in his rucksack alongside a garden trowel, he reversed the bike out of the hallway, ready to set off. He had decided Ecclesall Woods would be the best place to get rid of it. There were other candidates closer to home – Sheffield was well blessed with parks and woodlands – but he reckoned Ecclesall was the right mix of far enough away, had lots of secluded areas distanced from well-trodden paths and was quiet enough at this time of the evening to suit his purposes.

At the entrance to the public footpath, he stopped and dismounted. He was on a road that cut through the middle of the woods, with the imposing height of the trees on either side and the absence of street lighting making it feel desolate and intimidating, even though major clusters of houses were not far away. Martin was not spooked by it, though the blood was whooshing in his ears as the adrenaline flooded his body. This was just what he wanted. He checked both ways to see if any cars or pedestrians were around to notice him before turning off the front and rear lights on his bike and stripping off his helmet and bright yellow safety jacket, storing them away in the rucksack.

He pulled up the hood of his sweat top but did not cover his face with the scarf yet, just in case he met anyone on the path before he reached the point where he would disappear deeper into the woods to do the deed. He did not want to risk alarming anyone coming in the opposite direction with his full assassin get-up. If he did see anyone, he would have to abandon the operation for tonight. He could not take that chance.

There was no one around. He had got lucky. Martin checked all around him again and pushed his bike over the marshier ground and fallen branches to where he could dig unobserved and bury the gun where it would, hopefully, remain undiscovered for centuries.

He struggled through the debris and between the trees until he reached what he felt might be as good a place as any. He lay down his bike and walked on, a few paces deeper. Martin took a last look around and pulled up the scarf to cover most of his face. There was no sign of any living being, nor a sound other than the creak of the trees as the wind whistled and bent their upper reaches.

Taking a deep, fortifying breath, he pulled the rucksack off his back and kneeled on the ground to take out the trowel. The soft earth yielded willingly as he dug and he piled it neatly beside the ever-deeper hole, thrusting and scraping at the ground with almost frantic progress in his desire to complete the task as quickly as possible until he had dug so deep that he had to lay with his cheek practically against the surface to stretch and reach the bottom.

Breathing heavily and sweating from the burst of exertion, he rose on his knees and put his hands on his hips to allow himself a few moments of recovery. He looked down on the hole he had made. That should do the job. Once he had covered it over again, there should be no reason that he could think of why the ground would ever accidentally give up its secret. He laid the trowel down beside him and reached back into the rucksack, pulling out the bundle of blue material and unwrapping it to reveal the pistol.

Even though the sight of it no longer shocked him, he remained wary of it, as if it had an aura of destructive power. Martin certainly knew well enough now what it was capable of. He picked it out of the cloth and gripped it by the handle again, keeping his index finger well away from the trigger this time. He held it to eye height and twisted it in his hand, so that the light of the half-moon through the still bare branches of the trees glinted off the dark metal while he inspected its form for one last time. He shuddered, recalling what happened the last time. Time to bury this thing for ever.

Martin shoved the material into the rucksack but his heightened senses alerted him to another sound. He froze. It was coming from behind him, a shuffling, sniffling noise – like an animal. He twisted quickly, alarmed, and there, three feet away, was a black and white face. A dog. It looked straight at him, curious about what it had found but showing in its eyes that it was happy enough to treat it as a potential friend.

The surprise made Martin leap to his feet, gun still in hand. He heard the voice. A man's voice.

'Buddy, where the bloody hell are you going?'

As Martin spun, terrified, to where the voice had come from, he was suddenly hit by the stark white light of a torch, making him squint and pull up both arms to shield his eyes from the dazzling glare. He was held, exposed and powerless, in the beam for no more than a few seconds before it was extinguished again, leaving him back in the dark with the disorientating flash spots from the torch filling his vision.

He heard the voice again, yelping in panic, followed by the sounds of stumbling steps as the man fled through the trees as fast as he could or dared. The dog stayed for a moment or two longer, staring at the stranger, before seeming to realise that this newcomer was not, apparently, going to make friends and that the person who was its friend was rapidly getting further away, so it set off after the man.

Martin was left alone again, his eyes readjusting to the natural light and his mind adjusting to what had just happened.

Get away from here!

He scooped up the rucksack and threw the gun and trowel into it, attempting to fasten its clips as he scrambled back towards his bike, away in the opposite direction from where the man and his dog had fled.

Out of the woods and back on the main road, Yuvraj Patel darted behind the cover of a parked van and peered tentatively around it to make sure he was not being pursued.

He was blowing hard, from a mixture of agitation and being totally unused to taking a late-night dash through the woods, and there was mud on his hands and knees where he had twice tripped and fallen in his desperation to get away.

Buddy had quickly caught up and cantered easily to

join his master. He panted slightly, his tongue lolling beyond his lower jaw, but his eyes said 'That was fun! Can we do that again?'

Yuvraj was in no hurry. He stared, wild-eyed, towards the footpath entrance and pressed himself against the van for security. He stayed there for ten minutes, having to urge Buddy to stay quiet three times, before he began to feel reassured that the mad gunman was no longer on his trail.

He unzipped his coat and reached for his phone in the inside pocket. It was late and it was breaking their code of when they could and should not call each other but he had to speak to her now.

'Hello, Helena Morrison speaking,' she said flatly as she answered. He knew she was well aware who was calling. His name would have popped up on the screen. Darrell must be within earshot and she did not want to give anything away.

'It's me,' he confirmed.

'Oh, hi!' Helena replied, keeping up the pretence. 'Just hold on a sec while I move away from the TV.'

He heard her stand and start to move and heard her say 'Just council business, won't be long,' to Darrell as she closed the door behind her and headed up the stairs.

'Yuvraj, what the fuck?' she said with irritation as he heard her close another door.

'I know. I'm sorry.'

Something was wrong. She picked up on his anxiety down the line.

'What is it? What's happened?'

He was relieved he did not have to break through her

annoyance before telling her.

'He came for me as well,' said Yuvraj in hushed tones. 'He tried to kill me.'

Helena felt her heart leap into her throat but said nothing.

'He must have been watching me to get to know where I always take the dog for a walk at the same time of night and he was waiting for me in the woods. I saw him standing there with the gun in his hand and I swear he must have been ready to pull the trigger but I think I startled him by shining a torch in his face and I was able to get away. He was a short guy dressed completely in dark clothing and had a scarf or a neckerchief to hide his face. It had to be the same guy.'

The recurrence of the nightmare sent Helena dizzy and she fell into her office chair before her legs gave way under her.

'Oh god, Yuvie! Are you all right?'

Yuvraj glanced down at his palm. There was a streak of blood among the mud. He must have cut it on a stone or whatever as he fell.

'Yeah, I'm OK,' he said. 'Helena, I'm so sorry for suggesting that you were overreacting. You're right. This has to end now. First thing in the morning, I'm going to phone Cranford and tell him that we're out.'

14

They were definitely on the same page now. No amount of money was worth taking an assassin's bullet for.

Helena was still reluctant to leave Darrell alone in the house but Yuvraj argued that it was of paramount importance that they presented a united front to show Cranford they were absolutely not going to change their minds. She could see the sense in that. To reinforce the point, they decided they would meet at a pub roughly midway between their two homes and travel on together.

At the end of a jittery night, Yuvraj made the call first thing. Hardstaff was not happy. He did not want to give up his Saturday morning, but Yuvraj persuaded him that it was an issue of the utmost urgency which could not be resolved over the phone and he gave in. The closer it came to the key decision day for Swarbrook Hill, the granting of approval from the planning committee, even the nerves of the unshakeable Cranford Hardstaff were being stretched. There was so much at stake. No detail should be overlooked. Nothing should be taken for granted.

He said they should meet him at the Botanical Gardens at ten.

Helena and Yuvraj stood in front of the middle of the

three domes of the Victorian glass pavilions and waited. They had arrived two minutes early for the meeting and it was already fifteen minutes past the agreed time. Cranford was playing a little power game, no doubt.

Helena shivered, her hands thrust deep in the pockets of her dark grey winter coat, partly through apprehension but mostly because of the icy wind that had torn in from the north overnight, sending temperatures dipping. She stamped her feet, cursing herself for not having worn thicker socks, as she glanced repeatedly towards the entrance to the gardens.

'Where the hell is he?' she asked, not expecting a reply, and risked exposing her fingers to the biting gusts to tug her purple bobble hat further down over her ears.

Yuvraj was trying not to show how much he felt the cold, but he could not control the agitation that had been building within him all night and had started to consume him since he made the phone call. He felt it was his responsibility to take the lead in presenting their demands to Cranford and had been rehearsing what he would say over and over in his head but, because he was well aware how intimidating the veteran leader could be, he feared he might fluff his lines. Still, it had to be done.

He looked at Helena as she continued her foot-stamping jig, like a frigid flamenco dancer, and wanted to take hold of her so they could share what remained of their body warmth, but they dare not risk being seen. All their secrets had to stay that way.

A large figure emerged around the corner of the far pavilion and the chill cut deeper into Yuvraj.

'He's here,' he said.

Mark Eklid

Helena turned to see for herself.

'Thank god for that.'

Hardstaff was in no hurry. He wore a heavy black overcoat with a fur collar and his stern face peered from beneath a dark fur Cossack hat, making him look like Stalin's unkind uncle. They watched as he moved closer to them with the malignant threat of an advancing iceberg, their trepidation mounting as the distance closed between them, until he stood, large and imposing, in front of them.

'This had better be important,' he announced, making it clear they would not be offered an apology for having been kept waiting.

'It is,' Yuvraj replied, mustering his resolve. He checked around him for anyone close. 'Is this really a good place to talk? It's a public space.'

Hardstaff frowned. His predator instincts smelled fear.

'Hiding in plain sight,' he growled. 'Nobody bothers you here. They're too busy looking at the plants.'

A broad, discomfiting smile spread slowly across his fat face. 'Besides, I like it here. It's nature - the best kind of nature. Everything is kept together in orderly groups, there are proper paths and there are labels on everything so that you know what you're looking at. We should charge people to get in. Remind me to raise that with Parks and Recreation.'

Hardstaff turned and set off down the steps towards the path that split the large lawn in front of the pavilions.

'Come on, let's walk and talk,' he ordered. 'It's freezing and I don't want to spend all day in this fucking place.'

Yuvraj scurried after him and Helena followed, though

126

less urgently.

'There have been developments, Cranford. You were aware that a man with a gun appeared at Helena's door on Wednesday and shot her husband?'

Hardstaff ambled along the path, his attention seemingly more focused on the fountain and the faint sound of the water that trickled from its tiers.

'I heard, yes.'

'Well, the same gunman – we think it was the same gunman – came after me yesterday. He was waiting for me while I was out walking the dog.'

Yuvraj paused, expecting the impact of the news to strike home. Hardstaff sniffed the air and looked to the skies for a sign of rainfall.

'And…' he prompted, wearily.

That was not the reaction Yuvraj expected. 'And that means we think someone knows about Swarbrook Hill. Someone knows and they are warning us. We're being threatened, Cranford. Helena had a funeral wreath sent to her home.'

The council leader wandered on, unmoved.

'Helena and I have talked this through. We must heed the warnings. We have decided we are pulling out of the deal.'

Hardstaff came to a halt. He stared fixedly ahead, waited and then pronounced: 'No, you're not.'

'We have no choice,' appealed Yuvraj. 'Our lives are in danger. Surely you can see that? Both of us have been confronted by a man with a gun and he has already proved that he's prepared to use it. Helena's husband was seriously wounded and I consider myself fortunate to have escaped with my life last night. What will he do next time? Will he come after my kids? Someone knows we are not telling the truth about Swarbrook Hill and they're letting us know that we either come clean or they are coming after us. We've done everything you asked of us to push this project through, but this is too much. I'm not prepared to sacrifice my children to…'

Hardstaff turned suddenly, silencing Yuvraj with a burning laser stare.

'Will you just calm the fuck down?'

Yuvraj's head dropped. Helena stood defiantly straight, wanting to show she was prepared to meet his eyes.

'Do I need to remind you what is really at stake here?' added Hardstaff, softening his tone. 'This project has been six years in the making. Six years since the developers first approached the council to discuss taking two hundred acres of useless industrial wasteland off our hands and turning it into an idyllic new village on the edge of the city, providing 1,200 new three-, four- and five-bedroomed houses as well as retail units, leisure facilities, health services and a school. We have been through the full process of public consultation, environmental impact studies, geological studies, flood protection assessments – the full fucking lot. This is a one hundred and thirty million-pound project which will create thousands of jobs in its construction, open the way for the council to secure millions of pounds worth of central Government bonuses, generate three million pounds each year in additional Council Tax income and greatly enhance the prosperity of the city as a whole through the additional spending power of the new residents it will draw in. This is all win and all we have to do is make sure there are no more delays. If this project fails to gain planning approval at committee level next month, the developers will appeal, there will have to be a public inquiry which will no doubt recommend to the secretary of state that he grants the go-ahead and all that will have changed is that the developer will have seen millions more – tens of millions maybe – disappear down the plughole through wasted time. And that's the best-case scenario. Who could blame them if they don't just decide to pull out altogether?'

He paused, letting his words seep through, and glared menacingly.

'The developers approached me to recruit key council officials to make sure the planning application gets through committee with no further hitches. I've got the Cabinet on my side – I can handle the Cabinet – but the reports you two put to the committee will be crucial and the developers have been prepared to pay us a lot of money to make sure your reports are persuasively in their favour. Should they have to play it that way? No, of course they shouldn't. The planning committee should be falling over themselves to grant approval, but we all know there are too many fuckwits on this council who will gripe, object and block just because they don't like big businesses or because somebody has suggested that a colony of rare newts might be inconvenienced by building on this site. We cannot allow those people to carry other gullible committee members with them in the vote. We personally stand to make a lot of money from this and, let's be candid here, that is an attractive prospect, but if this planning application fails to win approval the first time we have broken the terms of our agreement and we make nothing. That is the stark truth. Remember that the next time you come to me with talk of getting cold feet but also remember this.'

He leaned forward, ready to drive home the weight of each of his next words with a jab of his forefinger.

'We are doing nothing wrong.'

The old statesman stepped back, satisfied he had nailed another keynote speech.

'Are we though?'

Hardstaff cocked his head towards Helena, who stared back, challenging him. He glared at her through half-closed eyes, but she was determined to make her point anyway.

'Are we doing the right thing? Should we be recommending to the committee that they grant planning approval?'

Hardstaff snorted disparagingly. Yuvraj moved to put a stalling hand on her arm but she shrugged him off.

'I think we all know that this is a troubled site. The surveys have found higher than acceptable traces of asbestos, arsenic, lead, radon gas – we would be exposing whoever buys houses on this development to major risks of cancer and God knows what other nasty health complications. And what about the mines? There's a maze of old coal seams under this site, full of toxic gases and dangerously polluted water that could be disturbed and not only provide major health hazards to anyone living there but it could get into the local eco system and poison the land and water for miles around. And that's without taking into account the historic unrecorded mine workings that the Coal Authority says we might also have to deal with. How can we, in all conscience, report to the planning committee and say: "everything's fine, go ahead," when there are still so many serious issues to address before approval should be granted?'

'*Might* be risks, *could* be problems – if we lived our lives to those rules, we would all be too scared to get out of bed in a morning. Look, if there are real concerns, we can attach conditions in the approval and then the developer will have to…'

'Have to what?' Helena interrupted. 'They promise: "sure, we'll do it" but no one would be there to make sure it was done properly. They would effectively become self-regulating. Where's their incentive to make sure the site is completely safe unless we delay approval until they do?'

'That's enough,' snapped Hardstaff. 'We've been through all this health and safety bullshit with the previous Head of Planning and Regeneration and it caused us months of stalling. That's why we had to get rid of him. I used my influence to get you into the post because Yuvraj assured me that not only were you a highly capable young officer but that we could rely on you to do what was necessary. You knew what you were getting into when you agreed to accept the deal on the table. It's too late to back out now. You're in this up to your neck, Ms Morrison, and I'm sure you are fully aware that corruption in a public office is a serious offence.'

'Are you threatening me?' she glared.

'I'm pointing out that we are all too far down the road to turn around and head back now. Just bear that in mind the next time you're bothered by your conscience.'

'Perhaps we should all take a breath,' said Yuvraj, stepping in to defuse the mounting antagonism between his two colleagues. 'Maybe we were a bit hasty in saying that we were pulling out.'

Helena felt a flash of anger but suppressed her instinct to rebuke him for his betrayal.

'But we still have the very real issue at hand of a man with a gun who knows our business and might just blow this whole thing apart, however united we are.'

Hardstaff tipped back his head, ready to pass judgement.

'So, what do we know? We have a rogue man who knows where to find both of you and has, so far, fired one shot – possibly accidentally, as I understand – and has followed up by sending a wreath by way of a crude symbolic warning. Have either of you any cause to believe this individual has solid information of our agreement?'

Helena was stony-faced and conceded nothing.

'Not as such, but…' offered Yuvraj.

'No written or verbal confirmation? No actual threat to expose us?'

'Well…'

'I think he has nothing. I think maybe we are dealing with someone who has a broad objection to the Swarbrook Hill development and understands the function of councils well enough to know that you two are key players in the process. Either that, or he is in possession of a small amount of information but cannot prove a thing. If he could prove it, he would have plastered it all over social media, taken it to the papers, TV, radio, because this type of person loves to be heard and if he's not even willing to put a conspiracy theory out there, it means he has nothing on us. He's trying to scare you into making a mistake – doing something rash. He's fishing. What do we know about him?'

'Helena's husband got the best look at him, isn't that right, Helena?' Yuvraj prompted, attempting to draw her into the conversation, but she was having none of it. 'He said the man had his face covered but that he was smaller than average – only about five feet. The man I saw was about the same height, which is why we think it was the same man. I didn't see his face either.'

Hardstaff's eyes narrowed. About five feet tall. Yuvraj was right about one thing, there aren't many grown men about who are around that sort of height. He could think of only one.

'That fucker!' he spat. The venom in his words took both Yuvraj and Helena aback.

'Do you think you know who it is?' queried Yuvraj.

'I might,' Hardstaff growled. 'Some little fucker who belongs to some piss-pot environmental protection group and has a vendetta against me because of that business with the tree felling a couple of years back. I bet he wants to rob me of my legacy project. He knows he can't get to me, but he thinks he can scupper my plans by getting at you two. That's what he's doing. He's trying to kill the project just so that I don't get the final credit I deserve for the crowning glory to a lifetime of service to this city. This is personal. He's out to get at me.'

There was a stunned silence between them as Hardstaff smouldered and the other two attempted to grasp what he had said.

'Can you be sure it's him?' ventured Yuvraj at last.

'I trust my gut,' said Hardstaff. 'It's him.'

'So, what do we do? Should we have him arrested?'

Hardstaff pondered the suggestion. 'We can't take that chance just in case he does have anything. I've got a better idea. He thinks he's got something on us, so we get something on him. I know somebody who can bring us what we want. Leave it with me.'

Helena stared at the old man. Has he totally lost it? She saw the festering resentment in his eyes and wondered if that was what a lifetime in local politics did to a person.

'That's it?' she asked. 'That's the plan? You dig around for dirt on someone who may or may not be the man who shot my husband and we're supposed to do what?'

'You do nothing,' he retorted. 'You carry on as normal and that means you prepare your case, as required, to recommend to the planning committee that they grant approval next month and, in the meantime, you act as if nothing has happened. If we can draw him out and make him make a mistake, all the better, but, for now, you fulfil your part of the agreement and I'll do mine. I'm going to shut this fucker Bestwick down.'

15

The phone vibrated with a low buzz on the bedside cabinet, chinking gently against the glass ashtray for a third and fourth time before a heavily tattooed arm reached grudgingly from under the duvet to grab it. The arm dragged it back under the cover and, from deep beneath it, came a muffled curse before the sound of the phone was silenced.

The arm, still holding the phone, reached out again, this time to throw back the bed cover and, in a single, decisive but hardly graceful movement, Wesley Hughes rolled sideways to perch upright, his short legs dangling several inches from touching the bedroom floor. He wore only a tatty pair of boxer shorts, the same he had worn and slept in for at least three days before that, and practically the only part of his petite, pudgy body that was not covered in ink, coarse black hair or both was the top of his head.

He jumped down from the edge of the bed and took a first laboured step towards the bedroom door as he lifted the phone to his ear with one hand and reached down the front of his boxers for a scratch with the other.

'Yeah?'

Wesley knew who it was. The name on the display was

'Foghorn'. As a security precaution – and partly to amuse himself – he had allocated all his business contacts code names of cartoon characters. Most were random but associating Cranford Hardstaff with a blustering, bombastic rooster made his moniker a particularly easy one to remember.

'I've got a job for you,' came the reply.

Wesley's movements became gradually less stiff as he walked to the door and eased down on the handle. He paused for a second, as the light of the day poured into the room through the open door, to look back towards the bed to where Beth lay motionless on her side, facing away from him, her bare shoulders exposed, apparently undisturbed. He stepped through the door and closed it behind him.

'You haven't paid me for the last one yet.'

'You are joking, I presume,' replied Hardstaff. 'I only pay when a job is done properly. The dim youth you employed managed to release the mice into the wrong shop. He was meant to infest the café so that I could get it shut down. If I'd wanted him to send them in so that they could chew through the covers of a few old Human League albums, I'd have fucking asked for that.'

Wesley walked down the stairs and into the front room, switching on the main light and leaving the curtains drawn. A low oval wooden table in the centre of the room was strewn with scattered magazines, unwashed mugs and unopened letters and he sifted through the mess, knocking a TV remote control onto the floor, before he unearthed an opened packet of cigarettes and a lighter. He took one of the cigarettes with his spare hand, put it in his mouth and lit it, drawing deeply so the end glowed red and the paper crackled as it was burned away. He held in the lungful until he felt its first stimulating tingle before releasing the smoke across the room.

'Out of curiosity, how did he manage to fuck up such a simple job? The instruction was that there were four shops in a block and he was to release the mice into the second one from the left. Where was the scope for error in that?'

The failure had angered Wesley too. His reputation was built on reliability. He didn't make mistakes. It was not unusual for him to bring in others – people he could trust – to assist in the fulfilment of contracts if they had skills he lacked but this had appeared such a straightforward job that he had handed it to one of the younger guys he sometimes used for fetching and carrying. That kid would not be given a second chance. Wesley did not accept incompetence and had made his feelings plain to the kid. He did not want to give bloated buffoons like Hardstaff the excuse to bad-mouth him again.

'He approached the shops from the back and didn't work out that the second from the left looking at the block from the front was the second from the right from the rear. He won't be getting any more work from me.'

'I should bloody hope not! Why the hell did you use him in the first place?'

Wesley felt his temper rise and took another deep, calming drag on the cigarette.

'Are you going to tell me what this next job is or not?'

Hardstaff muttered to himself on the other end of the line before he felt ready to issue his instructions.

'The target is the same,' he said. 'Because your minion

couldn't tell his left from his right, I still need him taken care of. I need you to get to him this time, rather than his café. He's proving an inconvenience to me by getting involved where he shouldn't and making out as if he has information he can use against me. I need you to find out how much he knows and make sure he keeps his mouth shut from now on.'

Wesley wandered to the sofa and sat down.

'What are we talking? Do you want him roughing up and threatening to keep him quiet? Does he have family?'

'How would I know if he has fucking family? Everybody has family.'

Wesley leaned to reach a glass beside the sofa and flicked ash into it, waiting for the voice at the other end of the line to come up with a more constructive suggestion.

'I'm tempted to suggest violence but I'm not sure it's the right option for now. Not until I know what he has. I want something that gives me a hold on him, but I don't want to make him a martyr. I don't want him showing his bruises on TV. We need to come up with something more subtle.'

Subtle. Valerie does subtle.

'I think I know someone.'

Hardstaff waited, expecting details.

'Go on,' he prompted, finally.

'A woman who has done jobs like this before. She's very persuasive. She lures them in, drugs them and gets them to tell her everything without them realising it. If you want material to guarantee this guy's future co-operation, I believe she also offers a video option.'

'I like it!' said Hardstaff. 'Drug him up to the eyeballs,

get the information and then film him handcuffed naked to a bed while your associate flogs him with a whip and feeds him slices of pork pie. Let's see what that does for his credibility with his eco-mentalist friends!'

Interesting. Wesley raised his eyebrows. Hardstaff seemed to have grasped the concept disturbingly quickly.

'Something like that,' he said.

'Sort it. I need it done quickly. And don't fuck it up this time.'

Hardstaff ended the call. Wesley took a last drag on his cigarette and dumped the butt in the glass.

What an arsehole.

He stood and wandered towards the table again, picking up the cigarettes and the lighter. He lit another. The chilliness of the front room made him crave a return to the cosy warmth of the bed and he climbed back up the stairs.

Beth was awake now. She was on her other side, facing him, propped up with her head resting on her open palm. He dropped the cigarette packet, the lighter and the phone on to the bedside cabinet and climbed back into bed.

'Give me one of them, would you?'

He leaned to pick up the packet and lighter and tossed them idly on to the duvet between them without a word.

'Thanks,' she said, sarcastically, and retrieved them.

'Who was that?'

Wesley rolled over, away from her, to stub out his cigarette in the ashtray and then pulled the duvet higher.

'Business.'

She sat so that she could light up.

'Another job?'

'Yeah.'

Since Darrell had phoned to suggest Wesley might know about their affair and that he might be the man who had shot him in the foot, Beth had been taking a closer interest in her husband's movements. She had been thinking a lot, too. The possibility that Wesley cared enough to be aware of what she was up to with Darrell still seemed unlikely to her. His inability to feel anything about anybody other than himself was one of the reasons she had launched the affair in the first place. The possibility of his being driven by jealousy to track down and threaten her lover seemed a remote one. No. He didn't have that in him.

But what she had thought a lot about over the last couple of days was just why she was still in this sham of a marriage. As far as she could tell, all he needed her for was to be part of his cover. She was his respectable teacher wife sharing his respectable, ordinary house in a respectable neighbourhood. Hadn't he encouraged her to go into teaching for just that reason? Stop the neighbours' tongues from wagging?

What do they do to be able to afford a nice house like that?

Well, she's a teacher and I think he runs his own business.

What sort of business?

I don't know but she seems right enough. I saw her at the parents' evening.

Oh! Must be fine then.

That was what he got from their marriage but what was in it for her? She was stronger now. She was no longer the messed up young woman he first met - the one who was so desperately in need of rescuing that she grabbed at the first rope thrown her way and had so eagerly hauled herself to safety. She had grown. She was no longer dependant – on him or all the stuff she used to poison her body with. She had started to think a lot more about her escape, but she needed to get at his money and, to do that, she needed him out of the way.

'Are you going to take me out tonight? You haven't taken me out for ages.'

'Can't,' came the reply from beneath the duvet.

'Why?'

'Busy.'

'You're always busy.'

'I'm a busy man.'

She sat quietly as the cigarette burned in her fingers. She didn't particularly want to spend the evening with him. She just wanted to know where he would rather be.

'You never tell me what you're doing.'

Wesley stayed silent and still.

'Why won't you tell me what you're doing?'

'Because you don't need to know.'

'It's because you don't trust me. Why are we still together if you won't trust me? You've never trusted me. You shouldn't live with someone if you can't trust them.'

Wesley turned quickly to face her. He was getting irritated now.

'I only trust people who are useful to me, people who serve a purpose. What purpose do you serve, Beth? You were a spoiled college kid who knew nothing and couldn't face having to do anything to make your way because you felt the world owed you a favour. You'd have been dead by now if I hadn't taken you in, so don't give me that shit. You should be grateful. If you don't like it, you can fuck off. Go back to sharing dirty needles with all your useless drop-out friends – if any of them are still alive.'

He rolled back over and tugged at the covers.

Beth was quietened. She was angered but mostly hurt by the assault. The truth hurt.

'I only want to feel like we mean something to each other. That's all. Just trust me with one thing. Tell me what you're doing tonight.'

She heard him release a long, exasperated breath.

'I have something I need to dispose of.'

A breakthrough! She had got through to him.

'What, a body?'

He responded with a contemptuous snort.

'Something someone needs to avoid from falling into the wrong hands, then. A gun. Is it a gun?'

No reply.

'It's a gun, isn't it? I bet it was used in a crime. Was it that jewellery shop robbery last month? The one where the couple who ran it were shot? I read that the wife was in a bad way. Are they using you to get rid of the gun?'

Still no response.

'I bet you're helping them avoid being caught in other ways as well. Are you hiding some of the stuff they stole at your lock-up?'

'Just drop it, Beth.'

She smiled to herself. He didn't like that she was figuring it out.

'Have you ever shot anybody, Wes?'

The covers were flung off and he jumped out of bed,

heading towards the en suite bathroom. There was no chance of any peace. He wished he had not given her even the slightest encouragement to pry into his business.

'No, but there's a first time for everything,' he mumbled as he trudged away.

Beth ignored the dig. She was pleased with what she had learned. That was useful information.

***

Helena and Yuvraj did not speak as they marched, head down, into the cold wind towards where they had left his car. She barely gave him time to press the keypad to open the door before she tugged at the handle on the passenger side and jumped in. It was cold outside, but she was warmed by the flush of fury.

'Maybe we were a bit hasty?' The words had been bubbling inside Helena and she threw them back in Yuvraj's face with the force of a slap.

Yuvraj said nothing as he closed the driver's door behind him. He knew she was cross.

'We came here to tell Cranford that we are definitely pulling out of his scheme because we don't want some lunatic stalking us and killing us and you let him walk all over you and then say maybe we were a bit hasty?'

He felt his ears beginning to burn. As soon as the words had left his mouth, he had realised he had left himself open to Helena's wrath.

'I was just trying to take some of the heat out of the situation. You two going at each other was helping nothing.'

'I was standing up to him, Yuvraj. He's a playground bully, you know that full well. We went to see him

143

specifically to tell him that we weren't going to let him push us around anymore and you tell him maybe we were a bit hasty? Do you realise how weak that made you sound?'

Yuvraj was blinking his eyes fast and shuffled uncomfortably.

'He thinks he knows who might be responsible. We should let him try to sort it out. We owe him that.'

'And what if this great gut feeling of his is wrong? What if there isn't somebody out there who will apparently go to any lengths to stop Cranford from having a full-sized statue of himself erected outside the town hall one day? Even if someone is that obsessed – and who could blame them, by the way? – what if Cranford is targeting the wrong guy?'

She leaned closer to him and glared into his eyes so that she could not be ignored.

'What if there's still a lunatic out there who will stalk us down and kill us?'

'Helena, let's just be calm about this. Don't be…'

'Hysterical? Should I not get hysterical? Please don't say I shouldn't be hasty.'

'Unreasonable,' he replied, choosing the word carefully and hoping it was the right one. 'Maybe we have found ourselves disturbed by the events of the last couple of days and perhaps we should look at it more reasonably. Cranford might be right. If this person with the gun had proof, wouldn't he have put it out there in the public domain already? Could it be that he is trying to get inside our heads so that we make a mistake or do something… illogical.'

'He's fucking succeeding if he's trying to get into our heads,' she replied.

'We can't let him. I say we keep as low a profile as we can for a while, prepare as normal for the planning committee meeting and let Cranford sort it out. There's still too much at stake here to throw it away when we really can't be sure we need to.'

Yuvraj dared to reach out his hand to touch hers. She did not shrug him off.

'Don't you agree?'

She stared blankly ahead, calmer now.

'I suppose so.'

He withdrew his hand.

'But you'd better be right.'

16

The experience in Ecclesall Woods had disturbed Martin. He had been caught in the act, gun in hand, and could only be thankful that the dog walker was not braver and the dog was not fiercer. It was also a blessing that he had the foresight to cover his face again, to disguise his identity, and though he felt confident the dog walker would not have been able to give much of a physical description to the police when he reported the incident – as he surely did – Martin had gone off the idea of burying the gun as a means of getting rid of it.

He needed another plan.

Later that night, as he calmed his nerves with a mug of lemon balm tea, he decided if burying the gun beneath the earth was not the solution, sinking it beneath the water might be. All the lakes and reservoirs nearby were just too far to cycle to, especially after a full day at the café, but the River Don cut through the centre of Sheffield and was deep in places.

He checked the map, retracing a day last summer that he decided to do the Five Weirs Walk, and tried to work out which section of the six-mile route might suit his purpose. His memories of the walk alone were not enough.

Looking for the best place to get rid of a weapon had not been on his mind that day.

Between Attercliffe Road and Effingham Street, he thought he might have found a good spot. He would try again the next night.

It was uncomfortable, Martin found, cycling with a World War Two German pistol stuffed down the front of your trousers. Another new experience in an increasingly bizarre period of his life. The front sight at the end of the long barrel rubbed against the inside of his thigh with every push of the pedals. He felt it chafing but resisted the temptation to readjust the gun's position in case any passing motorists thought he was trying to bring himself a totally different sort of relief.

There was a Tesco close by, where he could leave his bike and be fairly optimistic that it would still be there when he got back. Martin chained the bike and his helmet to the rack in the shelter, tugged down the hem of his dark fleece so it covered him to mid-thigh and put on the green cap he had kept down the back of his elasticated waistband before limping along the half-mile walk to the riverside.

Apart from the risk of being seen trying to get rid of the gun, or the outside chance that he might be knocked off his bike and have to try to explain why he was riding with an antique small firearm down his pants, the thing that bothered Martin most about what he was about to do was that he hated dumping the gun in such a beautiful waterway. Sure, the Don had endured much, much worse through the city's industrial age but nature had nursed it back to life. He had made a covenant with nature to protect it however and whenever he could and so this felt like a betrayal. Only after he balanced the potential of causing damage through pollution against the potential of being caught in possession of a weapon that had been used to inflict grievous bodily harm did he finally decide the trade-off had to be made.

The icy wind stung his cheeks as Martin headed into the face of it on the path alongside the busy road. The evening light was fading fast and headlamps burned brightly as cars and vans hurried home. He walked briskly, head down, and hoped he would be giving none of the drivers who were passing by reason to notice him.

Soon, he came to the fork in the road he was looking for and took the turn on to the riverside footpath. A hooped frame above the walkway made it appear as if he were about to plunge into an uncovered tunnel, with the chain of electric lights overhead reducing the ominous fear of danger lurking ahead that might otherwise have dissuaded Martin from taking his first steps along it. He took a deep breath and pressed on.

He could hear the murmur of the river to his left but see only glimpses of it through the thick bushes beside of the path. Peeking over the bushes, from the far bank of the river, were buildings that were once the crumbling remains of industry, many of which had been redeveloped for new purposes. Martin sheltered behind the peak of his cap, glancing up briefly to make sure no one was heading towards him or, worse still, lurking with the intent of doing him harm. It was late enough for the path to be well past its peak busyness but early enough to make it still reasonably safe to walk along.

At a point where there was a slight kink in the line of

the path, Martin stopped. There was a gap of a couple of metres in the bushes so that he could see the river clearly for the first time – and make sure there was no one to see what he had to do. He leaned against the metal railing, attempting to look as if he was casually inspecting the still waters three metres below his feet, while his eyes scanned the buildings opposite for signs of life and activity. He could see none. He stepped back and nervously peeked to either side in case anyone was heading towards him from either direction. No one was.

Yet he hesitated. Part of him was guiltily willing someone to come into view so that he would have to call the operation off, even though he knew this was something he had to do. His nerve was failing him. He moved forward to grip the railing again, desperate to summon the strength within but still powerless to act, all the time having to choke back the inner urge to walk – run – away from there immediately, all the time increasing the chances of being discovered hovering on the brink of a deed he dare not commit.

His heart beat faster than ever until he could barely see beyond blurs of shapes around him. Panic was engulfing him. Every fibre of his instinct was telling him to get away, reminding him that his last two attempts to challenge his core values of right or wrong had only landed him in deeper trouble, yet the tiny fading voice in his rational mind – the part that was beseeching him to go through with it – would not let him leave.

Finally, he snatched the gun out from its hiding place and gripped the handle of it in his gloved hand again. He held it in front of his face, feeling his eyes drawn by its mesmeric pull, aching to be able to release it as if every passing second was burning it deeper into his flesh and making it impossible to ever be free from. Finally, he found the strength at last to cock his arm back and send it spinning through the cold evening air to where it landed, with a hollow splash, in the middle of the river and was swallowed up for good.

Relieved but still choked by his anxiety, Martin was lumbering away along the path almost before the gun hit the water, stumbling into a trot until he realised, almost as he reached the footbridge, that he was heading in the wrong direction. He turned back towards where he had left his bike, willing his limbs to behave normally but refusing to look back at where the circle of ripples caused by the impact of the gun had now faded and died.

***

In a dark corner of a car park on the opposite bank, seventeen-year-old Chloe Wood was having difficulty controlling someone else's limbs. Specifically, the wandering hands of her boyfriend, Sam.

'Stop it, will you Sam!'

Sam was disinclined to obey. He reckoned she must have realised he had a bit of a kiss and a fumble in mind when he winked suggestively and led her by the hand to where prying eyes could not see. The rampant juggernaut of his teenage hormones had shot too quickly through the gears to pull up now.

'Pack – it – in!' she hissed at him through clenched teeth, trying to make it as clear as she possibly could that a line had been drawn.

He pulled his head away, resting his hands on her hips.

'Fuck's sake, Chloe. It's only a bit of fun.'

'It's not fun feeling your bloody cold hands on me. They're like ice blocks.'

'I know how to warm them up,' he said with a leer, launching another attempt at penetrating the outer defence of her hooded puffa coat.

She let out a small shriek, wrapped her arms around his neck and pulled him forward into a kiss, attempting to distract him. When, eventually, they came up for air, she glanced over his shoulder and noticed a small figure by the railing on the far side of the river. He appeared agitated.

'Look at that bloke over there.'

Sam was too preoccupied to give attention to anyone other than the person immediately in front of him.

'What about him?'

'He's acting strange. He looks like he's thinking about throwing himself in the river.'

Sam ignored the suggestion and grabbed a handful of her backside, pulling her closer in hope that he might get her focus back on the matter at the forefront of his mind. She slapped his hand away.

'Seriously, I think he might.'

'Let him get on with it then.'

Chloe wriggled free of his grasp just as Sam was sliding his right hand up towards his next intended target.

'Sam! Stop being a twat, will you, and look.'

He rolled his eyes. It was time to concede defeat, for now. He dutifully turned to where he was being directed, his body language spelling out that he was doing so because he had been told to, rather than because he cared.

The figure in dark clothing and a dark cap had stepped away from the railing, moving in small, jerky steps one way and then the other, like he was barefoot on hot bricks and could not work out which direction would give him his escape route. He lurched forward again and took hold of the railing as if his survival depended on it, rocking back and forth on his toes, before releasing his grip and lifting his jacket to pull an object from the waistband of his trousers.

'What the hell?' said Sam, captivated too now.

'What's he got in his hand? Is that a gun?' Chloe whispered.

'Shit!'

'Oh, god – he's not going to shoot himself, is he?' She recoiled, hiding behind Sam's shoulder at the prospect of what might happen but only far enough so that she could keep an eye on the figure.

Finally, the man drew back the object in his hand and threw it. They heard the splash and saw the man hurrying away.

'Come on,' said Chloe, taking hold of Sam's arm and dragging him across the car park towards the road.

'Where are we going?'

He resisted her attempt to take him away. Surely, the show was over and they could pick up where they left off?

'He's heading towards the footbridge to get over to our side. We need to get a good look at him.'

Sam did not understand her urgency. 'What for?'

'He had a gun, Sam. What kind of a person carries a gun and then throws it in the river? My dad's a police officer…'

'Your dad's a copper?' He wondered for a moment if he had done anything to the daughter to incriminate himself.

'… and I think he might want to know who this person is. If we can get a picture of him…'

The two of them quickened their pace, at least one of them eager to get into position before the mysterious man reached the other side of the footbridge.

***

Wesley Hughes stepped purposefully along the path, hunched under the peak of his cap with his hands in the pockets of his dark jacket. Being short usually made it easier to remain inconspicuous and he knew that after he did what he needed to do and crossed the river towards the centre, he could melt into the Saturday evening bustle and slip away unnoticed. All he had to do was keep his wits about him until it was done.

It was usually quiet in this part of the city at this time of day and he had not encountered anyone on the path so far, but he noticed someone heading towards him and cautiously dipped his head to shield his face.

The other person seemed unaware of Wesley's approach. He was of similar height and build, though slimmer, and appeared to be distracted by something, shaking his head and muttering as he closed the gap between them at a bustling pace. Wesley moved to one side, allowing plenty of room to pass by, but the other man ploughed on along the middle of the path, unaware he was on a collision course, until they were practically on top of each other.

In almost the last step, the other man realised there was

another presence on the path and diverted himself just enough to avoid contact, passing with a mumbled 'Sorry, 'scuse me,' and scurrying on his way again.

Wesley shot him a filthy glare and carried on to where there was a break in the bushes to his left, a point where there was a slight kink in the line of the path. He assessed in front, behind him and to the side before quickly snatching the handgun from the waistband of his trousers and flicking it, in one movement, towards the river, barely breaking stride as he walked on towards the footbridge.

He stepped out over the river crossing. Already, his attention was turning to what he needed to do next before he would return home. Suddenly, he saw a distracting flash of light in the corner of his eye and looked up towards it. A young girl and boy were posing with a phone for selfies – her pouting, him pulling a face of mock excited surprise. Wesley silently wondered why kids felt the need to take so many pictures of themselves and carried on towards the centre.

Chloe watched him go and began to thumb through her handiwork. The camera had not been set in selfie mode but had captured a sequence of movement as the short stranger who had thrown away the gun walked by them and looked straight towards their camera. They were good, clear images. Her dad would be pleased.

17

'I promise you I am *never* doing anything like that again.'

Evelyn sat in the armchair next to the bed and listened to Martin's tale of trauma and near-calamity, a suppressed smile playing on the corners of her mouth. He was so melodramatic, but he played the role of victim so well and that made him an excellent storyteller. She loved to listen to him talk, whether it was the latest gossip about customers in the café or the full harrowing account of how he – eventually – disposed of an illegal weapon.

'Well, it's done now,' she offered, deliberately minimising the extent of the emotional scarring he was suggesting he had suffered. 'It's gone and you don't need to worry about it anymore. That should be the end of it.'

'Thank goodness,' he replied, quietly. It had taken him a long time to feel normal again following the events of the previous evening and every stinging reminder from the sore patch of skin on the inside of his thigh brought it all back. Talking it through with Mrs Dawes had been a help. She was the only person he could tell.

Martin turned to look at the large clock on the far wall of the ward.

'I'd better be off. I'm sorry to have to cut you short

today, Mrs Dawes, but I've left Maggie on her own in the café and I said I'd be back by three.'

He stood and took his yellow jacket from the back of his seat to put it on.

'I'm so pleased to see you're able to get properly up and about now and it sounds like the physio is really happy with your recovery.'

Evelyn smiled, proud that he had acknowledged her progress.

'You'll be out of here in no time.'

Her smile slipped. 'Well, we'll have to see about that.'

'Of course you will.'

Martin zipped up his jacket and picked up his cycling helmet.

'You've not forgotten, have you?' she asked.

'Of course not. It might be a bit full-on early this week and I've got the accountants coming in on Tuesday, but I promise you, I will go to visit your ex-husband before the weekend.'

He leaned towards her and kissed her on the cheek.

'I'll see you tomorrow.'

She watched him leave. She always felt a little sad after he had gone but the closer she was to the end of her time in hospital, the harder it was. There might not be many more visits to come.

Thankfully, there were only two customers and their dog in the café when he arrived back. Maggie was busying herself by tidying away clean dishes and cutlery.

'Hi!' he breezed in from the back room after changing out of his cycling gear. 'Sorry I'm a bit later than I said I would be.'

'No bother.' Maggie was thirtyish and comfortably rounded. She had given birth three times in five years and had saw no reason why getting back to the same shape she was in when she was twentyish should even come close to the top of her priority list. 'It's been fairly quiet.'

Martin looked out of the front window.

'Get off home to the kids if you like, Maggie.'

She paused midway through drying a coffee cup with a tea towel.

'You sure?'

'Yeah. It's too cold out there for people to be out and about. I'll probably close up at five today.'

Maggie finished drying the cup and put it with the rest. 'I will, in that case. Thanks.'

She started to unfasten her apron on her way to the back room but then remembered.

'Oh, I took a message for you.' She picked up a piece of paper from behind the counter and handed it to Martin. On it, she had scribbled the name 'Valerie' and a phone number.

He stared at it quizzingly. 'I don't know a Valerie. Did she say what it was about?'

'Just that it was personal.' Maggie pulled the apron from over her head. 'She asked if you'd call back.'

He shrugged and pushed the slip of paper into his pocket.

Once the couple and their dog had left, it was quieter still. Martin finished the few jobs he could think to do and decided there was little point even hanging on until five to shut up shop. The temperature had barely struggled into plus figures all day and anyone with any sense was at home with the heating on.

After everything he had been through that week, a few hours at home listening to music with a couple of glasses of wine sounded like an appealing prospect.

The message. Might as well return that call and find out what this Valerie wants. Get that out of the way.

He retrieved his phone from the inside pocket of his jacket and keyed in the number Maggie had left him. The call was answered on the fourth ring.

'This is Martin Bestwick from the *Better World* café. I understand you called earlier.'

There was a pause, then a woman's voice, dark as liquid chocolate and smooth as pure honey, purred down the line.

'Martin, so good of you to return my call.'

OK, he thought. 'How can I help you?'

'We've never met, but I'm familiar with the wonderful work of you and your group,' she said.

So, it's group-related, nothing to do with the café.

'That's nice. I'm glad you appreciate our objectives.'

'I'd like us to meet,' she said, suggestively.

'Well, we have meetings every…'

'No,' the voice cut in. 'Just you. I'd like to meet you.'

'I see,' Martin replied, not seeing at all. 'Well, I…'

'I have something that will be of interest to you. Information.'

'Oh!' This was getting odder. 'What sort of information?'

'I understand you know about Cranford Hardstaff.'

He had not been able to hear mention of that name

without blushing since the beer can incident in the Peace Gardens the previous weekend. Even though he had not been responsible, he felt he had been blamed.

'I know a bit about him, yes.'

'I can tell you things about Cranford Hardstaff that will make your toes curl,' she promised, and Martin felt his toes curl at the prospect.

'Really?'

'Meet me at the *Chianti Club* wine bar on Division Street tomorrow at eight and I'll show you everything I've got.'

She hung up. Martin held the phone to his ear for several seconds longer, as if waiting for someone else to come on the line to explain what that conversation was about.

'Well, that was weird,' he announced to the empty café.

He had never heard of the *Chianti Club* and he had no idea who this woman Valerie was. Should he go there to meet her? He decided to go home, to think it over.

***

Even as he sat at the bar, nursing a soda and lime the barman had made unpalatable by putting in too much lime, Martin was still not sure he had made the right choice. Curiosity had got the better of him and now he perched on a tall stool, facing the main door, waiting for a strange woman to turn up with toe-curling information about the leader of Sheffield City Council.

In the context of everything else that had happened over the last couple of weeks, it was a situation that hardly even rated as odd.

Chianti Club was underlit and underpopulated. Apart

from three young men at the other end of the bar, drinking over-priced lager from long, thin glasses, and a couple in their thirties who seemed as if they had already run out of things to say to each other, Martin was the only customer. The interior design was more Lower Manhattan than central Sheffield. The walls had been stripped down to the bare brick and the furnishings looked as if someone had taken great care to make them appear old and worn. Part shabby chic, part nouveau desolate. The faint sound of avant-garde jazz gnawed away at the ear from an expensive sound system and practically the only lighting came from the glass-fronted cabinets behind the bar accommodating tall racks filled with wine bottles that no one appeared eager to sample. On a cold Monday night, it was not a place to be if you were already contemplating throwing yourself under a bus.

The security man on the door, his credentials fastened with a reflective green strap around his considerable right bicep, had looked down with distaste when Martin arrived in his deep red beanie hat, mid-blue all-weather coat and all-terrain hiking boots but let him pass without a challenge. Perhaps he realised that, rather than keeping out undesirables, he would be doing the bar a better service by attempting to throw people in.

Eventually, someone else did come in.

Martin noticed her first but one of the group of three men soon saw her too and alerted his two friends straight away. Even the male half of the bored couple chanced to lift his head, which had been dipped over a small glass of beer almost the whole time, to steal a glance and risk getting a kick under the table.

She clearly wanted to be noticed, pausing midway across the floor to flick the black cocktail jacket off her bare shoulders and reveal a red satin dress. It was cut daringly low at the neckline to reveal her full, pneumatic cleavage and high at the hem to allow complete appreciation for her spectacularly long legs. She folded the jacket over her arm and wiggled on red heels like a catwalk model, heading straight towards Martin, homing in like a hawk swooping for the kill.

She must be freezing coming out dressed like that, he thought.

Slowly and without seeing a need to check she had approached the right man, she parted her plump strawberry-red lips and breathed: 'Hi, I'm Valerie.'

She was mid-twenties and elegantly slender. Her smoky black mascara and shaped eyebrows framed the ice blue of her eyes, sparkling like a topaz and as ravenous as a wild husky's. She stroked strands of golden blonde hair behind her right ear to uncover the long, gold drop of her earring and stood so close to Martin that her perfume tingled his skin like soft kisses. She paused, waiting to see if he was capable of answering her greeting or would melt in a pool at her feet.

'Martin. Pleased to meet you,' he said and held out his hand to shake.

She took it gracefully in the fingers of her right hand and squeezed lightly.

He withdrew his hand. 'Could I get you a drink?'

'Vodka,' she replied, tilting her head slightly to the side, 'with two ice cubes.'

Martin glanced up to try to catch the eye of the barman,

who was pouring more glasses of lager for the three men. They had their eyes fixed on Valerie.

'I'll go to find somewhere we can talk more privately,' she said, picking up Martin's glass of soda and lime and, before he could object, carrying it away with her to a booth in the dingiest corner of the bar.

Obviously not hot on manners, thought Martin as he attempted to attract the barman with a wave.

Valerie bent gracefully into the seat of the booth. She glanced back towards the bar where Martin was still waiting to be served and unclipped her red clutch bag, taking out a small, folded piece of paper. Holding Martin's glass out of sight beneath the table, she unwrapped the paper and tipped in the white powder contained within it, stirring the drink with a plastic stick before re-placing the glass on the table.

She smiled to him as Martin joined her at the booth, picking up her vodka and, almost as soon as he had sat down, tipping it towards him.

'Cheers,' she said. Martin lifted his drink to chink hers and grinned, uncertainly. Valerie took a sip of her drink, but he did not.

'You said you had something you wanted to tell me.'

Even in the low half-light of their corner of the bar, he noticed the twinkle of her eyes. Do not hurry, they said. Allow yourself to enjoy the view for a while.

'All in good time. I thought we might get to know each other a little first. Tell me all about you, Martin Bestwick.'

'OK,' he replied. *If that's what you want.*

'Well, I'm currently single.' He instantly regretted leading with that detail. This already felt like he was a mouse being seduced into laying down on the trap and the inference of those words had not helped his chances of survival.

'I'm a part of the Sheffield Environmental Action Network awareness group, as you probably know, and I own a small vegan café called *Better World* in Broomhill. Apart from that...' His words tailed off as he felt himself dissolving in her scrutiny.

'A café, how interesting,' she cooed, and he wondered if she was actually interested or was being sarcastic.

'What about you? What do you do?'

'I work for myself,' she ran her fingers gently through her hair. 'I suppose you could say I specialise in personal services.'

Martin gulped. He could tell that he was being steered down a road he did not want to travel. He felt beyond uncomfortable. He needed to divert the conversation back on track.

'Look, Valerie, I appreciate your coming out to see me on a cold night such as this, but I have other things I need to do tonight, so if we could just...'

Martin was suddenly aware of a shape looming over him from behind. One of the three young men from the bar, tall and assured, was leaning casually with his elbow on the backrest of the booth, holding a half-filled glass of lager in his other hand. All his attention was on Valerie.

'Hi,' he oozed. 'I'm Alex. Me and my friends were wondering if you'd like to come over for a drink.'

Valerie picked up her glass and took a sip. 'That's very kind but, as you can see, I'm with someone.'

The man glanced dismissively at Martin and turned

back to her.

'Yeah, but wouldn't you rather be with me?'

She raised her eyebrows and gave the slightest shake of her head.

'No, actually. I wouldn't.'

Alex was not about to give up easily. Going back to his friends so plainly defeated was not an option.

'We're staying here for one more and then we're going to the casino. I've got a feeling that we'll have a good night. I think you could be our lucky charm.'

Martin shuffled in his seat. He hated men who treated women like objects.

'Look, the lady said she's not interested.'

The man sneered. 'I didn't ask you, short arse. I don't need a fucking leprechaun.'

'Hah!' Martin let out a single hollow laugh and grinned ruefully. 'You arrogant prick.'

Alex felt his ears redden. Nobody got to talk to him like that. In a moment, he considered throwing a punch but, instead, he picked up Martin's glass and threw its contents all over him.

Martin gasped. Even Valerie's cool was, for a second, disturbed. Alex loomed over the pathetic dripping figure beneath him but then felt the grip of a large hand on his arm.

'You – out!' growled the door security man.

As Alex was dragged away, Valerie cursed silently. *Shit. The drug.*

She swiftly dropped back into character and shuffled around the booth to offer comfort.

'Martin, are you all right? You're soaked.'

'It's OK,' he replied, soda water dripping off his nose as he brushed his coat with his fingers. 'It's one hundred per cent shower-proof.'

With a paper napkin off the table, she dabbed tenderly at his wet face and leaned towards him so that he could feel her breath on his damp skin.

Valerie's blue eyes fixed on his. His whole body stiffened. He was part spellbound, part terrorised. She was enthralling. 'Thank you for standing up for me,' she whispered, as he felt her hand delicately slide up the inside of his thigh.

The trance was broken. He jumped to his feet.

'That's, that's fine. Just fine. It's OK.'

Martin wanted to get away. Coming to the bar to meet this… siren was a big mistake.

'I have to go,' he blurted. 'If you have information for me, please tell me now because I need to leave.'

She leaned back in the seat. Engaging a man's complete attention was not usually so difficult. This was just a challenge, that's all. She still had faith in her natural abilities, even without the drug. Besides, she had other wraps. There would still be opportunities to placate him totally and have him entirely in her power.

'You can't go out into the cold all wet. My apartment is near here. We can get you dried off, then we can have a drink together and I'll tell you everything.'

He shook his head emphatically. 'No. I don't know what you game is, Valerie, and I would never judge you or your life choices, but we have to get this clear. You are not my type.'

She smiled, coyly.

'What type would you like me to be?'

'I don't think you understand,' he answered. 'You are *really* not my type.'

Realisation dawned and she nodded a rueful nod.

'Ah!' she said. That explains it. 'In that case, we can still go back to my apartment – as friends. The information will make it worth your while.'

'Forget it.' Martin began to back away. 'Quite honestly, I doubt there ever was any information and I have no idea why you would choose me to try to lure back to your place for a night of whatever but I wish I'd followed my instincts and phoned you back to call the whole thing off. Good night, Valerie. It's been… interesting to meet you and if there is something you need to tell me, please send me an email. The address is on our website.'

With that, he headed for the exit to walk home in soddened trousers.

Valerie watched him go. There was no point in trying to call him back. The demeanour she had maintained so carefully fell from her. She drained the rest of the vodka, picked up her bag and swore under her breath.

'Bollocks.'

She had failed. She had never failed before and she did not like the feeling.

18

Detective Inspector Jane Jackson of Sheffield CID sat behind her desk, carefully scrutinised the ten-by-eight print in her hand, and pulled a face of pained resignation. The image on the print was not the issue. That was clear enough. The matter she was agonising over was what she would be able to do with it.

Across the other side of the desk, awaiting the verdict, was Detective Sergeant Will Copson. Without a word needing to be spoken, he could see the way it was heading. He felt exactly the same way about it, but it had to go before the inspector for confirmation.

She sighed.

'I think we can be pretty sure it is Wesley Hughes,' she said.

'I reckon so,' nodded the sergeant.

'But what does it actually give us? All it proves is that he was on Effingham Street at a certain time of a certain day but that's it. The witness reported a possible gun sighting, but they couldn't be certain. Possible? I can't request a diving team to deploy on the strength of a *possible* gun sighting. What if it was a stick, or an old phone, or a bloody electric toothbrush – we'd look complete idiots and I'd get my arse kicked from here to Bramall Lane and back. It's not enough.'

She flung the print across the desk despairingly and Copson picked it up.

'I agree, ma'am,' he said with a grimace. 'Pity though.'

Jackson stood and wandered to gaze over the busy street below from the window.

'Too right. We've been after this slippery bastard for too long. He's the pilot fish that feeds off the parasites on the sharks' skin and keeps its teeth clean for the next time it attacks. If we can get to him, we might be able to get him to give up some of the bigger fish, but he gives you nothing to grab him with. This,' she waved her arm dismissively towards the picture in the sergeant's hand, 'doesn't get us close enough.'

'Righto, ma'am.' Copson turned to leave but the inspector called him back.

'She was the daughter of one of our officers, you say.'

'Yes, ma'am. PC Dave Wood of the road traffic division. His daughter.'

Jackson nodded. 'Get word back to him that we appreciate what she did. It's good work. Say he should tell her that if she ever wants to make a profession of it, she should give us a call.'

The sergeant smiled. 'Will do.'

***

Martin arrived back at the café from a trip to the suppliers. It had taken him longer than he had anticipated. The lunchtime rush was looming and he still had the visit from the accountant to look forward to. At this rate, he was struggling to get to the hospital this afternoon. He had not missed a day since Mrs Dawes was admitted and had pledged to be there every day, but she was a lot brighter now and didn't need him so much. She would understand if he had to give it a miss, just this once. He had warned her he had a lot on.

Tying his apron around his waist while mouthing greetings to two of his regulars, Martin stepped behind the counter. Maggie was spooning a portion of avocado and green bean pasta into a takeaway box for a customer and Kate was warming a jug of soya milk with a jet of hissing steam from the coffee machine.

'Right, what needs doing?' he asked.

Maggie shrugged. 'All in hand.' She looked up and gestured with a tip of her head towards a table to her left.

'Gentleman over there wanted to see you, though.'

Martin followed the direction of her nod towards where a man of around 50 years old, with pinched features and round metal-rimmed glasses, sat alone and looked towards him expectantly. Martin acknowledged the eye contact with a small sheepish wave and the man allowed a brief hint of a smile to curl the edges of his tight-set mouth for the most fleeting fraction of an instant in response.

'Who is he?' Martin whispered, attempting to do so without moving his lips in case it was obvious to the stranger what he was asking.

'How the bloody hell would I know?' replied Maggie, less subtly. 'He asked for you by name. He's been there three quarters of an hour.'

Ducking out was not an option but after scarcely escaping intact from the clutches of Valerie at the wine bar only a few hours earlier, Martin was suspicious. At least this guy didn't look like he was about to come on with a big seduction play. He dipped a little deeper into his reserves of resolve and stepped from behind the counter.

The man rose and extended his hand in readiness as Martin approached.

'Brian Gibbs,' he said. His handshake was firm and businesslike.

Martin sat in the chair opposite but said nothing. Whoever this guy was and whatever he wanted, he would have to make the first move.

'My apologies for arriving unannounced,' said Brian. He was well-spoken and measured but appeared slightly on edge. 'What I need to tell you is best imparted face to face and in an environment that offers total confidentiality. I reasoned that your business premises would be suitable.'

His narrow eyes darted from side to side and he leaned forward to add, in hushed tones, 'Are we able to speak freely here?'

Inside, Martin's spirits sagged. He had enough on without having to waste time on someone who behaved like he had just stepped out of the pages of a Le Carré novel.

'Yeah, no worries.'

'Good.' Brian adjusted his posture in his chair and stared intently across the table. 'I have information of the utmost importance for you. You must take this information and act with the greatest urgency or a calamity will ensue. Believe me, I do not overstate the magnitude of the situation. Unless you put a stop to what is about to happen, we will suffer an environmental catastrophe with consequences that will last for generations to come.'

Martin's interest was caught but his guard remained up. He had been duped by empty promises of extraordinary revelations one time too many in the last twenty-four hours already and it was going to take more than a trail of smoke to get him excited.

'I'm sorry, Brian, but I have no idea who you are and…'

Brian held up the flat of his palm. 'You're sceptical, I understand,' he said. 'I'm getting ahead of myself, forgive me. Let me tell you who I am.'

He eased back in his seat. 'I worked for twenty-six years as a planning officer for Sheffield City Council, serving the last twelve of them as what is now known as the Head of Planning and Regeneration. They like to tinker with the job titles every now and again. I think it gives some people the feeling that they are more important than they actually are.

'Anyway, I was forced to resign my position almost six months ago. I was foolish. I laid myself open to certain personal indiscretions in my private life which the hierarchy at the council became aware of. They told me they could prevent the information from leaking into the public domain only if I accepted an offer of early retirement and agreed to go.'

'Sounds like blackmail.'

Brian drew in a deep breath and held up his hands as if he were about to surrender. 'I had my family to think of. It would have destroyed them.'

Martin nodded that he understood the predicament.

'Anyway, prior to leaving the council a great deal of my time and the department's energy had been spent on the Swarbrook Hill project – have you heard of it? It's a two hundred-acre village development to the east of the city boundary on land that was former industrial premises and a landfill site.'

'We're aware,' said Martin. 'We were represented at the public inquiries and registered our concerns over some of the contamination hot spots found by the Environment Agency and the risk of pollution caused by disturbing disused mine workings. We won a few concessions and we're hoping the chief scientific officer is sympathetic to the issues we raised when he files his report to the planning committee. There are a lot more changes we'd like to see put into place.'

'Don't bet on it, Mr Bestwick,' said Brian, ominously. 'The top men at the council, and especially the leader, are particularly keen to get this through the planning stage smoothly and without delay. I shared many of your concerns and have tried to pressure the developers, at every stage of the process, to exercise due diligence over every important detail, but I believe my caution became an inconvenience to the council leader. I'm convinced that contributed to my premature exit from my post. I think he wanted someone in place who would be more prepared to turn a blind eye to some of the more contentious aspects of the project.'

Martin's attention was now completely engaged. 'That is worrying.'

'But that's not the worst of it,' Brian added, his

expression becoming graver still. 'Towards the end of my time in charge I heard tell of reports that pre-dated the investigations carried out specifically on this project. Very alarming reports. They were little more than rumours at that stage but deeply concerning rumours which, if proven to be true, would mean the entire development would have to be brought to a complete and immediate end. Unfortunately, my time in post ended before I could gather any evidence. I did raise the subject privately with the council leader and he denied there was any truth in my suggestions. He refused to allow me to pursue my inquiries officially. Again, I can't entirely rule out in my own mind the possibility that my fall from grace and my raising these concerns with Cranford Hardstaff were not unconnected.'

Hardstaff. That name keeps cropping up. Valerie had used it as a lure to get Martin to the wine bar and he speculated again what her motives might have been. He had less reason to be suspicious of the man now facing him across the table, but could he too be trying to snag Martin with a different sort of bait? Perhaps he should be more suspicious. What Brian had told him so far was alarming but where was his proof?

'What do you expect me to do with this, Brian? Blackmail, conspiracy, rumour – we can't base a campaign of resistance on that. We need evidence.'

'I'm coming to that,' Brian added with a self-satisfied grin.

'I fulfilled my end of the non-disclosure agreement I signed by remaining silent for the first five months after I accepted the council's terms, but my conscience would not rest. I was troubled by what I knew, dissatisfied by my actions, but then I saw you, Mr Bestwick, on the TV news one night, standing up to Hardstaff over the issue of a tree felling and you spurred me on, sir. I saw a man who was not prepared to allow himself to be pushed around by the powerful bureaucrats, no matter if it was at a personal cost, and I felt ashamed of myself. I vowed to do my duty, not as an employee of the council but as a servant of mankind and mother nature.'

He paused for dramatic effect. Martin, intrigued if a little bemused, waited for him to deliver the crescendo.

'I still had contacts. I approached one and he did me a great favour, at substantial risk to his own career, by securing me copies of the documents I needed.' Brian reached into a black leather case at his feet and pulled out a plain brown A3 envelope. He placed it carefully on the table like it was the crown jewels and patted it twice.

'Here they are,' he declared, proudly.

Brian kept his hand on the envelope, signalling that he was not quite prepared to surrender its contents yet.

'You have heard, I presume, of the Trent Coal Preparation plant in Nottinghamshire?'

Anyone involved in an environmental action group over the last half a century, especially in this part of the world, knew about the Trent Coal Preparation plant. One of the pioneers of developing smokeless fuel since the start of the twentieth century, their product had done so much to cut levels of the choking air pollution which hung like a permanent fog over so many industrialised urban areas but the processes they used created a different sort of danger.

An explosion in the late-1960s and a fire in the mid-1980s were, from an ecological point of view, two of the worst industrial accidents the UK had ever known. The highest ever levels of harmful dioxins, the toxic by-products of the plant's processes which have been shown to cause skin disease, cancers and infertility, were recorded in rivers and in farm livestock for miles around and for many years after.

'Of course,' said Martin.

'Then you will be aware that the manufacturing processes and incineration of chemical waste were shown to produce two hundred and ten different types of dioxins and that the plant was used to manufacture thousands of tons of toxic chemicals derived from coal tar heat treatment and refinery. They included the one used to devastating effect as a herbicide and defoliant by the USA during their chemical warfare programme in the Vietnam War – the one known as Agent Orange.'

'Yes, I was aware.' Martin acknowledged, soberly.

'The plant has long since closed and has been largely dismantled now, of course, but the company never revealed where they dumped all the contaminated debris and unwanted excess waste products, many of which can never be made safe. The report I began to investigate before I was removed from post was that one of their preferred dumping sites was former industrial land to the east of the Sheffield city boundary on the site now known as Swarbrook Hill. The rumour proved to be true and here,' Brian patted the envelope on the table again, 'is the proof.'

He sat back and observed, waiting for the full weight

of his words to settle. Martin stared blankly at Brian and then at the envelope. This was almost too much, the information too awful, the implications too dreadful. How could someone take all that in straight away?

'This went on for years in the days when these matters were far less stringently regulated than they are today – and it wasn't only waste from the Trent Coal Preparation plant that was dumped at Swarbrook Hill. The site was also used to dispose of thousands of tonnes of contaminated fly ash from a waste incinerator plant in London. Pure fly ash contains ten times more dioxins than was left in soil by Agent Orange, which has been shown to be responsible for a huge number of birth defects and disease in Vietnam. The waste plant was generating 20 tonnes of this every day and a lot of it ended up at Swarbrook Hill.

'If this building development is allowed to go ahead, they would be situating a community of 1,200 new homes on a time bomb. It is too appalling to contemplate what the effects could be if this dump site is disturbed by the construction work. One millionth of a gram of some dioxins are enough to kill a small rodent and there is Lord knows how much of this waste under the ground at Swarbrook Hill. I was in consultation with the developers almost from day one, six years ago, and I know their plans inside and out. If my calculations, based on the information in these files, are correct, then the school they plan to build will be slap bang on top of the main dump site. They cannot be granted planning permission. This development has to be stopped.'

Martin nodded. His mind was racing through the steps

he would have to take.

'We're only a small group but we have national affiliations, of course, and I'll have to consult with them to make sure we do this properly, but if what you are telling me is confirmed in these documents, this is huge.' He was talking through the thoughts that were bombarding his brain at the rate of a million a minute. Brian smiled. He got it.

'It's all here,' he reassured.

'Will you stand with us when we make this public?' Martin asked. 'Your story would lend us extra credibility.'

'No,' Brian gave an emphatic shake of the head. 'That is my one condition of releasing these documents to you. If certain people at the city council find out that I played a part in handing you this information, I have no doubt that they will attempt to blacken my name with the disclosures they are holding against me. I must protect my family from that. I would also be contravening the non-disclosure agreements I signed as part of my departure and that would threaten my future financial security as well. My name must stay out of this.'

Martin judged that a reasonable trade-off. 'Fine. We will protect you as a source.'

Brian held their eye contact for a second or two longer as he judged the value of the promise and then slid the envelope across the table.

'In that case, this is all yours. I hope you can use it to do much good.'

He stood and stuck out a stiff arm again for a parting handshake. With a thin, satisfied smile, he picked up his case and left.

Martin sat again and opened the envelope, scanning the top sheets of the hundred or so it contained. This would need far greater in-depth scrutiny. He took out his phone from his apron pocket.

'Vivienne,' he said. 'It's Martin. We need to call an emergency meeting.'

19

The adrenaline rush of the plans set in place the previous evening was still surging as Martin strode through the sliding doors of the hospital's spinal injuries unit and headed for the nurses' station on the ward.

'Hi, Suneeta!' he called cheerily to the sister behind the desk as he stepped briskly towards the familiar bay.

'Oh! Martin,' she called after him and beckoned for him to come over.

Martin made an exaggerated, extravagant spin turn back towards her and leaned on the desk with a broad grin.

'Mrs Dawes has been a bit down today,' said the sister warily.

'Oh!' His face dropped in concern. 'Is something wrong?'

'Not as far as we know. The physio says she's almost as good as new and occupational therapy are doing an assessment to make sure she has everything she needs for when she goes home, so she should be able to leave us by the weekend.'

He looked puzzled. That was good news, wasn't it?

'Any idea what's bothering her then?'

The sister wrinkled her nose. 'She won't talk to us

about it. I thought maybe she might tell you.'

'OK.' Martin turned to resume his journey to the bay, though without the same spring in his step.

By the time the end bed of the bay came into view, though, he was all sunny disposition again – at least on the outside. Evelyn sat up in bed, not in her armchair, as she had been the last time he saw her. Her head stooped and her expression sagged, making her appear somehow much older overnight. She didn't seem to notice him approaching, nor did she seem to care when she lifted her eyes wearily and realised he was there.

'Hi, hi, hi Mrs Dawes! You're looking wonderful today,' he lied, bending to kiss her cheek. She was unmoved.

He touched her hand. 'I must apologise for not being able to come in to see you yesterday, but it turned into quite a day. I've so much to tell you and you will not believe what happened. I was on the phone until half past eleven last night talking to the people in London who are going to come up to help us out over the next couple of days and... anyway! How are you?'

Martin tried not to make it too obvious that this was no casual polite request. She appeared gaunt and crushed. Even in the early days after the accident, when she treated him with thinly disguised disdain, her feisty spirit shone through. There was nothing behind those eyes anymore. She looked ready to give up.

There was no point in his attempting to pretend he had seen nothing out of the ordinary. He was worried. This was more than 'a bit down'.

'What's bothering you, Mrs Dawes? This isn't like

you. What's happened? You can talk to me.'

She said nothing but tilted her head slightly towards him and fixed him with sad, watery eyes for only a second before the effort of the gesture appeared too much and she slipped back into the same doleful pool of misery.

Martin gently rubbed the back of her hand as it lay limply on the bed.

'Please tell me what's wrong, Mrs Dawes. I want to help.'

He rubbed her hand again, as if attempting to gently coax it back into life, but spoke no more, giving her the space to consider his offer.

Without moving, she said finally in a faint, croaky voice, 'I don't want to go home.'

So that was it. He absorbed the announcement for a moment.

'Why's that?'

Evelyn appeared reluctant to explain. She wanted to tell him but was wrapped so tightly in the web of her darker thoughts of the last day or so that it was difficult to get the words out. She struggled to force her head free of her own binding and added: 'I don't want to be alone again.'

The words pierced him. He saw her deepest fears and the low ebb they had taken her to, and it was heartbreaking. But why did she think she was going to be alone again?

'You don't need to be on your own, Mrs Dawes. I'll be just across the road from you and I'll be able to pop over every day for a cuppa and…'

'You didn't come yesterday,' she said flatly.

'No, no, that's true,' Martin admitted. Was that what had brought on her black mood? It had been practically impossible for him to break free for even an hour with the way the day had taken an unexpected turn but the guilt he felt about her being in this hospital bed in the first place stung him again.

'I couldn't be here yesterday for a whole bunch of reasons and I'm sorry about that but I would have called in if I could and when you're back in your home and just across the road it'll be so much easier for...'

'Don't pretend, Martin,' she interrupted. 'I know how it's going to be. You only came to see me all this time because it made you feel better about causing the accident...'

'Mrs Dawes, that's not–'

'... and once they send me home, you'll get back to your normal, interesting life and you'll forget about me. You'll be free of me.'

'That's not fair and it's not true,' he said, firmly, trying not to show how much her words had hurt. 'I come to see you because we're friends. I know we didn't know each other before the accident but we do now and I'm not going to let that slide just because you're not in the hospital. I want us to stay friends and I promise...'

'You promised you were going to help me find my daughter. You haven't lived up to that promise, have you? Why should I believe you again?'

'I will find Tanya. I will.' His voice cracked through the emotion now welling inside. 'I can understand how much this means to you and I wasn't just saying when I told you I would do all I could to bring your daughter to

182

you again. If it's at all possible, I'll bring Tanya to you so that you can walk out of the hospital with her this weekend.'

'Are you going to see Frank tomorrow then?' She was angry now, confrontational.

Martin sighed. 'I can't tomorrow.' It pained him to make the admission and Evelyn tutted in an I-knew-it kind of way.

'I'll be at a press conference which is going to get national coverage tomorrow. We're going to break a news story that will expose a cover-up in the corridors of power and could save thousands, maybe tens of thousands, of people from being exposed to deadly contaminated waste. We might even be saving lives, so I'm sorry, Mrs Dawes, but tomorrow I'll be doing something I have to do and I wouldn't attempt to get out of it even if I could because it is so important – and not only to me. Some issues are much bigger than me and you but that doesn't mean I don't care about you anymore. We're friends now and that means friends for life. I will go to visit your ex-husband, but I'm afraid it will have to wait until Friday.'

Martin glanced shiftily around the other patients in the bay, suddenly aware that he had raised his voice more than he intended to, but it had to be said. For all the sympathy he had for her feelings, Mrs Dawes had to be put straight. To suggest he didn't care was going too far.

She lowered her eyes, sheepishly. Martin had never given her a telling-off before and she had deserved it.

'I'm sorry,' she mumbled.

'That's all right,' he replied. Neither of them looked at the other.

'I'm just scared,' she said. 'I've got used to the nurses talking to me every day and the physio people and the domestics and they're all so lovely to me. And I've got used to you coming to visit and chatting about your café and all the other bits and pieces and I'm scared that I'll only have my telly for company again once I leave here. I don't think I could stand that.'

'I won't let that happen.' Martin leaned forward to enfold Evelyn in a reassuring hug. 'I can't promise to be there for you twenty-four hours a day, but I'll never be further away than the end of the phone and there's no reason why we can't see each other every day. We can go to each other's houses – I'd love to cook a meal for you sometimes – and there's no reason why you can't come to me at the café whenever you fancy. Some of my regulars are dying to meet you. They ask about how you are all the time.'

They ended the embrace. Evelyn felt the dark mist clearing. She had been left with too much time to think and had not realised she had been painting herself into a corner. She saw that now.

'So, you've got a big announcement to make tomorrow, have you?'

Both of them were glad for the change of subject. Enough had been said. Martin lifted the top brown plastic bucket seat off the stack and brought it to the side of the bed.

'That's right. Big press conference. The people in London have got all the contacts and they say all the top media – TV, newspapers, radio – are going to be there. We're going to tell them how we've got documentary

184

evidence that tonnes and tonnes of highly dangerous chemical waste has been buried secretly at a derelict site in Sheffield over a period of twenty-odd years through the sixties, seventies and eighties and, you'll never guess, it's lying there in the ground where they're planning to start building a huge new housing development! Right on top of all this incredibly toxic contaminated waste! We're going to demand that all plans to develop the site are stopped immediately, pending a major inquiry to establish just how dangerous it would be to put people at risk by going ahead. Then we want to see an investigation take place to find out the extent of the official cover-up that must have been going on for years. We need to know how high up this goes. Historically, we have to be told who allowed the dumping to go ahead in the first place, why nobody has ordered that the site is made safe in the meantime and who, knowing that all this poison was lying just under the surface all these years, still gave the go-ahead for 1,200 houses to be built on top of it. Did the developers know? Was the council aware? This is absolutely huge, Mrs Dawes. It's by far the biggest thing the Sheffield Environmental Action Network has ever been involved in and the implications are massive.'

Martin paused. He had hardly drawn breath in his eagerness to hurry out the words that had been bursting for air all morning. He struggled to stop his emotions from bubbling over and choking his voice. He had to let her know how much this meant to him.

'This is everything I've dreamed of becoming involved in. We all start out wanting to save the whole planet when we join an environmental organisation, change the world, but, for groups like ours, it's not about coming up with a solution for all the world's problems. It's a matter of taking care of what happens on our own doorstep. That's our responsibility. We save the planet one piece at a time. I've always said that if we all play a part, no matter how small, we all make the ultimate aim achievable and this is our time to make a real difference. This is our chance to change our corner of the world for the better and for ever.'

Evelyn watched him like a proud parent. 'Good for you,' she beamed and shuffled to sit up straighter in bed, then added, 'Do you know what, I think I'd like to get up now.'

20

The late morning press conference had come to an end almost an hour ago and now the offices of Sheffield City Council were in a state of pandemonium.

One of the calls put to the media at that press conference had been a demand to find out who knew about the dumping of dangerous chemical waste on the site earmarked for a major new housing development. The media had, in turn, bombarded the council with calls demanding to be told how much they knew about it. At the council, however, top officials were chasing around in the frenzied hope of finding anyone who knew anything at all.

Or would admit to it.

Cranford Hardstaff knew plenty. He was just not saying.

He was, in fact, not saying much of anything to anybody. He said very few words to his assistant, Colin Perkins, when he was informed for the third time that the communications manager had requested guidance in putting together the council's response to the revelations of the press conference, but he had said enough to make it plain to Perkins that he would not take kindly to being asked for a fourth time.

As he fielded yet another call from a senior council official asking for an urgent consultation with Hardstaff, Perkins wondered, not for the first time, if he really wanted to be the senior assistant in the office of the council leader anymore.

Not only was Hardstaff in no mood to talk, he had hardly moved at all for the last twenty minutes. He slouched toad-like in his black leather executive chair behind the desk, his elbow leaning against the armrest as he gently rubbed his throbbing temple with a circular motion of his index finger. His eyes were fixed on the large TV screen mounted on the wall, waiting for the national news bulletin to end and for the local news programme to begin; smouldering, mulling, plotting, stoking his festering temper closer and closer to melting point.

As far as he had been able to establish, he had not been personally implicated in the allegations made at the press conference and he was waiting to see if his name would be mentioned in the local TV report. He knew it might only be a matter of time anyway. Hardstaff had been sure to make it widely known that he was a champion of the Swarbrook Hill project because he wanted to harvest the maximum credit from it when the plans came to fruition. The media knew that. That was why they would surely come hunting for him. Even if he could steer clear of initial scrutiny for his involvement in the scandal, he might not be able to hold them off for long because they would surely demand that someone was held responsible. There had to be someone to blame. If they ever found out just how much he knew, they would not stop until they had his head on a stake.

But if he could just hold them off for a while, be granted the chance to put out a response which hit the right levels of shocked concern along with a pledge of righteous determination to get to the bottom of such a serious matter, Hardstaff hoped he might yet avoid the worst of it.

If he could just buy a little time, they might yet be able to palm off the blame on someone else. A high-ranking council official who has since died, maybe. That was always a sound tactic. The dead cannot put their side of the story.

If he could just keep them from the full truth of how much he knew, make sure no one ever found out he had taken money from the developer on the guarantee that the project would pass through the council processes without anyone finding out just what lay below the ground on the site, he might yet avoid the worst of outcomes – disgrace, dismissal.

Prison.

For it to come to that, someone would have to talk. Helena Morrison and Yuvraj Patel would not talk. They had too much to lose because they were also in it too deep. Neither would the head of the development company give the game away and they were the only four people who knew the full extent of their private arrangement. Who else could denounce them?

Unless. Hughes had not reported back yet to confirm that the honey trap had been sprung and Bestwick's silence had been secured. He should have heard by now. If Bestwick really did have something on them then they had to guarantee that the danger had been neutralised.

They had to keep his mouth shut.

It had better have been done.

But even that would not save the project now. It was dead. That was for certain. The minimum the council would be expected to do would be to put the brakes on it and that, alone, would kill the deal with the developer. There would be no way the planning approval request would even get as far as the order of business at the next meeting of the planning committee, let alone that it would be granted. Hardstaff knew that Swarbrook Hill would not even be considered again until the full council established exactly what was under the ground on the development site and once they found that out – well, that really would be that.

Hardstaff knew he would, if necessary, fight with the ferocity of a cornered tiger to keep himself out of prison but the rest – the money, his legacy, his name in the Queen's Birthday Honours List – were gone.

He had been so close he could taste it. The more he thought about it, the more his bitterness grew and the darker his mood became.

His phone on the desk vibrated with an incoming call for the thousandth time in the last hour and, for the thousandth time, he refused to answer it.

It was the head of the development company. Again. He, too, would be wanting someone to blame and that meant he would be blaming Hardstaff. Hardstaff was not in the mood to be yelled at.

He glanced from the phone screen back to the TV. The opening titles for the local news bulletin were just finishing. Hardstaff reached for the remote control to take the volume off mute as the middle-aged male anchor with a sharp suit and easy smile was introducing himself.

'First this afternoon, it has been alleged that the proposed site for a new one hundred and thirty million-pound housing project in Sheffield is a historical dumping ground for dangerous contaminated chemicals.'

Hardstaff snarled. *Top story. Hadn't they got anything better?*

'Reporting for us at the hotel where a press conference to announce this discovery has been held this morning is Michelle Rogers. This all sounds pretty worrying, Michelle.'

The camera switched to a young woman with a suitably grave expression who was holding a microphone at just below chin level. In the background was a row of chairs behind a table on a raised platform in a vast room, with rows of other chairs set in front of it to accommodate the nation's media. The main event had plainly ended long ago, though several people could still be seen over her shoulder, tidying up discarded press releases.

'Yes indeed, Declan. The environmental group that hosted today's press conference said they had been handed leaked confidential documents which proved that highly toxic waste material had been buried in a landfill site on former industrial land between Sheffield city centre and Rotherham. Some of this waste, it was alleged, was left over from the terrible Trent Coal Preparation plant fire which, you may remember, caused a major ecological emergency across a large region of Nottinghamshire back in 1984. They said that tremendously dangerous chemicals were buried secretly over a period of twenty-seven years dating back to the late 1960s and that they are still under the ground. Adding to the concern raised by these leaked documents is that this historic landfill site has been earmarked for a development of 1,200 new homes, which, the group say, would be exposing thousands of people to serious and possibly deadly health risks.'

The camera shot panned back to reveal the man stood alongside the reporter. He was around four inches shorter than her and was standing self-consciously stiffly in a plain blue shirt buttoned all the way up to the neck. Hardstaff recognised the face. His face reddened and his knuckles whitened.

'With me here is Martin Bestwick of the Sheffield Environmental Action Network. Martin, this is a shocking claim. How worried should we all be?'

Hardstaff did not hear the response. He picked up a hefty glass paperweight, presented to him several years earlier to commemorate some notable anniversary of the Sheffield Glassblowers' Guild, and hurled it at the TV screen, shattering it in a fizz of sparks.

'I might have fucking known!' he yelled, as smoke rose from the broken screen.

Colin Perkins, startled by the crashing noise behind the closed door of the council leader's office, wondered if he dared go in to find out what had caused it.

***

Helena Morrison's phone had also hardly stopped ringing for the last hour but, unlike Cranford Hardstaff, she had not taken the option of ignoring it.

She knew, even before she answered the first call from

192

the deputy head of Planning and Regeneration, that it had to be fairly serious for him to disturb her during a period of personal leave. As the full extent of just how serious it was dawned on her, Helena felt the blood drain from her face.

What she had agreed to was to help gloss over concerns with the Swarbrook Hill site and though those concerns were significant enough to weigh heavily on her conscience, they were not in the same league as what she was now being told might actually lay beneath the ground. If she had known this level of danger had existed there was no way she would have agreed to go through with Cranford's cover-up. Not at any price.

Helena talked through tactical responses and damage limitation with the deputy and the planning committee chairman and then… Then it was obvious that she would have to go in. Personal leave or not, this was a full-blown council crisis and her leadership was needed.

Darrell said he understood. He was fine with being left alone in the house. Of course he was. He was perfectly capable of getting around on his crutches now and did not need Helena to be there twenty-four/seven, busying herself with pointless domestic chores and attempting to drown him in cups of tea. She realised that but it did not stop her feeling oddly vulnerable again as she left him alone for only the second time in the week since they got home from the hospital. There was a certain sense of safety in them both being there in the house, shut away behind a permanently locked door, and even though she understood that it would not make the slightest difference to their chances of survival should the gunman come calling again, there was a kind of comfort in them being there, together. Their marriage had not been an especially happy one for quite a while, but Helena believed the shock of the shooting had brought them a little closer together again.

Just as it was when she set out for the Saturday morning meeting at the Botanical Gardens with Cranford and Yuvraj, leaving Darrell alone was a wrench. Maybe part of that was because she still held herself responsible for his injuries but that was not the full story. Dormant feelings had been awakened. They were good feelings.

Since that Saturday morning meeting at the Botanical Gardens, Helena's affections for Yuvraj had been heading in the opposite direction. She was still cross with him for being so weak when they were meant to present a united front in standing up to Cranford. He had left her with no alternative but to allow the council leader one more chance to put the situation right his way, even though doing so was against her better judgement.

And what of that? It certainly didn't seem as if Cranford had the situation back under control. Not by any stretch of the imagination.

That made her even more angry with Yuvraj but his was the first number she called as soon as she set out in the car for the council offices at the town hall. They needed to talk.

He was already waiting for her in the Peace Gardens, huddled into a large overcoat and sitting on a bench. Though it was bitterly cold, it was better that they met outside. They did not want to take a chance on being overheard.

194

Yuvraj rose when he saw her walking briskly towards him and, when she was close, he instinctively moved to embrace her. With the slightest of moves, she backed away enough to make him realise that would not be a good idea. It was important they were neither seen nor heard.

'Hi,' he said, tentatively, and she returned the greeting with a glimmer of a smile. 'How much have you heard?'

Helena, standing still for the first time since she had finally managed to find a parking space, felt the judder of a shiver down her spine.

'Enough.'

'It's a shit show,' added Yuvraj, watching to make sure a young woman pushing a pram, the only other person in the gardens, was not heading their way.

'Have you heard from Cranford?' she asked. He shook his head.

'We can't rely on him to get us out of this mess. We have to watch our own backs and we have to be careful in case Cranford tries to pin part of this on us, don't you agree?'

Yuvraj shrugged and that made her cross again. She needed more than that.

'How much do you think Cranford knew?' she said.

He puffed his cheeks, avoiding eye contact.

'Fuck's sake, Yuvraj, talk to me, will you? We're already far too deep in this mess and that's when we only thought there were a few higher-than-normal readings and worries about what happens if the old mine workings are disturbed. This is a whole new level of dangerous now and if it's suggested we knew all this poisonous waste was on the site and that we were prepared to conceal that from the public in return for a bribe from the developers – well, I don't even want to think about what might happen to us then, to be honest. If it ever gets out how much we were complicit in the cover-up we are going to be left wide open to being roped in as part of a huge, horrible conspiracy and it will be impossible to make anybody believe we didn't know the full truth. At the very least we'd lose everything, and we might be looking at going to prison for a very long time. We cannot allow that to happen. It's up to you and me to get ourselves out of this mess now because if Cranford knew everything and they are able to prove that, we could be in serious trouble. I don't think we can trust Cranford to protect us if they come for him and so we need to get one thing clear from the start – we have to find out how much Cranford knew.'

Yuvraj listened, increasingly edgy and agitated. He could not meet the challenge in her desperate glare. He could not face her. He turned away and lifted his head to gaze towards the dismal grey skies.

'Talk to me!' she demanded. 'We have to get this right.'

He reached to wrap his hands around the back of his head. The pounding pressure within it felt ready to burst free.

'He knew.'

Helena was momentarily stunned. 'What?'

'He knew,' Yuvraj repeated. 'Everything.'

She stared at him, disbelieving. How could Cranford do this? She felt dizzy and lowered herself on to the bench seat, bending forward and breathing heavily to stem the rising anxiety that was squeezing her heart. For all three of them to be caught up in something that was worse than they imagined was one thing but for one of their number to knowingly mislead…

'How can you be so sure?' Suddenly, she realised. His certainty.

Yuvraj, in torment, paced and cupped his hands to his face.

'You knew as well.' She could see it now. An eerie calmness enveloped her. As awful as it was, they had arrived at the truth.

He had no will to conceal it anymore. That would be pointless. He nodded.

'You knew. Both of you knew what was down there and you lied to me. You told me that all we were doing was to not set any unnecessary alarm bells ringing, that all the problems with the site could be resolved and that by helping the planning application get through committee we would be doing the right thing in the long run because the project would be so good for the city. You told me it was all right for us to take the developer's money because no harm would come of it and it would give us the chance to make a new life together. Even when our lives were put in danger – Darrell was shot, you had a gun pointed at you – even then you didn't tell me the truth. Even then, you preserved the lie and stood by Cranford instead of explaining the full, ghastly seriousness of what was really happening.'

'I was protecting you,' he pleaded.

'Protecting me! You drew me into a conspiracy which could have put the long-term health of thousands of innocent people at risk and you say you were protecting me! You were using me, Yuvraj. You needed me to see your sordid despicable plan through to the end and you were so blinded by greed that you didn't stop to consider the position you were putting me in for a moment. Protecting me!'

'It was better for you that you didn't know the full truth. That way you would not have been so seriously implicated if it ever–'

'Oh, thank you so very much, Yuvraj! I'm sure that would make the police look at my part in this in a completely different light. Do you think I'm stupid? Are you that stupid? You're a man of science. You're the senior scientific officer for the city, for fuck's sake – you're supposed to keep the people safe from the sort of danger you were deliberately exposing them to by agreeing to be a part of this whole appalling business. How can you sleep at night?'

He sank on to the bench now and Helena instantly stood, unable to tolerate being so close. She wanted to scream. Or hit him. Or both.

'Could you really have started a new life with me, knowing what you'd done? Knowing that you'd lied to me from the start. Could you have lived with your conscience? Do you even have a conscience?'

She circled around him, ready to strike.

'Did you even love me at all?'

He wailed and slumped, burying his head in shame.

'Of course I love you. I did all this for us.'

She gazed at him scornfully, loathing in her eyes.

'I don't believe you. I could never believe you again. If we get through this without being thrown in prison – if –

I never want to see your miserable face again, do you hear me? We're finished. Goodbye, Yuvraj.'

Helena stomped towards the town hall. She had a job to do.

21

In the dream, Beth had been wandering around a strange building so real she could almost reach out and run her fingers over the rough texture of the old brickwork as she turned corner after corner on to corridor after corridor that led nowhere. She was desperate to pee but could not find anywhere to go. Doing it there and then was not an option because there were so many people about and it was bad enough that they might all realise she was still in her nightclothes. There had to be a room off one of these corridors. If not a bathroom, any room where she could just squat in a corner and…

Her eyes opened. She was in bed, immersed in the soft warmth of the duvet, with her knees drawn up as another wave of pain from her achingly full bladder demanded her urgent attention. Beth curled her body a little tighter until the discomfort rolled through. Though she knew the solution was simple and far more easily achievable than it had been in her dream, she could not face having to give up the soothing comfort of her cosy sanctuary just yet.

It was the only thing that felt right at that moment. Without it, all that would be left would be the clammy rumble of impending rebellion from her stomach and bowel, the taste of dry bile in the back of her throat, the furry numbness of her tongue as it attempted to revive her cracked lips and the rhythmic throbbing in her head which beat with each deafening surge of blood pumped by her overworked heart.

It had been a good night.

Unable to face the prospect of another night in alone, Beth had called Cassie, one of her oldest friends. It turned out that they both lately lamented the loss of their wild days. Not the ones where they pushed the stakes so far that they teetered on the brink of oblivion but the ones where they still believed they were indestructible. When they revelled in the notoriety of playing harder than anyone else and set out to stack their reputations higher and higher all the time, at every opportunity, never realising that what they were building was always destined to come crashing down around them one day. Back then, they didn't care. It was just having fun.

That was why they decided to meet up, that night, straight away. Beth changed, touched up her makeup while she waited for the cab to arrive and launched herself into the past. They hit every city centre bar they fancied, led on and then brutally put down every man who foolishly thought they might win favour for the price of a few drinks and had not stopped drinking until after two in the morning. It was reckoning time now, but it had been worth it.

Another cramping stab in her abdomen convinced Beth there was no choice but to emerge from the duvet this time and, with a great surge of willpower, she was out and on her feet. She picked up her phone to check the time. Eight minutes to one. She also saw that there had been two missed calls, both from the school. It was too late to call them back now and they would have figured out for themselves she was not going to turn up to work. It was not the first time she had been a no-show. Words might be said this time – but who cares?

While she sat on the toilet, she sipped at water from the glass she usually stood her toothbrush in, trying to suppress the urge to throw up. The faint trace of mintiness was not helping, in truth. Still, she filled the glass again, after relieving her strained bladder, and walked groggily back to her side of the bed to seek out paracetamol. The recovery process was under way.

Did it always used to feel this bad in the morning? Possibly not. She was out of practice, but she had proved she could still do it. She smiled to herself, recalling blurry impressions of the previous night, and reached for her phone again.

God I feel like shit! Let's do that again soon. How ru?

The text to Cassie whooshed away and Beth put the phone on the bed beside her, waiting for a reply, waiting for the storm in her guts to move on, waiting for the paracetamol to kick in.

She shivered. It was cold out of bed. She contemplated climbing back in but decided she might be better off staying up, now she had done the hard bit. Her clothes from last night lay discarded in a pile on the bedroom floor. She could not face dealing with them. Instead, she pushed herself back to her feet, opened the bottom drawer of her wardrobe and took out a thick green jumper.

Coffee. She needed coffee.

Beth aimed for the door, then edged shakily, carefully down the stairs.

Wesley was in his favourite armchair in the front room, reading. It was one of those historical biographies he was always ordering. He had on his thick-rimmed reading glasses. She reckoned he only read those big, hefty volumes because he thought they made him look clever. He ignored her as she weaved across the room to the sofa in front of the TV. Neither of them said a word. That wasn't unusual these days. They had an unspoken agreement to not speak much and it suited them both.

Beth slumped dramatically into the sofa with an intentionally audible exhale of air, stared into space for a few moments and grabbed the TV remote control off the chair arm, pointing it at the set and pressing the power button.

Loose Women. That'll do nicely. Wesley hated it. It would really piss him off. She turned up the volume.

He remained still, unmoved, in his chair, focusing only on the book, determined not to give her the pleasure of knowing she was getting under his skin.

Beth could, nonetheless, feel the rising heat of his annoyance. If she got up now to make coffee and left the TV playing to itself for a while, he would be bound to bite eventually.

But her phone rang. Maybe it was Cassie, calling to recap some of the previous night's highlights. It wasn't. The name on the screen said Darrell.

'Hi Darrell.' Her voice was croaky.

'Hey babe.' His was low and deep, as usual. She turned down the TV volume. This would be much better. 'Can you talk?' he added.

'Yeah, I can talk.' Surely her husband's interest was engaged now. 'How's your foot?'

Beth was, by now, convinced Wesley had nothing to do with the assault but she checked his reaction as she said the words, all the same. Not a flicker.

'Hurts like hell but I'll be OK. Are you on lunch?'

She lay back and ran her fingers through her short orange hair and curled her legs up on to the sofa.

'Nah, I gave myself the day off.'

They allowed a moment of silence to pass between them.

'Perfect. Helena's gone out. She said she'd be out all afternoon. Some kind of crisis summit at the council. I was hoping you would come over. We'd have the house to ourselves. I want you to make me feel better. My body needs you. It's been the longest time without you.'

'My body's missed you too,' she replied, staring straight at Wesley as she did. Challenging him.

'Good,' he purred. 'Come on over. I'm ready for you.'

Wesley took a bookmark off his lap and closed the pages over it. She watched, expectantly. But he was only pausing to take a cigarette from the packet on the table beside him and light it. He blew smoke towards the ceiling and opened the book again.

How irritating!

'You know what, I'm going to pass,' she said.

'Aw, come on babe.'

'No. I've been thinking about this for the last few days. It was fun and the sex was good and all that, but I think it's time to bring it to an end. I think we're done.'

'You don't mean that.'

'Yeah, I mean it. It's over, Darrell. Don't call me anymore.'

'Babe…'

'And don't call me babe.' She hung up and tossed the phone onto the sofa.

Wesley took another drag from his cigarette and said nothing.

'It's not easy to crush them but it's better to do it that way. Less painful on the long run, don't you agree, Wes?'

He turned a page.

'We were having an affair for the best part of three months, right under your nose if you'd been smart enough to notice. It was purely physical, but it was great. He's got a good body – tall, muscular, nice dick. Completely the opposite of you, actually.'

Wesley flicked ash into the ashtray.

'We had sex all the time. Lots of different ways, different places – in fact, do you remember when I told you I was going to Birmingham to meet a girl friend? I lied. I was with Darrell. We spent the whole weekend in bed.'

He cleared his throat and pushed the bridge of the glasses higher on his nose.

'I just told you I've been seeing someone else. Doesn't that bother you?'

Wesley took a last drag on the cigarette and stubbed it out.

'You screw who you like. Why should that bother me?' he said casually.

She was angry now. He was the one meant to be angry.

'Look at you. You've stopped even trying to be a proper man. You're pathetic. You're a pathetic, little, impotent…'

He folded his book, using his finger to keep his place.

'Then why don't you just go? Piss off now, but don't take anything other than what you had with you when you first came through that door. Let me remind you, that was nothing. You were nothing. In one moment of weakness, I let you drag me to the Register Office and that's the biggest mistake I ever made because you're a parasite, Beth. You make like you want out, but you haven't got the guts to leave because that would mean having to fend for yourself until you find some other poor sod to feed off. And you call me pathetic?'

He opened his book again, though it was more for show this time. He wasn't seeing the words anymore.

She sat stiffly, tight-lipped. If she got up and stormed out of the room now, that would mean he had won by having the last word. She wanted to come up with the perfect response to slap him down again but could not find one.

The ring of a phone broke the tense silence. It was Wesley's. He looked at the screen.

Foghorn.

He cursed under his breath. Hardstaff was the last person he wanted to talk to right now.

He was rising to his feet as he accepted the call and muttered 'Hold on' down the line before marking his page and leaving the book on the chair. Beth took note of his initial reluctance to answer. She listened as he climbed the stairs to seek the privacy of one of the bedrooms and then snatched up her phone, following him as quietly as she could.

'Yeah.' Wesley pushed the door closed in the room where he kept his computer.

'You've fucked it up again, haven't you?' There was even more spite in Hardstaff's tone than usual. Wesley thought he knew why.

'There was a problem.' Valerie had told him what the problem was. They hadn't anticipated that. Why should they have? You can't know everything about a target without running proper surveillance and background checks and he hadn't been given time for that.

'No shit.' There was no point trying to explain it to Hardstaff. 'People told me you were the best there is because you were reliable. I'm starting to think I was deceived. This is twice you've fucked it up for me. Perhaps I ought to start putting the word out that you've lost your touch.'

As much as he wanted to tell Hardstaff to fuck himself, Wesley knew that would not be a smart move. He could give himself the option of never doing work for the pompous bastard in the future but only after he had finished this job. His reputation depended on it and his reputation was everything.

'I'll put it right. I'm working on it.'

'Don't bother,' Hardstaff spat. 'The situation has moved on. He's screwed me over good and proper. The gloves are off. I want him taking care of, once and for all.'

Wesley was not easily taken aback but he was this time. He even questioned that he had understood the meaning right.

'You want him terminating?'

'That's exactly what I want. Is that an issue?'

'Not an issue. A bit of an escalation, that's all. It'll cost you.'

'I don't care. This fucker has already cost me a fortune and if he isn't taken down, I don't know what else he'll cost me. I need him out of the picture for good. All I need to know is if you're up to it and if you can get it right, for once.'

Wesley did not rise to the barb. He had to think about it. But what was there to think about? He could not have word getting out that he turned the job down. The circles he mixed in would not look kindly on such an apparent show of weakness.

'I can take care of it. I'll need a few days. This has to be done carefully.'

'Understood, but this is a priority job. Do it soon but not in a way that makes it obvious. Make it look like an accident or whatever, just not like a hit. Nothing to raise suspicion in case he's not working alone. And you do this one yourself. No palming it off. Nobody but you and me are to know about this.'

Hardstaff was rattled, Wesley could tell. Somehow, that made him feel a little better about doing it. He was back in charge.

'It's done. I'll handle it.'

There was no sharp rebuke this time. Wesley preferred this Hardstaff. He was vulnerable.

'Good. Let me know when it's resolved.'

He hung up.

Wesley lay his phone on the desk. He needed to

compose himself. He had never taken on a hit before. He was not completely sure how to go about it. This would have to be thought through properly so that there would be no way the police could trace it back to him. He was used to planning out his jobs meticulously, so that wasn't a problem. Get the planning right and the rest would be easy. There had been lots of jobs over the years he had taken on not knowing how to implement them, but he always found a way. This would be no different.

This would be his first hit, but what was it he said to Beth the other day?

There's a first time for everything.

Outside the door, Beth switched off the voice recorder on her phone and sneaked nimbly back down the stairs, her slender frame touching each step so lightly she made no sound at all.

If the recording came out as clearly as she could hear, pressed as closely as she dared to the slightest of openings in the door, it would be dynamite. This was her way out.

This was how she could get Wesley out of the way and help herself to his hidden cash without fear of reprisal.

This was her chance to start again and make sure money was not a concern.

He had told her she was free to screw whoever she wanted. Well, she had decided.

You. I choose to screw you.

22

Beth gave herself the following day off too but at least she paid school the courtesy of phoning in to lie about the reason why this time. If things worked out the way she planned, it would not matter for much longer anyway.

She caught the Supertram to the city centre and walked to the police station on Snig Hill. It was not a part of the centre she had been to before, at least as far as she could remember. Her focus previously had been avoiding having to go to police stations rather than seeking one out, but this was different. This was doing something that would work to her advantage.

The red brick and cold concrete police building loomed on the eyeline long before Beth had reached the bottom of Angel Street and she began to wonder if she had the stomach to go through with it. The large mural of an old steelworker's head, made from coloured bricks and covering the full depth of a four-storey gable end, was a welcome distraction. By the time she had finished musing about the stories she had been told of the times Sheffield was known the world over for its steel and how those stories felt so much like ancient history now, she was almost there.

A sign on the front of the building pointed her down a row of steps to the entrance and Beth braced herself, walking briskly to the main doors and inside.

'I'd like to talk to a police officer,' she said to the sergeant at the enquiry desk. He appeared to her so old that he should probably have retired by now, with his bald head and moustache streaked with more grey than dark hairs. Perhaps, she thought, it was an inevitable consequence of being a career policeman and he was actually a lot younger than he looked.

The sergeant scrutinised her with dark seen-it-all eyes. It made her uncomfortable, unable to hold eye contact, like he was able to gaze straight through her and see all her sins.

'Could I ask what you would like to talk to an officer about please?'

Beth inwardly scolded herself for being intimidated. She was doing them a favour, after all.

'I have information about the jewellery shop robbery, the one where the people were shot.' She leaned forward and spoke softly to try to make sure she was not overheard. 'And information about other crimes. Serious crimes.'

The sergeant nodded and picked up the phone on the desk in front of him.

'I have a young woman at the desk who would like to talk to an officer,' he said when his call was answered. He seemed to be paying particularly close attention to her hair colour as she glanced around her at the bustling activity in the room. 'OK, thanks.'

He slid a clipboard and pen across the desk to catch Beth's attention again.

'Could I ask you to sign in here, please? Somebody will be down to see you in a couple of minutes.'

The officer who bounced jauntily down the stairs to the reception to meet her was no older than she was. He wore plain clothes, with only the identity badge swinging on a lanyard around his neck distinguishing him from being mistaken for some young bloke who had just wandered in off the street. With his close-cut beard that was little more than dark stubble and carefully gelled dark hair, Beth thought he was good looking. His eyes were fresh and his smile easy.

'Hi. DC Harry Adams,' he said.

She shook his hand but did not reply.

He turned to the sergeant. 'Can we have room three sarge?'

The older officer checked his list and confirmed 'All yours,' offering Beth a badge with the word 'visitor' printed on it for her to wear around her neck. The detective constable watched as she pulled it over her head and gestured towards a door to his left.

'This way, please.'

The interview room was nothing like as foreboding as she imagined it would be. It was windowless and not a place a claustrophobic would want to be shut in alone for very long but it looked more like a display stand for an office furniture supplier's basic range than the spirit-sapping cold tile and bolted down fittings she was half-expecting. The DC invited her to sit on the blue steel-rimmed chair on the far side of the white-topped table and he sat opposite.

'Right,' he pulled a pad of paper towards him and

clicked down the top of his pen. 'Could I start by taking your details please?'

Beth hesitated. Part of her wanted to stand and leave, say she had made a mistake, changed her mind, but she also realised she had come too far to back out now. She answered his questions.

'And how can we help you Beth?' She watched him. Could she trust him? He seemed just like a nice, ordinary guy but he was a policeman and that was a hurdle she still had to clear. She decided to take a chance.

'I have information about that jewellery shop robbery last month. I think I know where some of the stuff they stole is kept and I think I know what happened to the gun.'

This time it was he who seemed to be weighing her up. *Was she for real?*

'OK, that's good. Can you tell me where the stolen goods are being kept?'

'It's a storage unit just off the Parkway. I have the details.'

The DC made a note. 'And the gun?'

'It's been got rid of, but I don't know where.'

He scribbled some more but slightly less enthusiastically. Maybe her information would not turn out to be as useful as he had initially hoped.

'So, can I ask how you came to know about the stolen goods and the gun?'

She pursed her lips. This really was the point of no return.

'It's my husband,' she said. 'He takes on work from criminals, you know, when they need to cover their tracks or need someone they can trust to dispose of evidence or take care of stuff until the heat dies down, that sort of thing. He's their fixer, their cleaner. They go to him because he's good at what he does.'

Beth hoped she had not come across as being proud of him.

'He's involved in lots of criminal activity, dealing with all sorts of low-life crooks, and I've known about this for as long as we've been together, but I've decided I can't keep quiet anymore. He should pay for all the bad things he's done.'

Adams checked over his notes again. Her surname. He was trying to join the dots.

'What's your husband's name, Beth?'

'Wes. Wesley Hughes.'

He wrote down the name and underlined it. It was not familiar to him, but maybe it would mean more to one of his more experienced colleagues.

'And how do you know the people involved in the jewellery shop robbery are using your husband's services?'

'He admitted it. As good as, anyway.'

'I see.' He was still unconvinced. Too much of this sounded vague, implausible.

'Just out of interest,' he added. 'How long have you known Wesley?'

'About three years. Just less than three years.'

'So why come forward now?'

Beth had hoped her previous silence would not lay her open to being charged with an offence herself. She had pinned her hopes on being protected by the strength of the information she could offer.

'I overheard him plotting to kill somebody.'

The young DC sat up straight. Interesting.

'I listened to him talking about it to someone on the phone. I recorded it.'

She rummaged through her bag for her phone.

'Would you like to hear it?'

DC Harry Adams went back upstairs to the CID offices. After playing him the recording, Beth had agreed to give him a copy and to provide a full formal statement. He held the signed papers in his hand as he scanned the room for someone to discuss it with.

Detective Sergeant Will Copson was on the far side of the office, leaning on the back of a junior officer's chair as they talked about something on the computer screen. Copson gave the officer two encouraging pats on the shoulder and began to walk away.

'Sarge,' Adams moved to intercept him.

'Harry lad. What's up?'

'I need a word. Does the name Wesley Hughes mean anything?'

The mention of the name seemed to change the DS's mood.

'He's been on the radar for a while. Despicable pond life that we haven't been able to pin down as yet. What have you got?'

'I've just been talking to his wife.'

'His wife?'

Adams nodded. 'She's just given a statement connecting him to the jewellery shop robbery and she played me a recording that implicates him in conspiracy to commit murder.'

'Really?' The DS smiled. 'Come with me. We need to take this to the DI.'

After they had both read the statement and had listened to the recording, DI Jane Jackson and DS Will Copson exchanged a look that said it all. It was the break they had been looking for.

'How do you want to play it, ma'am?' he asked.

She flicked through the pages of the statement again.

'With this and the statement from the witness who thought she saw him throwing the gun into the river – and the photos of him at the scene – I think we've got something to go on. The recording, I'm not sure. The voice she says is Hughes is fairly clear but it's hard to make out anything from the other voice. We'll need to see if one of the technical team can do anything with it to tidy it up a bit, but it might be useful to us.'

The DI closed the file with the statement in it and stood.

'I think with all this together we've got enough to justify sending in a diving team to see if they can recover a weapon from the area of the river where the witness saw him disposing of whatever it was – hopefully, the gun. Then I think we should apply for warrants to search the storage unit at the address Mrs Hughes has given us and his home. We see if we can find the gun, see if it matches the one used in the robbery and then we bring him in. Once we've got him in custody, we can execute the warrants and see what we find. That could lead us straight to the gang who carried out the robbery themselves. Also, maybe once we do have him in custody, we can get information off his phone which helps us identify who he was talking to in the recording.'

Copson and Adams sat opposite her, listening intently.

'I think perhaps we've got him this time,' she said. 'Then we'll see how much he values his own neck and how willing he is to give up the names of the people he works for. What Mrs Hughes has told us could turn out to be very useful indeed.'

23

Silverwood Court was not, as it turned out, a street name. Evelyn Dawes' estranged husband Frank lived, so it appeared, in a large, bright and modern retirement village with its own fitness suite, bar, restaurant and function rooms.

As he entered the lobby area, the rush of warm air reddened Martin's cheeks, prickling them back to life from the icy wind's deadening bite, but there might also have been another reason causing his blood to rise. Though he had tried not to think too often about the last time he had set out to confront Frank – the plan he now acknowledged was astonishingly, recklessly stupid, and the mortifyingly inept way he had handled it – the raw horror of that night came flooding back.

What on earth was I thinking?

Had he been given the right address, Martin was certain now he would not have gone through with the plan. He would have realised as soon as he checked it out on the map that there was no way he could. That would have saved an awful lot of anxiety and trouble.

But what if the falling branch had not stopped Mrs Dawes from coming here, as she had set out to? She must have been in a desperately unstable state of mind to think that threatening her former husband with a gun was her best – maybe her only – option. Would she have gone through with it?

He pictured her for a moment, sending terrified pensioners scurrying for cover behind the tall pot plants around the broad central ground floor piazza as she wielded the ancient Luger above her head like a modern-day Ma Barker, and he cringed. That was a prospect too appalling to contemplate – especially as, so it emerged, the gun did contain live ammunition.

The scene before him was considerably more serene. Martin had not expected it to be so plush. Raise the temperature outside by twenty degrees and throw in the faint sound of gently lapping waves and he might just have easily imagined he was in the reception of a four-star hotel, the type that specialised in offering oldies winter-long breaks in the Costas as a way of escaping the British freeze. The pace of the residents, none of them giving the impression they were in a particular hurry to get wherever they were going, was also positively Balearic.

There was a reception desk to the right and behind it sat a wiry middle-aged woman in blue-rimmed glasses. She wore a green fleece, protection against the occasional withering blast of cold air that announced someone had stepped through the main lobby doors. It had 'Silverwood Court Village' embroidered on the left and a metal name badge pinned to the right. She stopped what she was doing at the computer as Martin approached.

'Can I help you?' she asked with a textbook friendly receptionist smile.

'Hi. I've come to see one of your residents – Frank Dawes?' He did not intend the last part of his opening line to come out as a question, but he was still not convinced Evelyn's information was entirely reliable.

The name did not appear to ring any bells.

'Mr Dawes?' the receptionist repeated to herself as she conducted a brief mental search before turning to the computer for a more exhaustive one.

'I can't recall us having a resident of that name,' she mused as she scrolled down her list. 'We've got a Mr Davies.'

Martin shook his head. 'Definitely Dawes.'

'Hang on, I…' She spun on her chair to face the door of the largely glass-fronted administration office behind her and looked to see who was within beckoning distance.

'Charlotte, do you know if we've ever had a Mr Dawes with us?'

Martin suddenly realised there was another very real possibility. Given the age of so many of the people living here, they must have a fairly high turnover rate of deaths and newcomers, he thought. Could it be that Frank was no longer with us?

The woman in the office considered the question. 'It's not a name I've come across. Do you know the apartment number?'

'Do you know the apartment number?' relayed the receptionist, unnecessarily.

'I believe it's number fifty-two.'

She returned to her records.

'Fifty-two,' she said. 'Fifty-two. The resident in number fifty-two is called Frank Elliott.' She looked apologetically back at Martin as if to say, 'I know it's not the *exactly* the result you were after but it's the best I can do.'

It definitely was not the result Martin was after. He tried to consider his options and realised he might not have any. He had half-expected his efforts to hit a dead end and maybe this end was literally dead. That would not be easy news to break to Mrs Dawes.

At least the man in number fifty-two had the same first name. The trail may not be entirely cold.

'Are you sure he doesn't live here – or lived here fairly recently, like the last three years? I'm a friend of his former wife and she had a letter from her solicitor a couple of weeks ago which gave this as her husband's address and, well, it's very important that I find him.'

The receptionist's expression became grave with empathy, like she wanted nothing other in the world than to come up with the solution. She tapped at a few keys on the computer keyboard again, just to be sure, but could only draw another blank.

'Sorry,' she said, biting her lip.

Martin puffed his cheeks. There had to be a possibility he was in the right place. There had to be at least a trace of Frank Dawes.

'I'm sorry, I don't want to be a pain but, as I say, this is important. Is there a chance you could just ask this Mr Elliott if he had a wife called Evelyn? If the name means nothing to him, I must have been given the wrong address. I know it's a bit of a long shot.'

'I suppose I could…' She picked up the telephone and swiftly pressed four keys. 'I'll just see if he's in his apartment and if not, I could put out a call to the bar and restaurant areas in case he's – Oh, hi! Mr Elliott?'

She shot him an encouraged look. He's in!

'Hi. Sorry to bother you. It's Wendy at reception. Hi. I've got a gentleman here and he's trying to find someone he thinks might live here. He's been given your apartment number and, could I just ask, did you used to be married to a lady called Elaine?'

'Evelyn,' Martin corrected.

'Sorry, Evelyn.' She fell quiet, listening to his reply, and a smile spread across her thin face. 'You did! Was she? Oh, really? 1968? I wasn't even born then! Did she? Aw, bless!'

Martin waved to try to distract her attention from the unfolding life story. He wanted to see if this really could be his man.

'Could I speak to him?' he mouthed.

'Yes, I bet you were. Mr Elliott. Mr Elliott, the gentleman would like to know if he could speak to you. Yes, he's here now. Would you? That's lovely, I'll let him know.'

She hung up. 'He said he'll be down in a couple of minutes.'

'That's great. Thanks.' Martin was trying not to raise his hopes but at least this was better than no progress at all.

'You can wait for him over there if you like,' said the receptionist, pointing towards a lilac sofa opposite her desk. 'He might be a while.'

She was clearly used to dealing with older people.

He accepted the advice and took a seat.

This was about the first time in the last couple of days that he had time to do nothing. Since the mysterious Brian had come to his café to hand over those documents, it had been absolutely full on – the planning, the calls, the excitement. Then, after the press conference, there had been the interviews with all sorts of news outlets and more requests had still been pouring in as the rolling story gathered momentum. Their affiliated national body had begun the process of lobbying MPs to call for a national inquiry into what, it was now broadly accepted, was a huge scandal. This was big and getting bigger. It was tremendously thrilling to be a part of it.

One call he was contemplating, if he could find the time and the courage, was to get in touch again with the vampish Valerie. Though he had no regrets about making his excuses and leaving that night in the wine bar, there was just the smallest niggling thought that maybe she did have information that was useful to them. Could the toe-curling dirt she said she had on Cranford Hardstaff be tied in with the contaminated waste dumping site? If he could keep her at a safe distance, at the other end of a telephone…

But that was for a later time. His thoughts now had turned to the faint chance that he might be about to face the man Mrs Dawes had described as a spiteful monster. The man who had denied her access to their only daughter for no reason other than malice.

If he really was that man, Martin felt safer seeing him in a sedate retirement village for reasonably comfortably-off older folk than he had as he approached that door on a dark residential street. The wrong door, it emerged.

There had been nothing in what he could hear of the conversation with the receptionist to make him fear he was about to come up against a man Mrs Dawes believed was best tackled at gunpoint but there could be a possibility he would turn nasty when Martin asked him about why he had poisoned his daughter's mind against her mother. This would have to be dealt with delicately. He did not want to provoke an ogre.

With growing trepidation, he watched to see who would approach the reception desk.

A lady wearing a loose-fitting pink t-shirt with a towel around her neck, her face still carrying the faint glow of the recently exercised, wandered to the reception with no apparent purpose other than to have a chat. Martin took his phone from his inside jacket pocket to check if he had any more messages and, when he looked up again, a man was at the desk too, patiently waiting to attract the attention of the receptionist.

She managed to interrupt the flow of the gym lady long enough to point the old man towards Martin.

He was comfortably into his seventies but upright and slim, like he was reaping the benefits of a life of having taken good care of himself, and around five foot eight tall. His thick greying hair was combed back and he glanced curiously through gold-framed spectacles towards the figure on the sofa for only a moment before limping towards him, slightly lame on his left side. Martin rose to meet him midway. They exchanged tentative smiles and handshakes.

'I'm Martin. Thanks for coming down to meet me.'

'Frank. No problem.' He nodded towards Martin's bike

helmet. 'I see you've cycled here. You must be frozen.'

He had forgotten he still had it on. 'Yeah. It's a bit cold but it's OK once you get going.'

'They say it's going to snow next week. This weather's all over the place, isn't it? It was like spring a fortnight ago.'

Martin could have responded with something pointed about climate change and global warming but, instead, settled for a more neutral, 'I know. Crazy.'

They looked at each other slightly awkwardly, neither wanting to extend the small-talk stage but not sure how to move the conversation on, until Frank took the lead.

'Wendy says you know Evelyn. Is she all right? There's nothing wrong, I hope.'

Martin screwed up his face, as if he felt a jab of pain.

'She's fine, but the thing is,' he said, 'I don't know if you're the person I'm looking for. The Evelyn I know has the surname Dawes. I was looking for Frank Dawes.'

'Really?' Frank winced, the clear light in his brown eyes dimming slightly. 'That was my Evelyn's maiden name. She's gone back to using her maiden name, has she?' The news seemed to hurt him deeply. 'We broke up three years ago. We went through a rough time and Evelyn, well, it hit her hard. It hit both of us hard but…'

There were tears in the corners of the old man's eyes. He was the right man. Martin felt sure enough to want to talk it through properly.

'Do you think we could sit for a while?' he said.

Frank shook himself from the soreness of his memories. 'Sure. Do you fancy a cup of tea?'

Without waiting for an answer, he turned to lead them

towards the arcade of shops at the heart of the building. Martin unclipped his helmet to take it off.

'You know I used to do a lot of cycling, right up to when I was almost seventy,' Frank announced. 'I had to give it up when my hip packed in. I'm waiting for a new one.'

They stepped into a large, warm room which curved around the sweeping bar at its core. Well over half the tables and bays were already occupied as couples and groups talked, sipped at drinks or played cards. Gentle music, barely discernible, lingered in the background as if not daring to overstep its boundaries. Frank headed for a small circular table with two chairs.

Barely had Martin unzipped his jacket to put it over the back of his chair than a woman in a black and white checked apron came to their table, poised with notepad and pen.

'Evening, Frank. What can I get you?'

She was old enough to have been a resident. She most likely was. None of the people Martin had seen so far looked in the slightest ready to give up enjoying a normal life.

'Just a tea for me please, Gill. Martin?'

He had finished with his jacket and was midway to lowering himself into the chair.

'I'll have a tea as well please.'

'Milk and sugar?'

'I don't suppose you have soya milk, do you?'

The woman glanced over her shoulder as if the answer might be there. 'I'll have to check…'

'It's OK,' Martin interrupted. 'Just black, if not, and no

sugar, thanks.'

She smiled, scribbled the order and left them.

'So, how do you know Evelyn?' Frank asked.

'We're neighbours. She lives in the house opposite mine.'

'Oh, yes? Where abouts is that?' Frank leaned forward, his interest keener.

'Crookes.'

'Crookes,' he repeated, adding sadly. 'We lost touch.'

Martin nodded.

'But she's all right, you say. Have you seen her recently?'

'I see her every day,' said Martin. 'She's been in hospital –'

'Hospital!'

'– but, as I said, she's fine now and about to be allowed back home. She was hurt in an accident. Nothing too serious.'

Frank's face was etched with anxious concern. Beyond that, Martin could detect a depth of long-standing regret, stirred again by this unexpected visit and tormenting him again.

'So, why did she send you to find me? I've not heard from her for such a long time and we didn't part on the best of terms.'

'Well.' Martin steeled himself. This had to be said. At least he could see nothing in the man opposite to make him fear a violent reaction. Quite the opposite. He was practically pleading to be told.

'Mr Elliott, can I –'

'Frank. Please.'

'Can I be fr... Can I speak openly?'

He nodded consent.

'It's about your daughter, Tanya.'

'Tanya?'

'Mrs Dawes wants to see her again. She says she wants the chance to be able to set all differences aside and be reunited with her daughter.'

'She said that?' Frank bowed his head.

'Look, I don't know what went on between you and your wife and it's not my place to judge but I promised I would come to meet you to try to broker some sort of dialogue so that the three of you could maybe offer each other the chance of a fresh start. If you could have seen how upset it made her to talk about –'

The woman in the black and white checked apron, now carrying a tray, interrupted his flow.

'We did have some soya milk, love. I've put it in this little jug for you,' she said, transferring everything on the tray to the table.

'That's very kind. Thank you,' said Martin.

Frank said nothing. As the woman turned to leave, he buried his head in his hands. Martin did not feel the need to return to the point he was making. What he had already said was clearly having a profound impact.

'What did she tell you – about Tanya?' Frank said at last, his words muffled by his hands.

Martin hesitated, not sure what he was being asked to disclose. Was it a test to see how much of their private wrangling he knew about? There was no point being anything other than honest.

'She told me that when the two of you were splitting

up you had said something to your daughter to turn her against her mother. She said Tanya wouldn't return her calls anymore and that when she went to Tanya's home there was no reply. She said all she wanted was the chance to put her side of the story and explain that whatever had come between the two of you that...'

'Tanya died,' said Frank.

Martin was stilled, stunned.

Frank emerged from behind his hands and raised his head. His eyes were watery.

'She went on holiday with her new fiancé, Ryan. They went touring in the Caribbean for three weeks. It was the first time she'd had a decent break in years because she was always working so hard but Ryan persuaded her to go and we'd been encouraging her to allow herself to take a holiday for years. Anyway, she went. They were just a perfect couple, her and Ryan, made for each other. He'd done a fair bit of sailing in the past, so one of the things they decided to do was to hire a yacht and get around a few of the smaller islands but something went wrong. The boat went missing. Nothing was seen of it or them again. They just disappeared. Some said they must have been caught in a freak tropical storm. Nothing was ever proved. It'll be four years ago in September since it happened.'

Martin felt utterly foolish. He had taken Mrs Dawes at her word. He had no reason not to. You wouldn't just make up something like this, surely?

'Evelyn was devastated,' Frank continued. 'At first, she fought like fury for the authorities to keep searching because she refused to give up on the hope that they might still be found alive, however unlikely everybody told her that was. She and Tanya were so close, it destroyed her to think she had been taken from us and she wouldn't accept it. I suppose she had some sort of breakdown. She reached the stage where she convinced herself Tanya was still alive and that anybody who told her otherwise was lying to her, like there was a conspiracy to keep them apart. She wouldn't go to get help from a counsellor or whatever, somebody who could help her deal with everything she was going through, and she especially wouldn't listen to me. The more I tried to tell her to let go and that she should allow herself to grieve in the normal way, the more I became the enemy. In the end, it broke us.'

He hesitated for a moment before he could go on.

'She demanded a divorce and I gave in. I thought it might do even more damage to try to stop her going ahead with it because I couldn't get through anymore. The only thing I could think to do was to live in hope that, one day, the thick mist of all that anger, grief and confusion would lift and Evelyn would come back to me. I decided to respect her wishes to leave her alone and wait. When we sold the house, I moved to this place, but I took on a two-person apartment because I still believed that we'd be together again soon. I've been waiting three years.'

He sat motionless and quiet, contemplating.

'From what she told you, it doesn't look as if she'll be coming back anytime soon though, does it? Poor Evelyn. She's really had it rough and it must have been getting worse for her, not better. I should have done more to try to get her the help she needed.'

There was nothing Martin could think to say that would offer comfort. Clearly, they had both been through hell, even though they had been sent hurtling along different routes.

'I cannot imagine what you've been through, Frank,' he said sympathetically. 'Both of you. I can't say that I knew your wife at all before she had her accident, but I have got to know her since and I've seen a change in her. She didn't seem to want anything to do with anybody when I first started visiting her in hospital but, just recently, she's different. I got the impression she wanted nothing other than to shut everybody out before but now, well. She opened up to me the other day and told me that she's frightened by the prospect of being alone again. I think she sees the light again, Frank. She's due to leave hospital tomorrow and I think if you come with me to take her home, it'll mean the world to her.'

'Do you think so?' He wanted to believe that to be true.

'I do. I think she might listen now. I think, between us, we could help her come to terms with losing Tanya and get her the professional help she needs.'

Frank nodded and took a sip from his tea.

'What time should I meet you there?' he asked.

24

Crowd containment was not an issue. The only members of the public who seemed in the least bit interested were two teenage boys who had been intrigued enough to interrupt their Saturday morning bike ride and were watching from the footbridge, no doubt in the ghoulish hope that something grisly was about to be dragged off the river bed.

Nevertheless, the three officers of the Police Underwater Search Unit had taken great care to cordon off the area with white and blue tape that had 'Police Line Do Not Cross' printed on it, repeated at two-foot intervals. And just in case anyone had not noticed the tape or the large white lorry with 'POLICE' on the front and the crest of the South Yorkshire Police Underwater Search Unit above the yellow and blue checks running down the side, one of the officers was unfolding a portable blue sign informing passers-by 'Police Diving in Progress Keep Clear'. Had there been anyone passing by, they would have been in no doubt that they were required to stay back.

The operation had taken over the whole of the car park from which, a week earlier, 17-year-old Chloe Wood and her affectionate boyfriend Sam had watched a man throw what they thought might be a gun into the river from the footpath on the opposite bank. With the photos Chloe took tying in with the information Beth Hughes had given them, suggesting her husband Wesley had been given the job of getting rid of a gun used in a violent armed robbery, the CID had taken the decision to send in the divers.

While one of the officers was completing the task of tape and portable sign deployment, another was running through the final safety checks with the colleague who was just about to enter the near-frozen waters of the River Don. The diver gave a thumbs-up to indicate that he was getting a good flow of air from the two grey tanks on his back. He took measured steps in his black drysuit towards the slope of the riverbank, through a small gap in the car park perimeter wall, bending his head to watch the fins on his feet through the slightly steamed visor of his full-face mask.

He jumped, feet first, the metre and a half from the car park level into the water and stood, waist-high, to make sure the other officer was ready to reel out the yellow safety rope that was attached to the diver's suit. The river was not fast flowing at the part they were to search, falling as it did between two of the weirs on the Five Weirs Walk, but it was deep in the middle. The diver checked the stability of his mask again and plunged forward, breaking the surface. Soon, all that could be seen of him was a trail of bubbles around the yellow rope.

Little more than ten minutes later, he bobbed back into view and raised his right arm.

'He's got something,' said the officer on the other end of the yellow rope.

'Is it the weapon?' asked the other, stamping his feet to revive them.

'It's *a* weapon. Are you going to get it from him or what?'

The policeman stiffly made his way to the gap in the perimeter wall and backed down a metal ladder so that the diver, having swum to the bank, could drop his find into a clear plastic evidence bag.

'I'd say this hasn't been down there for long at all, I think we have a winner,' he said as he climbed back to the car park. 'What do you reckon?'

His colleague took the bag and held it to eye level with his spare hand.

'Looks good to me. Signal to Phil to come out. It must be bloody perishing in there.'

The signal was given.

'Nice and quick, that's what we like. Whose turn is it to get the teas in?'

25

Martin paced outside the entrance to the spinal injuries unit, nervously switching his cycle helmet from one hand to the other and habitually tucking his hair behind his ear, which he tended to do when he was on edge. He had strayed too close to the entrance doors once, triggering them to open automatically, and didn't want anyone inside to think he might have done it deliberately. He had since restricted himself to a narrow two-metre corridor away from the sensors, making him appear like a fretful animal trapped behind an invisible force field to keep him from pouncing on hospital visitors.

He had no idea how Mrs Dawes was going to react to seeing her ex-husband again. The very mention of his name always stirred animosity in her, as far as he had seen, but if what Frank Elliott had told him was true, her anger was a symptom of deep psychological trauma caused by the tragic loss of her beloved only daughter. She had lashed out at Frank, irrationally blaming him as the cause of her despair, and Martin feared what seeing him again would do to Mrs Dawes. Not only that, he also knew that they would have to confront her with the truth of Tanya's death and he could think of no easy way to do that. They would have to help her deconstruct the conspiratorial stories she had invented for herself to save her from dealing with the finality of her loss and it scared him to think how she might respond to that.

Could her fragile psyche stand it?

Martin had spent another half hour with Frank the previous evening, after they had agreed a time to meet at the hospital. Frank had talked some more about Evelyn and Tanya and had told him that his last attempt to get in touch with his ex-wife through their solicitors – it always had to be through their solicitors, she insisted – had been to seek consent to donate the money from Tanya's estate to the legal aid fund set up in the tragic couple's names. That letter, Martin guessed, must have been the one that inspired Mrs Dawes to set out into a stormy night to threaten Frank with a World War Two pistol.

He decided not to mention this.

Martin had warmed to Frank but, when he returned home, he went straight on his laptop. It was not that he did not believe what he had been told, it was because he was curious to see what else he could find. The reason he had not been able to come up with anything previously was he had always searched for the name Tanya Dawes and Tanya Dawes, he now realised, had never existed. She was always Tanya Elliott.

It was all there for him now, from the first reports in the Manchester press of the mysterious disappearance of two partners from one of the city's legal firms, to news of the increasingly desperate search, which had also been picked up by the national media, and, finally, the grave acceptance of the couple's inevitable fate. Martin sifted through it all, suffering the sadness of it like a personal bereavement in fast forward. There could be no doubt the version of events Frank had told him had been accurate. Now they had to face the tragedy of the version Mrs Dawes had created for herself and that might be even harder to bear.

Martin had arrived at the hospital early, just in case Frank was early too. He did not want the old man to go in alone. He checked his watch. Four minutes until the time they had agreed.

He saw a man approaching and identified him first by his distinctive limp. As he came closer, huddled into a heavy overcoat with his head overshadowed by a trilby hat as he stooped into the face of a chill wind, Martin became more certain it was Frank.

They acknowledged each other with a nod and a gloved handshake. Frank's expression was pinched and pained. They both knew that what they were about to do might have consequences they could neither predict nor control.

'It's not easy getting parked at this place, is it?' said Frank, attempting to break the ice of their shared apprehension.

'I don't know. I always bike here,' Martin replied, raising the helmet in his hands as proof.

They looked at each other, mutually reluctant to take the next step, until Martin suggested, 'Shall we go in?'

There was no one to greet them this time at the nurses' station, so Martin led the way straight on to the bay.

Evelyn was sitting in her armchair, clutching, in anticipation, the handle of the overnight bag in which she had packed all the things Martin had brought her from home over the last 18 days. Sister Suneeta was chatting to her as she stripped the bed. The old lady was cheerful, but her face dropped in an instant when she noticed the two men cautiously approaching her corner of the bay.

The sister noticed the change and turned to see what had caused it.

'Oh, hi Martin. Big day today. She's ready for you,' she said, attempting normality.

But the smile of response was forced and who was this other man? Suneeta glanced back towards Evelyn, whose eyes fixed, half-scowling, half-fearful, on the stranger. Whatever was about to be said here would only be said once she was out of the way and the sister stopped busying herself with the bed.

'I'll leave you to it,' she said to Martin. 'Just let me know if there's anything you need. Would you like me to pull the screens around to give you some privacy?'

'It's fine thanks,' he replied.

Something was definitely not right. She left, ready to keep an eye or an ear on what might be about to happen from a discreet distance.

'Hello Evelyn,' said Frank.

Her gaze was unbroken. His unexpected appearance disturbed her.

'What are you doing here, Frank?' she asked.

'He's come to take you home. We're both going to take you home,' Martin interjected.

She snorted. 'Not likely.'

'Evelyn, I –'

She cut across Frank's words as if he was not there to fix angry eyes on Martin.

Catalyst

'Why did you bring him here? You know what he did to me.'

The accusation of betrayal in her tone was clear. He edged closer and sat on the edge of the bed beside her.

'It's all right, Mrs Dawes. I know about Tanya. I know what really happened.'

'What are you talking about?' she spat out.

'The accident, Evelyn,' Frank said softly as he, too, moved closer to her chair. 'We lost Tanya in an accident three and a half years ago. Don't you remember? She and Ryan went to the Caribbean on holiday and they went missing. They were never found.'

Her eyes darted and she blinked rapidly.

'What rubbish has he been feeding you? It's all lies. My Tanya is perfectly fine, it's just that he doesn't want me to see her anymore. Get him to tell you where she lives now, Martin. He knows.'

Frank bowed and Martin feared he might soon buckle. Every slashing word from the old lady appeared to wound him deeply but the inner strength that had helped him absorb so many blows through the last three and a half years was not spent yet.

'There is nothing in this world that I would love more than for the three of us to be together again and I know you know that's true, Evelyn. If I could give my own life to bring her back, I'd take the deal in a heartbeat, but wishing like that isn't going to change a thing. There was nothing anybody could have done to stop Tanya being taken away from us and nothing either of us can do now to change that, however much we want to. We could never stop loving Tanya, but we have to accept that she's gone,

Evelyn. We've lost her.'

The words echoed around her mind and struck strands of her consciousness that had been buried away for years. Outwardly, she was still hostile but, inside, the thaw had begun.

She looked at Martin. 'Is that true?'

He nodded, sadly. 'I read all about it myself last night. After I went to meet Frank, I did some searching on the internet and saw all the articles that were in the press at the time. I'm so sorry, Mrs Dawes.'

Evelyn's head was swirling with the confusion of the new information and the supposed reality she had lived by for so long. She wanted to fight the contradiction, deny what she was being told, but, deep within, she knew she should not.

'I don't understand,' she said.

Martin shuffled close enough to touch her arm.

'Look, I don't really know about these things but it looks to me as if you have been through a terrible, terrible shock and it affected you much more deeply than you might have realised at the time. But that's OK because there are experts who can help you come to terms with everything you've been through and you've got the two of us to support you. Frank and I will be there for you whenever you need us. You don't have to face this alone. You need never be alone again.'

Tears welled in Evelyn's eyes. 'So, Tanya's gone?'

Martin did not need to respond. She knew it for herself. It was true. She was powerless to fight it anymore.

Frank leaned forward to hold her hands as they tightly gripped the handles of the overnight bag.

'We still have each other, love. These past few years have been rough, and I know it's been even harder for you, but we still have the chance to get through the worst of it if we do it together. Let's take care of each other again, Evelyn, like we always used to. We were a good team, you and me.'

Echoes of a life long forgotten flashed before her again. Good times. Happy times. The times before... before...

Frank squeezed her hands. 'Would you like us to take you home now?'

She looked deeply into his lined face and saw again the man she once loved, the man who stood by her for forty-eight years. He was beside her again.

'Yes,' she said, timidly at first but then, more assuredly, 'Yes. I'd like that.'

26

A subtle feint and sharp change of pace were all the player needed to buy a few inches of open ground and send the ball fizzing low over the surface into the penalty area. The big defender was caught off-balance, hurried into a less solid connection on his attempted clearance than he wanted as he tried to change direction quickly, and was only able to divert it away from goal towards the edge of the box. On another day, that might still have been enough to clear the immediate danger, but he was unfortunate this time. The ball went straight to an attacking player. He took one touch and, before other defenders could rush out to close the space, struck a shot that ripped into the top corner of the net.

The home supporters rose as one to let out a roar of jubilation. The TV commentator screamed the name of the ecstatic scorer, who, arms raised, dodged between crestfallen opponents to sprint away from the pursuit of happy team-mates.

Darrell Morrison, however, did not move. The goal did not prompt so much as a flicker of a change in his blank expression as he lay on the sofa, listless and lethargic.

He had been this way for two days, since Beth told him

it was over. Dumped him.

The foot was healing nicely, according to the nurse who had changed his dressings the previous day, and he was able to get around the house much more easily now that he had been issued with a hard boot, but he wanted no more than to lounge on the sofa and allow any TV programme, as long as it did not require him to think, to drift in front of his eyes.

Darrell was not usually one to feel sorry for himself, but this was different. It was not just that he had been dumped, though he ached for the touch of Beth's willing, youthful body and craved release from the torment of tracing the lines of the tattoos on her abdomen and her thighs every time he closed his eyes. It was what the end of the relationship meant that really hurt.

He was thirty-seven years old. Being with Beth made him feel young. What did the future hold now? Middle-aged and past it. He might never know the pleasure of the touch of younger female flesh again and that made him sad. He had risked everything to be with Beth – not least his job as their liaisons became ever more reckless – but he hadn't cared. Part of him wanted them to get caught, so that it would force him to quit his marriage and his job. He knew it was a fantasy – a hopeless one, as it turned out – but the thought of being made to leave in disgrace to take up a new life with Beth, scratching a living by working bar jobs or waiting tables, and having her, that body, all to himself was one that had been hugely appealing. He would have been poor but alive.

It had occurred to him that he might have to leave that school anyway. He could not stand the thought of them still working together, awkwardly shuffling around the same staff room, knowing that he could not have her anymore.

Helena had not been around much to notice Darrell moping on the sofa, basking in self-pity. She probably wouldn't have cared anyway if she had been around, but she hadn't – as usual. Yet he had enjoyed the few days they spent together after the shooting. They were tight again, free of other distractions, but that had not lasted. Even though she was meant to be taking personal time off to be with him, she had spent just about the whole of the last two days at work because of the fall-out of the news report that had dominated the local headlines since Thursday. She was working now, upstairs in the study, even though it was a Saturday.

What happened to their marriage? They used to be happy. Once.

He heard her coming down the stairs and hoped she was heading for the kitchen or was about to tell him she had to go out again, anything as long as she left him alone, but the front room door opened and she came in.

'Budge up,' she said almost cheerfully, waiting to sit on the far seat of the sofa, where Darrell rested his injured foot on two cushions.

Reluctantly, he shuffled his body upright as she picked up the cushions and sat. Darrell propped himself on his arms, ready to swing around and give her more space, but she touched his leg to stop him and, without saying a word, encouraged him to put his foot on her lap. He did not resist.

Helena gently stroked the clean white bandages. He

watched her. She looked so tired.

'What's the score?' she asked.

He examined the screen to read the match information in the top corner.

'Err, two-nil. I've not really been watching it to be honest.'

She nodded. He knew that she had no real interest.

'You seem a bit flat,' she said.

'Well, you know.' He gestured with a tip of his head towards his foot and hoped she had bought the excuse.

They sat in silence for five minutes, both staring blankly at a football match that might just as easily have been a re-enactment of the Battle of Little Big Horn as far as either of them cared but looking at the TV served as a diversion for them, so they could both pretend there was another reason they were in the room together. The sharp blast of the referee's whistle brought the game to an end and they were alone again.

'We need to talk,' she said, forcing out the words before she could change her mind.

Inwardly, he sagged. The last thing he needed was one of Helena's 'this is how I feel, tell me how you feel' attempts to counsel some sick aspect of their failing relationship. He didn't think he could stand that, but he was trapped.

'I've been seeing someone else.'

Darrell was shocked. He gazed at her through narrowed eyes. *Seriously?* Her attention was still outwardly fixed on the TV. She *was* serious.

'It's been going on for eight months and we loved each other – or at least I thought I loved him. Anyway, it's over now. I found out that I didn't really know him at all.'

He was stunned, rather than hurt, by the revelation. He had been so obsessed by the need to conceal his own affair that he had not even contemplated that Helena might have another man in her life – and she had been living the lie for so much longer! He and Beth had only been seeing each other for weeks, since the start of the spring term.

'Jesus!' He was struggling to find words to say. 'Eight months! I mean, what…? Who is he? Do I know him?'

She shook her head. 'Some guy I met through work. Who he is isn't important.' Helena made herself turn to give him the respect of eye contact.

'I'm so sorry, Darrell. I've been an idiot.'

He made a half-angry you-can-say-that-again noise of feigned disgust, but he knew he could not be truly outraged. That would be hypocritical. It came more from bemusement. He had been unfaithful to her but had never thought Helena would do that to him.

'That's not all,' she added, solemnly, and he stared at her again.

What else?

'You know this furore about the dangerous chemical waste at the site of the proposed housing development?'

He nodded vigorously. 'That's why you had to go back to work, right? Haven't you been part of the team trying to work out how it nearly got through the process without anybody knowing?'

'I have,' she said, as if there was a large 'but' on the way. 'But what I haven't told anybody yet is that I'm more a part of the problem than the solution.'

'What do you mean?' He was being forced to see

Helena in a whole new light and had no idea what she might reveal to him next.

'You were working on that housing development, weren't you? Did you see this coming?'

She hesitated. This was less easy to admit to than the affair.

'Worse than that, I'm afraid. I'd agreed to take money in order to make sure the planning application got through the committee stage.'

'Jesus!' He almost shot out of the chair, bad foot or not. 'Fuck, Helena! How could you? I mean, this is just... fuck!'

'I didn't know how serious the contamination was.' She was desperate for him to see it more closely from her side. 'If I had known the full extent, I would never have agreed to go along with it, I swear. The other two who were a part of this – one of them was the man I've been seeing – they didn't tell me everything. They told me there were only moderate levels of contamination on the site and that the benefits to the city generally far outweighed the potential risks. They kept me in the dark. I got played.'

The explanation appeared to calm him a little, but not completely.

'But you took a bribe! You put your duty second to money, Helena. This is so wrong.'

She shrugged. 'I know, I know. I should never have agreed to go along with it. I haven't taken money yet because it all depended on the planning application going through and obviously that's not going to happen now, but that's not the issue and you're right, I know. Like I said, I've been an idiot.'

Darrell's brain was in overdrive, trying to take in all the implications.

'So, what happens now?' he asked.

'Now? Well…' That was the question that had consumed her practically every waking moment since she had confronted Yuvraj. She knew what she had to do. What she didn't know was what they would do with her.

'I've decided to come clean. I've just been writing out my letter of resignation and I'll hand that in on Monday when I go to see the council's Monitoring Officer and basically tell him everything I know. Then, I guess I'll have to do the same with the police because they're bound to look to prosecute once the full facts come to light. As for what happens to me, I don't know. Obviously, I'm ruined professionally but I deserve that. Whether or not they believe me when I tell them I wasn't fully aware of what was going on and whether or not they give me credit for coming forward and telling them everything they want to know, I suppose we'll have to wait and see.'

Darrell buried his face in his hands. He had wanted Helena out of his life for so long but her going to prison? Now that he faced losing her for real, he could not stand the thought.

'I'm sorry, Darrell. I've made a right mess of this, haven't I? I'm sorry for everything you're going to have to go through and,' she gently wiggled his injured foot on her lap, 'I'm sorry for this.'

He stared at her, puzzled.

'How is that your fault?'

'The warning was meant for me,' she said. 'It was all linked in with the contaminated site. We think the man who came to the house was connected to one of those radical environmental groups who found out what we were planning to do and was looking to scare us into stopping. I tried to get the other two to back out because it was getting too dangerous, but they wouldn't listen. In the meantime, it looks like the environmentalists decided to take the decision out of our hands and they've done what they set out to do. They've killed the project stone dead. I think when the man came around that night it was to confront me, but you got dragged into it and got shot and that's all my fault. It's bad enough that you were hurt at all, but I don't know what I would have done if the bullet had done even more damage. I don't think I could have lived with myself. I don't know how you can forgive me, Darrell, but you should know that I'm truly sorry.'

He hadn't properly heard everything she said. He was confused.

'Hang on, hang on. The man with the gun was looking for *you*? I thought he was warning me.'

It was her turn to fail to understand.

'What would an environmental activist want to warn you about?'

'I didn't know he was… I thought he was…'

Helena was stilled. This time, he needed to come clean.

'I've been having an affair as well. Her husband is a bit of a gangster and I thought he'd found out about us and, you know.' Darrell made a gun with his hand by sticking out his forefinger and fired it by making a 'pow' noise.

'*You've* been having an affair?'

She didn't know whether to feel appalled or relieved.

'Who with?'

'One of the other teachers,' he said, bashfully.

Helena took a few seconds to reflect on this new information and laughed out loud.

'So, we've both been having affairs with people we work with. I suppose that makes us a couple of cliches!'

He did not share her amusement at first but then hesitantly cracked a smile.

'Yeah, I suppose it does.'

She composed herself again. 'Are you still seeing her?'

'Nah,' he shook his head emphatically. 'It's over. She dumped me, actually. On Thursday.'

'Thursday? Must have been the day for it.'

Darrell cocked his head, inviting further explanation.

'That's the day I found out the truth. I dumped him, actually.'

He smiled. 'Nice one.'

They sat quietly, each of them in their thoughts, both lighter for the loss of their burdens.

'What have we done to each other, Darrell?' she asked, wistfully.

He thought. 'I guess we just stopped trying hard enough.'

They fell quiet again, until he suddenly sat forward and held out his open palm for her to take. She accepted the offer.

'It doesn't have to be too late for us,' he said.

'Ah, but I think it is,' she replied and she sighed deeply. 'These next few months are going to get messy and you shouldn't have to go through that. I've already put you through enough. You should get away now, before the shit really starts to fly, start again somewhere else. Pretty soon,

I could end up in prison anyway and even if I manage to stay out of it, things will never be the same for me. I'll never be allowed to forget what I've done.'

She withdrew her hand and he eased back into the sofa.

'No,' he said. 'I'm staying here. I'll stand by you, whatever happens.'

Helena rubbed his leg. 'You don't have to say that.'

'I mean it,' he pulled a stern face to underline how serious he was. 'We're in this together, whatever they do and whatever they say. I love you, babe.'

She smiled at him and tears welled in her eyes. He meant it, all right. She knew him. They had lost touch with what had made their connection special for too long but there it was again, the tiniest red glow of an ember in a fire they had both feared would never warm them again. It was already more than she dared to believe she deserved, but how she needed it.

Past the choking tightness in her throat she managed to squeeze the words, 'Thank you.'

Nothing more needed to be added. They were one again.

27

Detective Inspector Jane Jackson of Sheffield CID called the sergeant through to her office as soon as she began sifting through the usual Monday morning backlog of emails and memos and noticed that one of them included a photo attachment of the recovered handgun.

'Glock 17 – the 9mm semi-automatic of preference for the discerning modern violent criminal,' she announced with a smile as Detective Sergeant Copson closed the door behind him. She was in a good mood. It was far too early in the day for the nourishing effects of a weekend off to have been worn down by the daily grind.

'More or less exactly where the young lass said she saw it being thrown into the Don,' confirmed the sergeant.

'Very good,' she nodded. 'It certainly doesn't look like it's been down there a long time – have we been able to get anything off it?'

'Afraid not. I should imagine it was given a thorough cleaning before it was thrown away, but we nipped it down to ballistics yesterday and they were able to test-fire it OK. They're seeing how it matches with the bullets recovered at the jewellery shop robbery scene and they've said they should be able to get back to us with the results this afternoon. It's looking promising, I'd say.'

'I agree.' The inspector eased back in her chair. 'With this and the photos and the recording, I think we've got enough to go on, so let's bring Hughes in. Send someone to the house and if he's not there, I'd like us to watch the house and the storage place so we can take him wherever he shows up first. The search warrants are ready, yes?'

'For the house and the lock-up, yes ma'am.'

'We'll give them a good going-over as soon as we have him in custody and see what we can turn up. Hopefully, something that will lead us to the jewellery shop gang but, if not, I should think we'll come up with enough for us to put Hughes away for quite a while.'

***

Wesley Hughes was not at home when the police came for him. He had left early in the morning. Since accepting the assignment from Hardstaff four days earlier, he had been preparing meticulously; watching his subject, following him, studying his movements, noting his habits, and now he was ready. There was more surveillance to do, just to be extra certain, and then he had an appointment to collect the gun he needed to do the job. It was on. He was going to do it that evening.

This would be his first hit, but Wesley already had the feeling he might develop a taste for more. Providing services for his clients to assist in the smooth running of their businesses had always been both lucrative and satisfying for him. The stakes were always high because he knew his clients would not allow a margin for error and that it would not only be his professional reputation that would suffer blows if he became sloppy, so he never neglected the small details and always got the job done well. That was why so many of the influential figures in the South Yorkshire underworld came to him. He was the best.

Working for other people had always been enough but since agreeing to dispose of his first live body, Wesley had seen other possibilities for expanding his criminal portfolio. Sure, it meant taking on more risk than he usually did but the sheer thrill he had felt in preparing for this job was like nothing he had ever known before. He was about to execute the crime rather than just clean up after it and that was a far more gratifying prospect. Once he had his first kill on his CV, he could offer a whole new stream of usefulness to his clients in the future.

The principles of paying attention to planning and preparation had been the same and facing the responsibility of being the one to pull the trigger did not bother him at all. Even as he watched his target going about his daily business at the café, working behind the counter or chatting to customers, he felt no pity for him, no pang of guilt for the life about to be snuffed out. It was a job. It had to be done quickly and cleanly and now Wesley knew when his best opportunity to achieve that would be.

Every day shortly after 7 p.m., when the last customers had been served, the target would say goodbye to whichever staff member had been on that day and follow them to the door to flip the sign from 'open' to 'closed' but would never lock the door at that point. He then liked to make himself a coffee and sit, always at the same table, to work on his laptop for half an hour. Then he would clip shut the laptop, wash his cup in the sink and take the laptop and a blue bag containing the daily cash takings with him into the back room. Approximately six minutes later, he would emerge in his cycling gear, set the burglar alarm, push his bike out of the front door, lock the door and cycle off in the direction of Witham Road.

It was a routine. Routine was good. It made him predictable. Predictable made him easy prey.

It was 6.53 p.m. Wesley was parked across the road from the café – not directly opposite, where he might be noticed, but close enough to be able to see through the large front window as the last drinks were drained, the last customers made their way into the cold, dark evening and the last plates were cleared away. The very last ones.

He watched as the waitress buttoned her coat across her large bosom and smothered him in a brief hug before setting off to catch her bus, not realising she was deserting him to a bloody fate. He, blissfully ignorant, waved her on her way with promises that he would see her again the next day. Promises impossible to keep. The door was shut, the sign switched to 'closed'. It was time.

Wesley was far more composed than he thought he might be. He had considered that there might be a few signs of apprehensiveness – first night nerves, if you like – but there were none. He was calm, focused. Maybe he had a natural calling for this kind of work.

He opened the car glove box and pulled out the weapon he had collected from his contact in the afternoon. It felt good in his hand – a .22 calibre revolver. Revolvers left no ejected spent cartridge casings for him to be concerned about and, besides, they just looked better than the semiautomatics. He had given it a thorough check when he collected it but that was to establish its functionality. Now, as the blood surged through his body and his senses soared to greater heights than he had ever known before, he saw its deadly beauty too. The grain of the dimpled wooden grip, the curved spike of the trigger, the whir of the drum with its full burden of bullets and the eager hammer, ready to propel the shot down the chunky, stubby barrel to fulfil its mission of ripping through flesh and bone.

Wesley leaned forward to secure the gun down the back of his jeans waistband and looked towards the café again. The target was on his way to the usual table, cup in one hand and laptop tucked under the other arm.

The pale yellow of the streetlights showed no signs of any other person on the road as he twisted in his car seat to check all around him. The plan was set. It was twenty metres to the café. He would burst through the door, deliver the killer shot from close range – a second should not be necessary from that distance – walk behind the counter to grab the blue bag with the cash, so that the raid would look like a robbery, switch off the lights and leave, closing the door behind him. As long as no one heard the shot, or heard it and did nothing about it, it could be hours until the body was discovered and, by then, he would be long gone.

Job done.

He climbed out of the car and pulled on his dark cap, glancing up and down the street one more time. He pushed his hands deep into the pockets of his jacket and started walking, up the pavement on the opposite side from the café.

Suddenly, there she was.

From the side road just above the café emerged a woman, walking purposefully, her long, auburn hair flowing like a flame behind her in the cold breeze of the evening. She headed down the street, past the row of four shops.

Wesley cursed under his breath and walked on, burying his chin into his chest to conceal his face from this potential witness, walking beyond where he had intended to cross.

It was an unwanted complication but might not be a problem. He stepped on, towards the sound of the cars on the main road, and calculated the point at which he would turn around and check, making sure the woman had carried jauntily along her way past the shops and out of his way. Then he could cross and go back to the café.

He stepped back into the shadows between streetlights and turned to look. The woman had not walked past the shops. She was at the café door. She was knocking on it. Shit!

Wesley felt his heart pounding. Calm. Stay calm.

If I walk away, complete a small circuit of side streets, by the time I get back in sight of the café again, she'll be gone. She'll realise that she's too late for her cappuccino, apologise to the target and leave. It's still on.

He cursed silently again and moved. Best not to loiter. Don't attract attention, stay in the shadows. But he was angry at this inconvenience. He was way beyond prepared for what lay ahead, he was positively looking forward to it, relishing the moment he could squeeze the trigger and take the life, and now this woman had put herself in the way. All he wanted now was to do the job and get out. She had reduced it to a chore. She had spoiled his moment.

As the café came back into view, he glanced up anxiously. Not only was the woman still there, she had moved inside and was talking to the target. For a brief, spiteful moment he contemplated taking them both, but reason re-emerged to suppress this rash instinct. It would be too messy. That was not the job. It was not what a professional would do. A professional would cut his losses and try again when the odds are back in his favour.

And so Wesley turned and walked, head down, back to his car.

28

Martin looked up from his screen when he heard the knock on the door, expecting it to be one of his regulars tapping to wave hello on their walk home, but he did not recognise the middle-aged, long-haired woman who was gazing at him through the glass, her expression stern and serious.

'I'm sorry, my love, we're closed,' he called, spelling out the words with exaggerated mouth movements in case she could not hear him properly, pointing to direct her to the sign on the door just beneath her eye line.

But she either did not understand what he was trying to tell her or already knew. She stood at the door, waiting, shoulders hunched and shivering, staring towards him.

Martin closed the laptop lid. She was far too well dressed to be one of the homeless people who occasionally came by late in the day in hope of being given food that might otherwise be binned, and she was clearly not going to leave without him telling her she should to her face.

He opened the door and felt the growing cold of the evening burst through.

'We're closed, I'm afraid,' he repeated firmly but politely. She was unmoved.

'Mr Bestwick. I want to talk.'

Martin looked deeply into her green eyes in case they held any clue that would remind him of when he might have met this woman before, but he saw none. He felt he had no choice but to open the door wider and allow her in so that she could explain herself.

'Would you like to sit down?' he asked.

'I'd rather stand,' she replied coldly. 'I'll not stay long.'

'OK.' He instinctively backed away, suspicious. Something about her made him feel uneasy.

'How can I help you?'

She paused, glaring at him as if she knew he was setting a trap for her.

'Let's not be coy, Mr Bestwick. I think you know why I'm here.'

He was thrown by the abruptness of her tone. He had no idea who she was or what she might want.

'I'm sorry, but I…'

'Fine. If that's how you want to play it, I'll spell it out. My name is Helena Morrison. I'm the Head of Planning and Regeneration for Sheffield City Council, or at least I was until a few hours ago.'

Now Martin had an idea of the broad ballpark of why this woman might be here, though he was still struggling to think precisely why she should have called on him. Perhaps she felt compelled to give him a piece of her mind.

'I don't want to argue with you, Ms Morrison, I simply did what I had to do.'

'Don't give me that pious bullshit, I'm not here to enter into a debate. I've come to strike a deal.'

'A deal?' His curiosity was engaged.

'This morning, I resigned my position with the council. I also supplied the Monitoring Officer with all the information I had and gave a statement under caution to police fraud squad officers. I've done what you wanted me to do, Mr Bestwick. I named Cranford Hardstaff and Yuvraj Patel as the main protagonists in the conspiracy and, for the record, I'd like you to know that I was very much the junior partner of the gang of three in the deal on the council side of things. Hardstaff recruited Yuvraj and Yuvraj recruited me but neither of them trusted me enough to tell me anything more than they felt I needed to know. You'll just have to take my word for that. I should add that none of this is public knowledge yet and so I would respectfully ask that you hold back from putting any of this information into the public domain until the police have had the chance to do their jobs. This is between you and me for now.'

She waited, wanting his acknowledgement.

Martin was so taken aback by the barrage of unsolicited information that it took him a moment to mutter, 'Yes, of course.'

'I've come clean, Mr Bestwick. The Swarbrook Hill project has proved to be a disaster, a monumental waste of public money and council time, but it will never be revisited, not until such a time as the land on the site can be declared safe and I can't see that happening at any stage, can you? I've done all I can, Mr Bestwick, and now I want your word that you'll leave us alone.'

'Meaning what, precisely?'

He was trying hard not to make it obvious that he had

no idea what she was talking about.

She glared again, irritated that he was making her do this the hard way.

'No more visits, no more threats. You stay away from me and you stay away from Darrell.'

Darrell? Morrison? Wasn't that the name of...? Oh, god!

Panic gripped him. This was what he had feared – his stupid, stupid actions on that awful night catching up with him – but how could she have traced it back to him? She had been the one who had come to make all the concessions so far when, really, he was the one totally at her mercy.

'I didn't mean to shoot him. It was an accident,' he pleaded.

'And I suppose you didn't mean to send the wreath either.'

A wreath?

'Don't play me for a fool, Mr Bestwick. I've had enough of being treated like an idiot by people. All that matters to me is that we draw a line under this whole business between us now.'

'That's it?'

'Yes.'

Martin was not yet reassured. He was on the hook and could not believe she was willing to let him go. Surely, she should want revenge.

'If you know it was me, why didn't you go to the police?'

For the first time in their exchange, Helena smiled. She had considered doing just that.

'Let's just say I wish you hadn't shot a hole in my husband's foot, but I appreciate your spirit. You were prepared to make a stand and act on an issue you felt passionate about and so, while I don't like your methods, I admire your principles. Too many of us stand idly by and wait for someone else to get things done but you took on the responsibility and, well, you've succeeded. Without you and your group, the planning application for Swarbrook Hill might well have been passed by the council next week and who knows how much damage could have followed, to people's health and to the environment? You've helped avert a crisis, Mr Bestwick, and you've also done me a great favour on the long term by preventing me from becoming even more deeply entangled in a deceit that, had I known exactly what was at stake, I would have regarded as utterly vile. You might also have saved my marriage, by the way.'

She wandered to the counter and idly picked up a leaflet advertising the café's takeaway service. She pushed it into her coat pocket.

'So, to answer your question, I decided that if I were to hand your name to the police and stop you from doing more good work in the future that would be nothing more than vindictive and selfish on my part. If you promise that you're finished with us and if you promise that you won't resort to terrorising anyone else in the future, I'll promise to keep our secret. Do we have a deal?'

Helena held out her hand. Martin moved forward and gripped it.

'Certainly. It's a deal. Thank you.'

'Could I just ask,' she added, 'how did you find out

about us? As far as we were concerned, all this was contained within a tight circle, so who let you know the real story behind Swarbrook Hill?'

Martin backed away again.

'Oh, I couldn't possibly… It was information given under strictest confidence.'

There was no way he would allow Brian Gibbs' name to be dragged into the open.

'Hmm. Fair enough,' she said. 'I was just interested. There must have been a point at which you finally had enough knowledge to go public but, before then, you must have had an inkling or else you wouldn't have tried to scare myself and Yuvraj into blowing our cover. I was curious as to how you were put on to us in the first place and whether one of the others had cracked and given the game away.'

He stared blankly back, impassive.

'No matter, I was interested, that's all.'

She remained still, offering a final opportunity for him to tell her more, but he gave her nothing.

'Well, I've said all I came to say, so I'll leave you alone.'

'How is he?' Martin had wanted to check on his victim's recovery but there had been nothing in the news lately. 'Your husband, I mean. How is he?'

She appeared touched by his interest. 'He's fine. No long-term damage done. Thank you for asking.'

Helena half-turned to go but stopped.

'Just a friendly word of warning. Hardstaff really has it in for you. The last time I saw him he mentioned that he wanted to do you harm. I think we all understand that

Cranford is a bit of a loudmouth who likes to throw his weight around, but he's also got a nasty streak and I wouldn't put it past him to try something once this thing blows up. I'm sure the police will come looking for him soon but, in the meantime, you might just want to take extra care.'

With that, she turned the doorknob and braced herself to face the cold again. Martin followed her to the door and clicked over the lock.

Her final words had chilled him. Much of what she had said before that had astonished him.

So, Hardstaff *was* implicated in the scandal. Martin felt vindicated for going against his natural inclination to look for the best in people because he had always thought there was something intrinsically bad about the council leader. He did not understand why there was so much venom directed back his way, but it looked as if Hardstaff was going to get his comeuppance and that was good.

He wandered back to his table but had no will to re-open his laptop and finish the day's business. It could wait until he was home. He picked up the computer and his cup and emptied away the cold coffee in the sink.

Martin thought again about Helena Morrison. Their paths had crossed because Mrs Dawes had been momentarily confused and had given him the wrong address. What were the odds that it would be *her* address and that their paths would cross again because she was caught up in the scandal he had played a part in uncovering?

It could have gone so terribly wrong for him if she had told the police he shot her husband, but Helena sounded almost grateful for the way events had unfolded.

How on earth had he helped save their marriage?

It was weird how things worked out sometimes.

He grabbed the blue cash bag to lock in the safe and walked into the back room to get ready to leave.

29

The house was in total darkness with the curtains undrawn when Wesley pulled up on to the driveway. Beth was clearly not home. He was grateful for that. He was in a foul mood.

The drive home had been spent wishing the woman at the café a wide scope of dreadful ills. She had frustrated him. She had cheated him. He almost wished he had taken a shot at her before he left, just to make her aware how angry she had made him. The only way he had been able to calm his rising temper was to remind himself that he would be able to return the following day and get the job done properly, without interference. The plan was still sound.

Maybe it would be even more pleasurable next time. Nothing worthwhile ever came easy, right?

But all he wanted for now was to take out his frustration on a bottle of whisky and to be left alone. Beth could stay away for good if she wanted. Perhaps she had got the message at last.

He lit up a cigarette as he locked the car door and drew deeply on it, fishing in his pocket for the house keys. The alarm had been activated. Wesley took that as a sign that

Beth had not yet been back after work. Her failure on a regular basis to bother setting the alarm when she left the house was one of the many ways her behaviour irritated him.

There were three letters on the mat, and he picked them up after switching on the hall light. All junk. He tossed them back on to the floor. Even throwing them away was too much of an effort right now.

Wesley sucked on the cigarette again and felt for the gun tucked into the back of his jeans but changed his mind and left it there. He would have his first tumbler measure of whisky first and then go to put it away in the safe, ready for tomorrow.

But as he reached around the corner in the front room to turn on the light there was a knock on the door.

He swore and stopped. He was not expecting anything to be delivered or for anyone to call. Ignoring it was the most appealing option, but he decided to answer it instead. If it were someone offering to power-jet clean his driveway or give him a quote for new windows he would give them an almighty mouthful. Perhaps that would make him feel better.

He did not recognise the man in the dark overcoat with a pulled-up collar and a sneering, superior expression but Wesley saw the two uniformed policemen behind him and figured out the rest.

Fucking great.

'Hello Wesley,' he said, pulling out a warrant card to flash far too quickly for anyone to possibly study its authenticity, even subliminally.

'DS Mitchell. We want a word.'

'I can give you two.'

Wesley poured all the contempt he could muster into staring the officer straight back in the eye and casually flicked the cigarette out through the open door, just missing the three of them.

'Hilarious,' replied the policeman, mirthlessly. 'Don't bother taking your coat off, you're coming with us.'

'No fucking chance.' The gun. Wesley felt the gun pressing against his lower back. There was no way he could let them take him in with an illegal firearm down the back of his jeans.

'We can do the arrest here if you like,' said Mitchell.

'You're going to have to.' Wesley was out of options. This was his final bluff.

The officer gave a resigned sigh. 'OK. Wesley Hughes, I'm...'

Desperately, Wesley grabbed the edge of the open door and swung it violently in an attempt to slam it shut, but the policeman reacted far more quickly than he had reckoned on, fending it with an elbow. The blow made him yelp but he pushed back against the door to barge through in pursuit of his man.

Wesley had backed away only a couple of metres down the hallway and, realising his gamble to buy a few valuable seconds to conceal the gun had failed, he reached for it anyway. He did not know if he intended to use it to hurt the three policemen or just to keep them at bay. He had not been given the time to think it through. He drew it from behind his back and pointed it towards them, his finger tightening around the trigger.

Mitchell did see the gun. Had he been presented with

the same situation in a theoretical scenario he might have opted for a different response but, in the heat of the moment and with the momentum of his lunge through the doorway behind him, he hurled himself forward, seeing nothing but the outstretched arm holding the gun and wanting only to grasp it.

As his left hand caught the underside of Wesley's wrist and deflected it up, the trigger finger pulled beyond the point of harmless resistance and the gun fired, sending a bullet over the policeman's shoulder to lodge in the wall.

The two uniformed officers flinched instinctively, protectively, before charging to the aid of the detective sergeant, whose dive had taken him bundling into the body of the much smaller man, propelling him backwards and pinning him to the floor with a lung-emptying thud and the crack of ribs. The force of the impact, more than the grip of a hand around his wrist, dislodged the weapon from Wesley's hold and it skidded away across the laminated flooring.

As his two colleagues moved in to manhandle Wesley onto his front so they could click on the handcuffs, allowing themselves the rewarding extra joy of wrenching their assailant's arms painfully behind his back just a little more acutely than they needed to, Mitchell attempted to recover his breath and climbed stiffly to his feet. The sounds of the explosion of the bullet and the hiss of the pellet as it whizzed past his left ear came to him as a delayed reaction. That had been too close. Only now, it frightened him.

He gathered his composure and gaped through wide, scared eyes at the pathetic figure with his head pressed against the wooden floor, shackled and beyond resistance, and saw how his life might easily have changed in an instant. He was tempted to aim a kick at that exposed side to punish him for his recklessness but knew he could not. He was better than that.

There was a greater satisfaction to be had.

'Wesley Hughes,' he said. 'I am arresting you on suspicion of conspiracy to commit murder, resisting arrest, perverting the course of justice and assisting an offender. You do not have to say anything, but it may harm your defence if you do not mention, when questioned, something which you later rely on in court. Anything you do say may be given in evidence. Do you understand?"

They did not wait for a reply. The two uniformed officers were already dragging Wesley to his feet ready to take him to their car.

Mitchell reached in his inside pocket for a pair of blue latex gloves and an evidence bag to gather up the gun. He looked down at his hands. They were shaking. He told himself to forget about it. There was work to do.

***

Detective Sergeant Will Copson breezed into the interview room with a brown card folder in his hand. He was looking forward to this.

'Morning Wesley. How are the ribs? Did you sleep well?'

Wesley sat in handcuffs on the opposite side of the white-topped table and refused to rise to the bait. The doctor who examined him in the holding cell suggested maybe three ribs had been cracked by the impact of being tackled to the floor the previous evening but brushed aside any notion he needed to be taken to hospital. In actual fact, Wesley had been far too uncomfortable to get any sleep but knew he should not expect any sympathy for that.

Beside him sat a grim-faced lawyer, already aware that his client was on a hiding to nothing on the strength of all the information provided to him that morning. It had been difficult to come up with much cause for optimism in their briefing before the formal interview and the best tactic he could suggest was to say nothing and hope the police would not be able to make at least some of the charges they were preparing stick. Wesley had not struck him as a man likely to be very talkative anyway.

Copson pulled up his chair and lay the folder on the table. The audio disc had already been set up by the young detective constable who was waiting for the prompt from his sergeant to start the recording. In turn, the four men formally identified themselves for the recording and Copson leaned forward, ready to hold court.

'I'm told you put on quite a show last night, Wesley. We were already looking at a pretty impressive charge sheet and now, well, I think you're going to keep the CPS busy for a week.'

The two men opposite remained impassive. He hadn't expected a response. He just enjoyed saying it.

'But let's forget about last night for now, there are one or two other matters I'd like to talk to you about. Let's start with the armed robbery which took place on...'

The officer opened his file to read the information he had prepared.

'...February the 22nd this year, at the premises of A

and H Gul Jewellers on Attercliffe Road in Sheffield, which resulted in the serious wounding of both Mr Abdul Gul and Mrs Husna Gul and the theft of over £140,000-worth of gold and jewellery. Mrs Gul was left critically ill from gunshot wounds but has, thankfully, made a good recovery. Can you tell me anything about that robbery, Wesley?'

Wesley stared back blankly, his expression unmoving.

'No comment.'

'Were you there when the robbery took place or was it just your job to clean up after the gang? Did you agree to handle all the loose ends for them until the heat had died down?'

'No comment.'

Copson pulled a ten-by-eight photograph from his file and slid it across the desk.

'I'm showing the accused a photograph of a Glock 17 semi-automatic handgun which was recovered from the River Don close to the premises of Worthington Car Supplies Ltd of Effingham Street in Sheffield on Saturday, March the 28th this year. Do you recognise the gun, Wesley?'

'No comment.'

'Well, we have two witnesses who saw you throw this weapon into the river on the evening of March the 21st. One of them even took your picture.'

He brought out another photograph from the folder and slid that over the table too.

'I think she captured your best side, don't you?'

Copson allowed the weight of the evidence to sink in. There was no point giving Wesley an opportunity to deny it was him because it so clearly was.

'We sent this weapon to our ballistics testing laboratory and they were able to ascertain that the bullet they test-fired under controlled conditions matched exactly the bullet that was pulled out of Mr Gul's shoulder and so I think we can safely assume the gun you were seen throwing into the river is the gun used in the armed robbery. Is there anything you'd like to say about that?'

The man opposite him remained tight-lipped, unflinching.

'I thought not, but you might like to consider that if you gave us the names of the people who carried out the robbery, maybe that would be looked at favourably when it comes to time to weigh up your part in this. Do yourself a favour here, Wesley. There's nothing to be gained by taking the whole of the blame for this on your shoulders.'

'No comment.'

'Never mind, we've got teams ripping apart your house and going through everything at the storage unit rented by you, under a false identity, on Broad Street. I'm sure they'll be able to come up with something interesting, don't you?'

The fact that the police knew about the lock-up concerned Wesley more than he was prepared to show. Their discovery of it meant trouble. They must have been watching him.

'I'll leave you to discuss your position on that one with your brief in a little while. There's another small matter we need to discuss. Who were you planning to murder?'

Wesley puffed his cheeks as if the whole business was beginning to bore him.

'I don't know what you're talking about.'

'So, you normally carry a gun down the back of your jeans do you? Were you just about to set out to do it when we came to pick you up last night? Is that why you were carrying the gun?'

'These are dangerous times. You can't rely on the police anymore,' he replied with a grin.

Copson ignored him.

'Who phoned you up asking you to kill someone, Wesley? Are you going to give us his name or are you going to take the full rap for this one too?'

'No comment.' He was rattled again. How did they know about the phone call?

'Shall I remind you about the conversation – just in case it's slipped your mind?'

A glimmer of fear flickered in Wesley's eyes.

'Do us the honours would you please, DC Wright?'

The young officer pressed the button to play the recording passed to them by Beth. The second voice was clear, the first just about clear enough to make out what was being said.

'I want him taking care of, once and for all.'

'You want him terminating?'

'That's exactly what I want. Is that an issue?'

'Not an issue. A bit of an escalation, that's all. It'll cost you.'

The recording was stopped. Wesley's face darkened. There was only one way they could have got hold of that.

'That fucking bitch.'

Copson grinned broadly.

'Who's on the other end of the phone, then? Who wants

who taken care of?'

It was all Wesley could do to stop himself yelling out or attempting to kick the table loose from its fixings. He knew Beth was a self-centred, vindictive cow but didn't think she could ever pull a stunt like this.

'No comment,' he snarled through gritted teeth.

Copson left him to stew for a few moments more, relishing the suffering he had inflicted. Maybe by making him realise he had been the victim of betrayal it might put him in the mood to do a bit of betraying of his own. It was time to let him ponder that.

'I think that's enough for now,' he said. He reached across the DC to prepare to stop the recording.

'Interview paused at 10.27 a.m. DS Copson and DC Wright leaving the room.'

He pressed the button with a flourish.

'Come on George, let's give them a bit of privacy. They've lots to talk about, I suspect.'

As he walked back into the main CID office, DC Harry Adams saw the sergeant and walked towards him. He was keen to pass on what he had found.

'About Hughes's phone, sarge,' he said.

'Yes, Harry. What have you come up with?'

'Well just about all the numbers were unregistered and we haven't been able to get a trace on them.'

'That's no great surprise.'

'But this is an interesting one,' added the young constable. 'The one called "Foghorn" in the contacts list. We've been able to come up with a name for that number. Cranford Hardstaff.'

Copson screwed up his face. The name was familiar but

was seemingly out of context here.

'The council leader?' he asked, knowing it was unlikely there might be a second person of that name.

'That's the one,' confirmed Adams, eagerly. 'And the really interesting part is that his is the number that called Hughes closest to the time Mrs Hughes made her recording of the conversation.'

'Good lord!' said Copson. He often told his junior officers that the job will never lose its capacity to surprise you but even he had not seen that one coming.

He nodded, chewing over the information.

'We'd better invite Mr Hardstaff in to explain himself, I reckon.'

30

At the same time as her husband was having a short-tempered post-interview exchange with his lawyer, Beth Hughes pulled up in a taxi to find that her home had been transformed into a scene from *CSI Miami*.

She didn't notice what was going on at first, but then the taxi driver said, 'Aye, aye, somebody's been having a bit of bother,' and that had prompted her to look up from her phone screen.

There were two white vans and a patrol car in front of the house. The driveway was cordoned off with yellow tape and an officer in a bright hi-vis jacket was stationed, arms crossed, in front of it.

Beth was still, up to that point, feeling woolly-headed from the night before, when she had left straight from work to meet up with her friend, Cassie, for a few drinks – or at least that had been the plan. A few soon became a lot and she had last seen Cassie at whichever one of the city pubs it was that she first got chatting to that guy at the bar while she was ordering another round and after that... She assumed Cassie had made it home all right, but Beth had spent the night at the guy's place in Gleadless. Her memories of the night itself were a bit vague but she woke just after eight and soon realised there was little point even pretending she had any intention of turning up at work that day.

She had sex with the guy again, largely because he was awake first and seemed keen, before quickly showering and ordering the taxi.

'Drop me here,' she ordered, and the driver pulled in. She paid him and got out.

It was too cold for the neighbours to be on the street, but she could see plenty of inquisitive eyes keeping a close watch through windows. So much for the outward air of respectability she and Wesley had so carefully nurtured.

The officer at the tape surveyed her challengingly as she walked briskly towards him.

'I need to speak to whoever's in charge. This is my house,' she told him.

He stared at her, weighing up whether or not to believe her, before turning to hail a female officer who was working just inside the open front door.

'Sal,' he called, and she turned to face him. 'Could you get the sergeant? This lady says she lives here.'

Beth shivered uncontrollably as she waited. Of course, she could guess what had gone on, but the timing had surprised her. She hadn't expected them to come for Wes so soon and, when they did, she thought she might be given some notice. Clearly, the information she had provided put her in less of a privileged position than she had imagined.

A plain-clothes detective, wearing blue latex gloves and holding a clipboard, emerged from the house. His sour expression, as he walked towards where Beth waited at the tape, said everything about how much he felt this interruption was a less than valuable use of his time.

'I'm the officer in charge. You say you live here,' he announced. 'Could you tell me your name, please?'

'I'm Beth Hughes,' she replied. 'What's going on?' She could practically feel the disdain in the detective's bearing. He was making no effort to disguise it. Beth was guilty by association.

'We have a warrant to search this house for evidence of criminal activity. I'm afraid you cannot be allowed in until our search is complete.'

'But this is my house,' she protested. 'I need to get some things.'

'Not possible, I'm afraid.' There was no scope for negotiation in his bearing.

'How long are you going to be?'

'I can't say,' he answered sternly, before his attention was distracted by a call from a colleague at the door of the house. 'Now if you'll excuse me.'

Without waiting to be excused, he headed back to the house. Beth watched and felt the blood drain from her already paled face.

What the other policeman was waiting to show the detective was a blue metal security box. Beth knew what it was. Wes had used it to store a few thousand pounds in cash and some documents. Important documents. The stuff related to his criminal contacts was of no interest to Beth, but the account details were. Those were the funds she intended to divert as soon as Wes was out of harm's way, to set her up nicely for the new life she had planned without him. They must have taken up the flooring in the conservatory and discovered the sunken hiding place.

Beth's intention was to recover the box as soon as she had word that Wes was under arrest and take it to where it would be safe for a day or two, just until she was ready to leave and start again. She had decided to head to Portugal. That would be far enough from possible danger, in case Wes figured out how the police had come to know so much about his affairs and asked an associate to exact a little retribution.

But now the box was in their hands. She had nothing, apart from what was left of her month's salary in her bank account, and that would not keep her for long in the Algarve.

She had to get away from the house, though she had no idea where she would go. She turned and left, walking so quickly she almost broke into a trot, just as the first flakes of snow started to fall.

31

The first wispy flakes soon gave way to a swarm of fat white icy blobs which fluttered gently down through the still air from slate-grey skies. They dazzled and disorientated unwary motorists, drew excited small children to the windows of warm rooms and elicited mounting dread in the minds of office workers who still had hours to go before they would have to tackle the journey home.

The snow fell and fell and fell, overwhelming everything beneath it in a thick white blanket. It fell all through the afternoon and all through the evening, then all through the night, making roads indistinguishable except by the lines of abandoned vehicles. People, ill-prepared and unsuitably dressed, trudged their slow progress through the deep, sapping mass, dreaming of the relief of when they would be able to sip hot tea and swap nightmarish tales with their loved ones about their severely disrupted commutes.

It curtailed plans, knocked out communications and brought the whole infrastructure to a standstill, and still it came down, until it looked as if the whole city was sinking into the earth under the weight of it.

Grim-faced weather forecasters tried hard not to revel in reminding viewers they had predicted its coming and were declaring it the heaviest single day's snowfall to hit the region since 1963, warning ominously of more to come. Sombre emergency service leaders were summoned to implement well-laid plans for getting aid and assistance to those who would soon be cut off.

One such person was Cranford Hardstaff, though he had no desire to be rescued. He had realised it might be wise to disappear from public view as soon as he was made aware of Helena Morrison's Monday morning appointment with the Monitoring Officer. That could only mean one thing and he had no intention of staying around to face the consequences.

Hardstaff had the ideal hideaway. It was a cottage set back off the main road from Buxton to Ashbourne, in the heart of the Derbyshire Peak District. He and his wife had bought it years ago, back in the days when they still could see a point in making decisions for a better life together, and he had managed to hold on to it through the acrimonious divorce wrangling as her solicitors clawed away large chunks of the considerable wealth he had built up through his businesses.

He never talked to anybody about the cottage and certainly never invited anyone to make use of it, even though it stood abandoned for most of the year. It was his private haven and now it was coming into its own.

As soon as Hardstaff caught the scent of revelation in the town hall air, he had abandoned his office, collected everything he needed from home, stocked up with a few days of basic supplies and set out for the cottage.

After a couple of days shut away, with the phone turned off and the world unaware of where he had gone, Hardstaff reasoned it would be safe to either drive south and get on a ferry or head for one of the quieter airports and catch a flight to his place in Italy. There he would stay, live a carefree Tuscan life and try to forget all about his crumbling empire in Sheffield.

But on the day before he planned to make his move, Hardstaff found himself marooned in a sea of white. It was soon so thick on the ground that it was pointless to attempt to drive away, even in the Range Rover. The radio told him that the airports were closed and even the major roads were impassable. He fumed with the frustration of his extended isolation and when an environmental expert was interviewed on the news programme, speaking about how the severe weather snap was unquestionably another sign of the damage of climate change, the radio was sent flying with a crash against the thick stone cottage wall, never to crackle to the sounds of the airwaves again.

For five more days, Hardstaff remained in his secluded hiding place, snug but most definitely stuck. The constant orange glow from the wood-burning stove was his only companion as he wiped away condensation from the windows and peered for signs of a reprieve, only to be greeted time after time by the same leaden skies and the occasional further flurry of snowfall.

His only contact with the outside world came through a small television. Hardstaff had never been a big TV watcher, dismissing the vast majority of its content as 'frivolous shite', but it became his routine to switch on for the regional news programme every evening. The weather dominated the bulletins and he was lifted by suggestions that what they irritatingly referred to as 'The Big Freeze' might be about to break, but that was not all he was interested in.

There appeared to be no developments in the Swarbrook Hill collapse fallout, which Hardstaff regarded as helpful for his chances of getting away, once he had the chance.

But he was concerned that there was still no announcement of the mysterious death of a certain well-known local café owner. Surely Hughes must have done the job by now?

As he came to terms with his imposed solitude, re-reading every book in the cottage and working his way steadily through the contents of his drinks cabinet, a sense of calm contentment also descended over Hardstaff, the likes of which he had not experienced for many years. The control he had wielded for so long was not his anymore but surrendering it no longer felt such a wrench. He was beginning to look forward to his Tuscan retirement.

On the sixth day, Hardstaff awoke to bright sunlight bursting through the gap at the top of his curtains. He peeled them back to reveal the confirmation of clear blue skies for the first time in what seemed an age. The temperature was up. The lines of snow on the branches of trees and on top of walls were thinning, eroding the thick carpet on the ground with drips of melting ice. The thaw had come.

He smiled. About time. The freezer was almost empty and the stock of tinned food was running low. He would not have been able to stay in isolation for much longer and now nature had done him a favour, for once. He spent the rest of the day preparing to leave for good. If the forecasts were accurate, he might be able to set out the following day.

Hardstaff turned on the TV to watch the news for what, he hoped, would be the last time. A diet of reports from closed schools, interviews with worried pensioners and stories of communities chipping in was starting to annoy him. But he wanted reassurance that the weather had turned for the better and so he turned on the TV to play in the background as he tried to create a palatable meal from the last of his dried pasta, a small tin of baked beans, two frozen hash browns and the remains of a jar of pickled onions.

His culinary creation was soon interrupted.

'Your headlines tonight,' announced the woman on the sofa who was wearing a dress in a green, white and black pattern that looked like it was based on a failed test card experiment from the 1970s.

'One top council official resigns and two others are suspended in the Sheffield new homes site scandal.'

Hardstaff, about to pour the pasta into a pan of boiling water, stood with his arm suspended in mid-act as he listened to the list of the rest of the top stories before putting the packet down to turn up the TV volume.

Alongside the woman on the studio sofa was a younger man of Asian heritage who sat as stiffly as if he knew he was not meant to be in the camera shot but had been caught out by the timing of the start of the programme. He clenched the pad of paper on his lap with both hands as he faced the camera.

'Our top story tonight is news of the first council officials to be implicated in the Sheffield new homes site scandal and among them is the long-serving council leader, Cranford Hardstaff. An internal inquiry was launched last week to look into allegations that key council officials knew the planned site of the one hundred and thirty million-pound Swarbrook Hill project on the city boundaries was the historic dumping ground for thousands of tonnes of dangerous chemical waste and this is the first confirmation of the people who, it seems, will be the focus of that inquiry. Michelle Rogers is at Sheffield Town Hall for us. What else can you tell us, Michelle?'

The reporter, her cheeks glowing red under the camera lights, appeared grateful that the producer had decided to come to her so early in the programme. With the temperature plummeting under clear skies, plumes of steam from her breath rose into the frigid air when she began to talk. Two boys made rude gestures at the camera over her shoulder as they passed by.

'As you said, Ravi, Sheffield City Council announced they were to launch an internal investigation into the revelations surrounding the Swarbrook Hill development eleven days ago. Nothing more has been made public about this process since until the council issued a press release today to confirm that council leader Cranford Hardstaff...'

Stock video footage of Hardstaff at an official function was cut in to the report as soon as she mentioned the name, which did nothing to lift the mood of the man himself, watching in his cottage.

'… has been suspended from his duties until further notice, pending the outcome of the council's inquiry. Senior Scientific Officer Yuvraj Patel has also been suspended, while it has been confirmed that Helena Morrison, the council's Head of Planning and Regeneration, has handed in her resignation.'

The camera shot returned to the chilly reporter.

'This announcement adds fuel to the suggestion that certain council officials knew more about the history of the proposed housing site than they had been prepared to share with their council colleagues. It may be some time yet until we learn of the outcome of the council inquiry. The issue is, as we know, also likely to be the subject of a wider government investigation as well as possible police action, but we should stress that, as yet, no charges have been brought.'

'Bloody right you should,' growled Hardstaff.

'With me now is Martin Bestwick from the Sheffield Environmental Action Network, the organisation which first broke the news of the dangerous contaminated waste buried on the site where hundreds of new homes were to be built.'

The reporter turned slightly to her left and the camera shot panned back. The chunky blue woollen hat, topped by an exceptionally large pom-pom, looked almost comical on Martin's head, but Hardstaff was not laughing.

Under any circumstances, that man was the last person Hardstaff wanted to see on his TV screen. For him to be invited to pass judgement at this moment of his public humiliation was close to unbearable. Yet there it was again, the face he had come to despise. As if that was not bad enough, the sight of it this time sent Hardstaff into a fury far greater than it ever had before. It was worse than having to listen to him spouting his eco-mentalist bollocks on the television again. Worse than being taunted with reminders of the damage inflicted in the last few weeks. Worse even than the fact that he had taken on the great council leader – and had won.

Worse than all of that. Bestwick was obviously and most definitely not dead.

Hardstaff released a primal scream that might have shaken the foundations of a less substantial building and would have startled people in a radius of hundreds of metres, had there been anyone that close.

He stared at the screen, incredulous.

How is this man still alive? I hired someone to kill him. What more does a person have to do to wipe this smug little self-righteous bastard off the face of the earth?

'Martin, the fact that the council has taken these steps has been greeted as a sign that the authority is prepared to get to the heart of this controversy. How do you feel about it?'

Martin nodded sombrely and the pom-pom on top of his head shook.

'We certainly welcome the news, Michelle. The more we probed into the background of this scandalous betrayal of public trust, the worse it became and these are three names we fully expected to see mentioned in connection with the cover-up. The steps the council has announced today are in line with information we have received since we launched our call for a full public inquiry. So while we support the council's internal findings, we will not be completely satisfied until the full extent of this dreadful episode is completely out in the open and action is taken to make those responsible pay for what they have done.'

'Do you think that should include criminal proceedings?'

'If inquiry findings point towards that as appropriate, definitely. These people are public servants who were supposed to act in the best interests of the people who pay their wages and were meant to keep them safe. What we have seen here is that certain officials appear to have been motivated by more selfish aims and have been prepared to recklessly endanger public safety. Don't forget, we are not only talking about the hundreds of people whose health would have been put at risk if they had bought houses on this site, we're talking about the hundreds of thousands who would have been affected by what would have been a major ecological disaster.

'If it is found that these three individuals took decisions knowing the likely consequences, then we think the judicial system has a duty to make them pay. What we have seen today with the naming of these three officials is that the culture of corruption in the city council goes right to the top and so while we are encouraged by the steps the council has taken today, we fear this is only the tip of the iceberg.'

Hardstaff watched silently, each word feeding his anger like a steady trickle of petrol on burning tinder. He jabbed at the power button on the remote control and the screen went blank but he could not tear his eyes from the TV. It held him, trance-like, petrified. He was so enraged that his body had shut down. Had anyone been with him, they would surely have taken cover for fear he was about to combust.

'And can I just add one more thing, Michelle?'

Hardstaff knew he had turned off the TV but there was Bestwick's face again. It leered at him in extreme close-up, filling the picture so completely that it seemed he might pop the membrane of the screen and emerge into the room itself.

'Stick that up your arse, Hardstaff! I told you I'd ruin you. How does it feel, loser?'

Hardstaff blinked. The TV was turned off. Of course, he had not seen that last part. The little bastard was inside his head.

He's taken everything and now he's taking my sanity.

Trembling, the broken council leader grabbed hold of the TV, jerking the cables from the back of it until it was untethered and he could carry it. He opened the door and cast it as far as he could. It landed with a soft whump on the snow-covered grass.

Hardstaff closed and locked the door behind him. He was panting, even though the effort had not been so great.

On the stove, the pan of water had almost boiled dry.

32

It took the rest of the night and the remaining two-thirds of a bottle of scotch for Hardstaff to calm himself. The more he drank, the more clearly he began to see again and the more he saw, the more deeply he resented the man he held responsible for his fall.

Less than a month ago, he had no idea who Bestwick was. Even after the incident where he had raked up the business with the tree felling yet again, Hardstaff regarded him as no more than a buzzing pest who needed swatting away, but he had underestimated his enemy. Though he could not have known from the start that this undersized environmentalist carrot-crunching fanatic was actually a dangerous revolutionary intent on bringing about his downfall, Hardstaff had not acted quickly enough to crush him. He had let him grow too powerful and, when he had decided to take decisive action, he had made the mistake of trusting others to do it for him.

Wesley Hughes had let him down. Hardstaff was paying the price for that.

There was no doubt that, had Bestwick been standing in front of him that night, Hardstaff would happily have torn him apart until all that remained was a small pile of fleshy waste for the foxes to gorge on, but that was not an option. He had missed his chance. It was too late.

The realisation of defeat consumed him and the drunker he got, the more painful his sense of loss became.

The bright light of morning stung his eyes as Hardstaff roused, flat out on his front with his face fixed to the pillow by a clammy pool of cold dribble. It had been after two when he had finally stumbled to the bedroom and collapsed, fully clothed, on to the bed rather than in it.

Closing the curtains had also been beyond him and though the sunshine through the window warmed his skin, his feet and fingers were numb with cold.

Hardstaff rolled on to his back with great effort, turning his head away from the painful light, the large dome of his belly rising and falling with each breath. For a few scrambled moments, he was not even aware of where he was or how he had got there but as his awareness dawned and memories of the previous night flooded his mind again in a dreadful rising tide, he almost craved a return to that brief blissful state of ignorance.

'Oh, god!' he groaned.

He pawed at the duvet over the other half of the double bed and pulled it over himself to try to get the deep chill from his bones but his toes began to cramp through cold, forcing him to writhe with all the grace of a stranded manatee until he could flatten his feet against the floor and ease the pain. With the duvet still wrapped around him, Hardstaff attempted to stand on legs that, from the shins down, seemed to belong to someone else, and slowly shuffled towards the door.

The main room was chilly. The wood-burner, which he had forgotten to stoke, had burned itself out. Hardstaff headed for the kitchen area and stopped briefly, confused as to why there was only a tangle of unconnected leads where the TV had been.

'Oh, yeah,' he said to himself as he remembered and carried on his way to fill the kettle so that he could make coffee. Black coffee. The last of the milk had long since been used.

On the counter he saw the almost empty jar of pickled onions and his stomach churned. He threw it into the bin.

After a shower and three coffees, Hardstaff reached a decision.

Today was the day he left all this behind, as planned, and headed for Italy. The snow ploughs had cleared the main road the day before, the snow in the cottage grounds was much softer and more yielding now the weather had broken and it would be far easier to dig out the car and clear two lines of tracks on the driveway. His bags were packed and ready to load into the boot.

This was not the future he had imagined for himself but it was the way things had worked out. Hardstaff told himself he had to swallow his pride and cut his losses. It was his best option.

Before tackling the task of shovelling, he thought it might be a good idea to get the fire burning again, so that he could warm and dry himself before he set out on his long drive.

The temperature outside was hardly lower than it was inside the cottage but it was a crisp, clean cold. Hardstaff gulped in a large lungful of the fresh air and was invigorated by it, feeling its refreshing properties through every fibre of his hungover brain.

He retraced what had become a well-worn path through the snow to where he stored the logs for the fire and took one off the top of the pile, standing it on the flat stone ready to chop, then picked up the axe from where he had left it the last time.

Hardstaff lifted the axe, his hand snug around the shaped dark wooden handle, and felt the weight of the thick steel blade, dense dark grey until it tapered towards the shiny silver of its keen sharpened edge.

A man could do serious damage with a weapon like this, he thought to himself. Serious damage.

He gazed down at the log, which would soon be split into four parts, helpless to resist against the force of the blade, and, for a moment, he saw the head of Bestwick where the log had stood. Beseeching eyes begged for mercy, though their desperation betrayed the knowledge that he knew he would receive none. Hardstaff raised the axe and brought it down with retributive force. The wood cracked and splintered, the two halves rocking gently on the flat rock as they fell.

Hardstaff glistened with the immense satisfaction of the blow. He stood up one of the halves of the log and rained the axe down on it again. The thrill of it surged through him and he brought out another log to split. Then another and another until he had far more kindling than he needed for his fire but he now had so much more than that on his mind.

'Why not?' he said out loud.

Before he headed to Italy, he could make a diversion to

Sheffield, find where Bestwick lived and take the revenge he so completely deserved.

Hardstaff caught the glisten of the sunshine on the edge of the blade in his eyes. He wanted to smash it down on that head right down the line of that stupid centre parting so that it split his thick skull and spilled its worthless contents over the floor of his dingy hovel.

He would find the address from the text message he had sent Hughes, overwhelm the little fucker as soon as he answered the door and use the axe to give him what he had been asking for. The police would not have a clue who had done it and even if they did, he would be safely hidden away in his Tuscan villa in no time.

Who did you think you were kidding, trying to convince yourself you could disappear and leave unfinished business behind? You would never have been content, knowing that he'd got away with causing you so much grief. That man has stolen your legacy, Cranford. It's your right – no, it's your obligation – to take retribution. That's why you ordered him to be killed in the first place and the only mistake you made was to put your trust in a third party. If you want something doing properly, do it yourself. Isn't that what you've always said?

'Bloody right,' he snarled.

33

The house was dark and quiet. Hardstaff trod carefully through the slushy snow on the rising path to the front door but had little hope there would be a reply if he knocked, so he did not even try.

Never mind. I can wait.

It'll be worth it.

He considered what to do next as a gust of wind disturbed the last stubborn brown leaves on the beech hedge which divided Martin Bestwick's home from the one next door. In the old clothes he kept at the cottage for when he needed to do manual work outside and with five days of stubble on his chin, he looked such a contrast to the image of the statesman he had always sought to portray to the outside world. He was happy for the disguise. He had taken a chance by bringing the Range Rover back into the city where so many people wanted answers from him, especially as it had a distinctive personalised number plate, but the roads, clearer of snow than they had been out in the countryside, were quiet and he had made the trip without attracting unwanted attention. He left the car parked down a quiet side road a short walk away, where he hoped it could not be spotted by a passing patrol car. Doing what he needed to do and getting away without being noticed at all was crucial.

His only stop on the way in had been at a quiet rural garage, where he filled up with diesel ready for the drive south and turned on his mobile phone – just long enough to check if he still had the text to Hughes with Bestwick's address. It was still there and though he realised he should probably have deleted it long since – just to be safe – he was grateful he hadn't. He memorised the address, deleted the text this time and turned off the phone again.

Hardstaff sized up the silent old brick detached house in front of him. Ideally, Bestwick would have been home but his absence opened other options.

Perhaps, if he could break in somehow, he could be inside waiting when Bestwick did return. Maybe he could position himself in an armchair, casually leaning his head on hand in a thoughtful pose with the axe menacingly on his lap, like a Bond villain. Or he could wait to pounce behind an internal door, with maniacal eyes, like Jack Nicholson in *The Shining.*

Heeeeeere's Cranford!

It was an enticing fantasy but breaking through the external door with the axe would not exactly fit in with the hoped-for element of surprise and Hardstaff was well aware that the days when he might force open a downstairs window and squeeze his large belly through the small gap were long gone.

He had to find somewhere to hide. Somewhere he could watch the house and remain out of sight, so that when Bestwick arrived he could go through with the plan as he had conceived it.

Knock on the door, barge through, pull out the axe he had secured with his trouser belt and strike.

Then back to the car, find a quiet pull-off about an hour's drive away where he could change into normal clothes and dump the old ones, then off to Folkestone for the Eurotunnel.

Thirteen hours after disembarking at Calais, he would be at the villa in Tuscany. It would be a long time on the road but he could always sleep in the car if he needed to and he was excited by the prospect of the trip, rather than daunted. It felt like an adventure.

He edged back down the slippery path to the road and looked both ways. To his right, the road fell towards the city centre and options for cover were few, other than in people's front gardens, but to his left was a T-junction. On the opposite side of it was a row of bungalows behind a neat long privet hedge and then an entrance to a driveway.

He headed towards there. The driveway led to a council-run care centre but what had caught Hardstaff's eye was the curved high stone wall to the right of the driveway, protecting the boundary of the centre's grounds. A cluster of tall old oaks waved gently in the wind behind it, their branches reaching over the wall as if trying to escape its restraints.

Hardstaff stood at the wall. The view to Bestwick's house from there was unrestricted and as long as the ground on the other side rose high enough to allow him to peer over the wall, he could watch completely hidden from sight. He walked up the driveway to find out what the view was like from the other side of the wall.

The ground under the trees was still deep in virgin

snow which had drifted with the wind against the wall. Hardstaff sunk mid-calf with every laboured step but, when he reached the point of the wall closest to the main road, the reward was that it came only to shoulder height. He could see the house easily. Perfect.

He created a small clearing in the snow from where he could stand and watch for however long he needed to, without fear of detection. The tall trees creaked above him but their noises gave nothing away as he set himself for his vigil, rubbing his gloved hands and kicking against the wall occasionally to keep warm, dipping low whenever he saw a car or a pedestrian approaching.

Even in so many thick layers, the cold began to penetrate to his bones but Hardstaff was alert and eager. Clearing the snow from around the car and on the drive at the cottage had been made much more of a trial by his alcohol excesses of the night before but he had slept for three hours in his chair by the wood-burner after that and awoke feeling much better. He was even able to tolerate the thought of food, and so he had made his delayed meal of pasta, baked beans and hash browns before setting off for Sheffield.

Locking the door felt as if he was bringing an era to a close. The next person to enter the cottage would be the estate agent, after he issued the instruction to sell from Italy, but Hardstaff felt no sadness in that realisation. He was still in control. They had exposed him and sought to shame him but they had not managed to bring him down. He was still free to do as he liked and Bestwick was soon to feel the power he still wielded.

He was too smart for them all. They would not conquer

the great Cranford Hardstaff.

He pulled back his sleeve to look at his watch. It was a few minutes before eight. He had been there for over an hour. Though his commitment to staying for as long as it took remained firm, he wished Bestwick would do the decent thing and come home to be killed soon.

As the darkness fell deeper, the cold bit harder and Hardstaff stamped to get the stiffness out of his knees. There were still no lights on at the house and as the hands on his watch crept slowly closer to half past eight, Hardstaff began to wonder if his victim was going to return home at all.

But then he saw the single light of a bicycle weaving up the hill and a figure in a bright yellow jacket dismounted outside the house. Hardstaff's eyes strained to be sure it was the right man but there was no need. The figure pushed the bike up the path towards the front door.

It was him.

Give it a minute, he told himself.

But he was impatient to get it done now, the final act of closure before he headed away to make a fresh start. He restrained his impulse to move for a few seconds more until the thumping surge of eager anticipation coursing through his body could be denied no longer.

Let's go!

The roads were quiet and the weather still, as if holding its breath in anticipation. Hardstaff trudged the short distance from his hiding place, hunched with his hands deep in the pockets of his overcoat, feeling the ease of movement slowly return to his chilled legs, his teeth gritted in resolve for the task ahead.

The bottle green wooden front door was in front of him again and he raised his hand to knock, but stopped. Maybe the door did not have to be opened for him. He gripped the rounded brass doorknob and twisted it slowly. Must not make a sound. Surprise will add an extra layer of satisfaction to the kill.

The doorknob creaked, barely noticeably, in his hand until he could turn it no further. Hardstaff pushed tentatively against the door and it moved – no more than a few millimetres, but it moved. It was unlocked. He pushed again, a little more forcibly this time, and the door opened.

Hardstaff eased the heavy old door open wider until he could step through it and into the hallway. The house was dark and cold but, ahead and to the right, light seeped through from the crack of a door leading to one of the lower floor rooms. Beyond it was the sound of activity – drawers being opened and pans being set down on hard surfaces.

Hardstaff grinned and his pulse quickened. There. Bestwick is through there.

He slowly pushed the front door closed behind him so that it held against the frame. No point shutting it fully and risking making a sound.

The stairway was to his left and, leaned against the same wall, was a bike, with a helmet dangling by a strap from the handlebars. Good. The helmet would have offered no protection against the axe but he was happy it would not be in the way at all.

He took a first step towards the room and his oblivious prey. The chipped mosaic Victorian tiled flooring absorbed the impact of his vast weight without offering a clue of his advance, but he stepped as lightly as he could anyway until he was almost there at the door. He was so close that the light from inside shone in a broad strip against the length of his body. So close that the sounds of movement from the room filled his senses. So close that he could almost taste his revenge.

Hardstaff flicked open the buttons of his overcoat, a gunslinger relishing the final moments before the rush of proving once again that he was not a man to be challenged. His fingers tightened around the wood of the axe handle where it met the heavy metal blade and he pulled it carefully free of the belt around his waist, holding it firmly in his left hand.

Ready to strike. Ready to make that bastard pay.

He leaned against the door, poised to burst through, drew a final deep breath and flung it open, stepping into the room. There will be no escape this time.

The man in the yellow jacket was on the opposite side of the room but he was not taken by surprise. He was not petrified. He was not helpless.

He was not Bestwick.

He was pointing a handgun at the intruder.

'Armed police. Drop the weapon. Now!'

Hardstaff was frozen. He stared blankly at the figure opposite, who stood arms outstretched with two hands wrapped around the weapon that was aimed at the torso of the intruder, his stare uncompromising and steely down the line of the barrel. He had been outflanked. He was the predator but he had walked straight into a trap.

'Drop the weapon!'

From behind him, Hardstaff could hear heavy footsteps advancing through the front door and he turned to see two more armed officers, wearing bulky protective vests over their black combat jackets and squinting down the sights of menacing black submachine guns. They yelled commands so loud and urgent that he could hardly make out the confusion of words but he understood their meaning.

Hardstaff bent his knees deliberately, cautiously, to lay the axe on the floor and rose slowly upright again with his hands raised.

'Hands on your head. Do it!' commanded the policeman in yellow.

As Hardstaff did as he was told, other officers surged into the room. One wrenched Hardstaff's hands behind his back to secure them in handcuffs while another collected the axe.

A third stood directly in front of the deposed council leader. DS Will Copson wore a protective vest over his normal clothes and stared deeply into the eyes of the subdued but resentful face before him. This was his moment of victory.

'Cranford Hardstaff. I am arresting you on suspicion of attempted murder…'

'Woah, woah, woah!' interrupted Hardstaff and Copson fell quiet. 'You don't think I was intending to kill him, do you? I'm a politician, not a maniac. I'm a man of peace. I was coming here to clear up any misunderstanding and bad feeling between myself and Martin and the axe, well, that was a sort of joke. Bury the hatchet, see? I wouldn't do anything as stupid as…'

'Save your breath, Hardstaff,' said Copson firmly. 'We've had surveillance cameras on this house since Mr Bestwick came forward to tell us he believed you intended to make an attempt on his life and so we saw you creeping about the place earlier this evening. We watched you go and find a hiding place to wait for what you thought was him coming home, so don't give me that garbage. We know what you've been up to. We've already secured a full confession from your accomplice, Wesley, and we know all about your sordid dealings at the council. You're finished, Cranford. Not even a professional bullshitter like you can get out of this one.'

With the formalities of the arrest completed, Hardstaff was led from the house by officers holding him by the arms. The flash of blue lights from the police cars on the street made him blink as he emerged into the cold evening and he bent his head to avoid the glare of their scrutiny, meekly allowing himself to be directed down the path and towards the open back door of one of the waiting cars.

As a hand was placed on his head to encourage him to dip and climb inside, Hardstaff glanced upwards again. On the steps of the house opposite stood a frail old woman, wrapped in thick clothing but still cowering against the chill of the night. Beside her, his arm pulled closely around her shoulder in comfort and mutual support, was a short man with straight dark hair and a straggly beard. They were both glaring at him: terror, not triumph, in their eyes.

Hardstaff saw him but could not muster even a final defiant flare of hatred to launch in the direction of the man who had brought him to this.

What was the point?
It was over.

34

'Good turn-out again.'

Vivienne moved beside Martin and slipped her arm around his. They looked out over the community hall together with satisfied smiles like proud parents as the banks of chairs slowly emptied and inquisitive newcomers picked through the information leaflets that had been laid out for them. A queue of at least twenty waited patiently for Diane and Richard to process their new membership application forms.

They had anticipated the surge in interest at the April meeting, coming as soon as it did after all the publicity of the Swarbrook Hill exposé, but there were even more new faces at the May meeting, if anything. The achievements of the Sheffield Environmental Action Network were there for all to see and, if the numbers in the hall and the traffic to the website were anything to go by, people wanted to associate themselves with a group that got things done.

'We're going to have to think about finding an even bigger venue in the future at this rate,' said Martin.

Vivienne laughed. 'The days when we were all able to fit around a table in a small corner of your café seem a long time ago.'

'You're not wrong,' he agreed. 'It's been a crazy couple of months, hasn't it, but we always said we thought we could make a real difference one day and, well, here we are.'

They watched the activity of the room in silence for a few happy moments more. So many opportunities lay ahead of them, so many plans waiting to be pursued. This was worth every ounce of the effort they had put in through the early days. Their voice, at last, was hard to ignore.

'Have you heard any more about the trial date?' Vivienne asked.

Hardstaff. Martin had been so afraid of that name in the days after Helena Morrison had visited him at the café and left him with a warning. It still send a shiver down his spine, even since the night of the arrest.

'Not a thing. It'll be some time yet, I guess. They're probably still counting how many charges they're going to try him for.'

'You're OK, though?' Vivienne was happy to hear his attempt at disarming humour but clung on to nagging concerns for her old ally.

'I'm fine, honestly,' he said, attempting a reassuring smile. 'I'd be lying if I said I'm completely over it because I still don't like to be on my own in the house. It feels like he's still there, you know? Lurking in dark corners. I've taken to leaving all the lights on, which is no good for my carbon footprint but I need it for now. I'll get over it, I guess.'

'You know there's always a spare room at my place,'

she said.

'Thanks,' he gripped her arm tighter to show his appreciation. 'It's only a short-term thing, I'm sure. I have to get used to being back to normal some time.'

A familiar elderly couple, hand in hand, were moving towards them and Martin's face lit up with delight when he saw them.

'So glad you could make it,' he said, hugging them in turn.

'Vivienne, I'd like you to meet two very special friends of mine. This is Frank Elliott and this is... well, what should I call you now? Mrs Dawes or Mrs Elliott?'

The old lady shot him a mildly reproachful glance.

'Evelyn. You should call me Evelyn.'

The couple exchanged handshakes with Vivienne as Martin continued the introductions.

'Mrs... Evelyn used to live opposite me but now she's moved in with Frank. How is life at Silverwood Court?'

'It's lovely,' she said. 'There's so much going on all the time. It's great to have so many new friends but we still want our old ones to stay in touch, don't we Frank?'

'Absolutely,' he confirmed.

'In fact, I've looked into setting up a vegan cookery group at the Court and I wondered if you'd be able to come by and give us a talk.'

'I'd be delighted to,' said Martin and he hugged Evelyn again.

Over her shoulder, he spotted a lone figure, lingering nervously at the back of the hall. He was slim and petite, dressed in crisp dark jeans and a dark blue jacket. His light-brown hair was streaked and styled in a new way now and his skin was tanned but Martin knew him in an instant. It had been twenty-one months, one week and six days since the split.

After almost eighteen years together, what was to one secure and blissful had become to the other stifling and unfulfilling. He wanted to travel. He wanted to sell up and, after they had seen the world, he wanted them to buy a bar on a beach and share a new life in the sun. But Martin did not want that and so they had to accept, reluctantly, painfully, that they had reached the end.

But there he was, barely daring to attempt eye contact, yet desperately wanting to be noticed. Not brave enough to be the one to make the next move, yet risking so much by being there at all. Wanting to stay, but ready to go. Waiting for a sign.

'Jody?' Martin said quietly.

'Pardon?' asked Evelyn as she broke from their embrace.

'Er, sorry, but I've just seen someone… We've not seen each other for…'

The three others watched his face with curiosity, wondering what had brought on this sudden change in his behaviour, but Martin barely knew they were there anymore.

'Can you excuse me for a minute, I just have to…'

And he left them there, striding with increasing purpose across the hall towards his past and a new future.

Acknowledgements

If I have learned anything from writing and self-publishing three novels it is that the description of an author as independent is fundamentally flawed. There is no way you could do it all without relying on others.

It's one thing to come up with what you think is a good idea. It's quite another to write about it and sound as if you know what you are talking about.

I had to lean on several people to fill in the gaps in my knowledge with *Catalyst*.

My Derby Telegraph colleague Eddie Bisknell was a huge help in keeping my fanciful plot lines within the bounds of reality and sparked good ideas for how the story could be developed. For further understanding about the workings of councils, I was also able to call on not one, but two Ken Currans (junior and senior) and both proved valuable.

The Derby Climate Coalition has been fighting the good fight since 2005 and their chair, Peter Robinson, was patient in explaining their operation and their relationship with other groups. I would heartily recommend you check them out.

I am lucky not only to have a wonderful and supportive family but also to have people within it who hold really useful information. So, thanks to my private medical specialists, partner Sue and son Jack, and my police procedural consultant, little sister Jane.

For finishing touches, Heather Fitt was just the type of attention to detail editor every writer needs and Andrew

Rainnie again produced an eye-catching cover design.

Despite supporting the wrong football team, my fellow Sheffield author Anita Waller has proved she has sound judgement as a generous source of advice. She has provided much inspiration and encouragement.

I'm grateful, too, to good friends Anne Meadows, Ruth Broadbent and Victoria Wilcox for reading through and amending the first draft and to the members of the ARC group for volunteering to check out the final draft before the button was pressed to go for publication. It is so reassuring to have you all there.

As I write, my next novel is already on the way. No doubt, I will be calling on the help of many of you again.

Also by Mark Eklid

Sunbeam
Published November 2019

John Baldwin has been on a downward spiral to self-destruction since the day he witnessed the murder of his best friend, Stef. It has cost him his marriage, his business and his dignity.

One year on from the day that turned his world upside down, he sees Stef again. John fears he has finally lost his mind but Stef is there to pull his friend back from the brink, not tip him over it. He offers John a fresh start; a new destiny.

John rebuilds his life. He has everything again but there is a price to pay. The killer is still on the loose and Stef wants revenge.

Reviews for Sunbeam

A plot that is so full of unexpected twists and turns that the reader is left guessing until the final page.
Derbyshire Life magazine

A massive five stars from me, loved it.
Anita Waller, author

More twists and turns than a Scalextric race track.
Clare Naylor, Amazon review

Family Business
Published June 2020

Family historian Graham Hasselhoff thought there were no skeletons in his cupboard. That is, until the day he met the son he never knew he had.

Getting to know Andreas, who is now the boss of a road haulage firm, soon leads him to a trail of arson, beatings, mysterious warnings – and murder.

Can his son really be behind this deadly business?

Graham has to quickly work out if Andreas is an impetuous eccentric – or a dangerously ruthless criminal.

Reviews for Family Business

Fabulously well written and totally original.
Veronika Jordan, book blogger

The twists in the plot left me guessing at several outcomes but I was not prepared for the ending. Wow!
Maggie, Amazon review

This is the first book I have read by Mark Eklid and it certainly won't be the last.
Teresa Ryder, Amazon review

For news of where to buy all of the author's works, visit his website, markeklid.com